Evil Crimes

ALSO BY MICHAEL HAMBLING

Michael Hambling

EVIL CRIMES

Detective Sophie Allen Book 6

Revised edition 2024
Joffe Books, London
www.joffebooks.com

First published in Great Britain in 2017

Cover art by Nick Castle

ISBN: 978-1-83526-858-2

To my wife Margaret and my three sons, Stephen, Malcolm and David.

PROLOGUE

November 2015

'Now. Let's jump now. Let's do it.'

He looked at her, at the gleaming eyes, wild with a passion that was beyond anything he'd experienced with anyone before. She shouted the words and they rose above the noise of the roaring wind and crashing waves that struck the rocky shelf on which they stood.

'Now's the moment. Let's do it.' She turned to face him. 'We agreed.'

He took a deep breath. 'Okay. Take my hand. We'll do it together. That will make it more special.' It was hard to hold himself here, on the edge of this rocky shelf, battered by the wind, his face lanced by the sea-spray as if hundreds of tiny needles were being flung at him. As each moment passed, he felt his resolve weaken, his uncertainty grow. He looked at her again, and then he noticed it. Or had he imagined it? A sly look of triumph that was there and then gone? What was happening? A germ of doubt was growing inside him. He could feel it gnawing at his soul.

'I said take my hand. We'll jump together,' he repeated, and tried to hold her gaze. Her eyes flickered everywhere but

1

at his. 'That's what you suggested. You said we'd end it all still touching each other. Surely that's what you want, isn't it?'

She nodded energetically. He could hardly hear her words above the roar of wind and wave. 'Yes, yes. It's what I want. For us. This life is no good any more. It's going rotten on us and we have to end it. We have to jump.'

'So take my hand. What's holding you back?'

'You jump first and I'll follow you. You're my true love, the one I'll always follow. You go first.'

'No!' he shouted. 'It has to be together. It has to be both of us at the same time. What's wrong?' For the first time he could sense something different in her. And yet it had been her idea to end their turbulent, passionate affair in this way. She'd planned it down to the last detail. The place, here on Dancing Ledge, and the wait until the weather was right, on a grim, stormy day. All this despite his own doubts. And now, when it came down to it, something in her was changing.

'Take my hand,' he shouted again. He needed to be sure.

She came close, her long, red hair blowing wildly in the wind. And then he realised. She'd bought a parking ticket. Why had she done that? Why had she bothered if they were both going to be dead within a couple of hours? It had taken them an hour to walk here along the coast path from Durlston Castle. He looked at her again. She could make it back to her car before the ticket became overdue. What was going on? Too late. He felt her hand push into the small of his back and he plunged forward into the wild water.

* * *

The young woman, her hair still blowing wildly in the wind, moved closer to the edge of the shelf and peered into the maelstrom below. His body twice struck the rocky outcrop with sickening force and then vanished. She put her mobile phone away and pulled her collar up. She tucked her long locks inside the soft corduroy material and curled her lip.

'Did you really think I was going to kill myself for you? Fucking loser.' She spat into the foam, laughed and turned on her heels. It was a long walk back to the car, parked in a secluded corner at the Durlston Country Park. Better get a move on.

CHAPTER 1: DISCOVERY

Tom Davis was depressed. This was one of the worst tasks in the world, and one he never thought he'd have to perform. Yardley Cottage was just an empty shell now that Eddie was no longer there, filling its rooms with her lively personality. It was a mere container, echoing nothing back to him, answering none of his questions, responding to his thoughts like the lifeless pile of bricks and plaster which, he finally admitted to himself, was exactly what it was.

He held the mug of tea in both hands, as if it were too precious to handle carelessly. He supposed that was true, in a way. He'd given Eddie this very mug as a birthday present a mere five months earlier, knowing that she'd appreciate its intricate floral design, traced out in orange, yellow and deep red. Had he sensed, even then, a shadow cast across her normally cheerful persona? There had been something, he was sure of it. Something had touched her. Something had blunted her keen interest in him, that sibling care she'd bestowed on him ever since they'd grown up together in a small town not dissimilar to Dorchester. She'd always been the big sister, and had stepped easily into an almost parental role after the car crash that had taken their parents away. And now, who was there to take on that role? No one. He felt as if he were on his own for the first time in his life. He ached for her presence.

He replaced the empty mug on the low table, stretched and looked around him. How much more was there to check before he could get the house clearance people in? He'd worked through the financial papers, bank statements, insurance claims and other assorted administrative details in the weeks following her death. Death? It was hardly an adequate term for the totally unexpected tragedy that had hit him like an express train. Even now, four months later, he couldn't quite bring himself to use the word suicide. It choked him just to think of it, his darling Eddie choosing to end her life like that. The worst of it was that despite weeks of talking to Eddie's friends, neighbours and acquaintances, he was no closer to understanding why she'd chosen to take her life. No one had a clue, least of all the neighbour who had discovered her body. They were all as bewildered as he was. Unless, of course, someone did know, but was refusing to let on. Tom scratched his dark curly hair. That would be the truth of it, of course. Someone probably did know but had decided to keep quiet for reasons of their own. Maybe they'd judged that the truth would be too cruel, that it would shed a different, less perfect light onto his idolised older sister. Maybe he'd been wrong about her for many years, blinded by the unswerving loyalty that he'd always felt towards her.

He glanced out of the window. The sun was edging out from behind a cloud, its rays falling onto some late flowering dahlias and making them glow. Time to get busy again. There was just the little upstairs desk to check, the one occupying the far corner of Eddie's bedroom. He'd had a quick look immediately after her death, checking for any important documents, but they'd all been filed in the bureau in this sitting room. He sighed, rose, and forced his limbs to move. He really didn't want to do this, but who else was there? He certainly didn't want strangers rifling through her personal papers, documents and diaries. It had to be him, and it had to be now. This was to be his last day in Dorchester, where Eddie had seemed so happy. He needed to travel back to London tomorrow. Work would be piling up on his desk and, in today's economically challenging times, he couldn't afford to be seen to be slacking, not in the cutthroat world of financial planning.

The morning sun shone bright into her bedroom, but it still seemed lifeless. Tom started work on the small bureau, methodically sorting through its contents. He put aside the papers that Eddie had kept from their parents' deaths, decades before, then started checking the rest of the contents, neatly divided into topics. As he already knew, all of the business documents had been kept downstairs. These were more personal items: letters, cards, photos and diaries. He'd already glanced through them soon after her death and found nothing untoward. He laid them out on the bed, arranging the diaries in chronological order. Strange. Eddie appeared not to have kept a diary for the current year. Maybe it was because she was already fighting depression. Even the previous year's had been sparse, with only the occasional short, almost cryptic entry. He continued to sift through the small pile of contents. Then he came across a small notebook with a floral cover, lying at the back of the drawer, previously hidden under the other documents. How had he missed it during his earlier visits? He'd probably been too tired, too preoccupied. He flicked through the little booklet. He couldn't make much sense of it at first. Most of the pages were blank and only a few contained short comments, written in a spidery hand. Tom took the notebook across to the window in order to see more clearly. He stood reading the sparse entries, and a feeling of unease started to grow within him. What was this? What had been going on?

He took the small notebook downstairs, sat down and read through the entries once more. He felt tense, almost nauseous. So Eddie *had* been emotionally traumatised in the weeks prior to her death. Tom was angry with himself because he'd somehow missed this notebook in the days following her suicide, when the police were still involved in probing her life. Why hadn't this innocuous looking jotter been placed in a more obvious spot, maybe with the other diaries? And then the realisation hit him. Eddie had planned this. She'd deliberately kept the notebook apart from the other diaries, almost hidden at the bottom of the drawer. But why? There was only one possible reason. She was worried that the wrong person might get hold of it. It had been carefully placed for him to find, and he'd let his sister down by failing to spot it earlier. Four long months had passed. Who would be interested now? Surely not the police, busy with a hundred and one other cases while grappling with the consequences of staffing cuts. But who else was there?

Tom extracted his wallet from his jacket pocket and searched through the contents. There it was, the card given to him by the police officer who'd been in charge of the brief investigation into Eddie's death. He took out his mobile phone.

'Can I speak to Sergeant Simons, please? It's Tom Davis.'

* * *

'So where are we off to, boss?'

George Warrander followed the stocky figure of Sergeant Rose Simons, who was hurrying down the steps to the car park behind Dorchester police station, their current base. George was a young constable still in his probationary year as a uniformed officer in the Dorset police force.

'The west side of town. There was a suicide there, back in the early summer when you were on leave. A middle-aged woman living alone. The closest family member was her brother but he lives in London. He's just phoned to say he's discovered a diary or notebook, or something like that. He said it's a bit suspicious.' They reached the car. 'It'll be a wild goose chase, but we've got an hour to kill before we're needed back in the town centre. It was a choice between going out to visit him or listening to the boss at the station droning on about new initiatives to improve how we interface with the public. No contest, particularly since our Mr Davis is a good-looking guy who doesn't seem short of a bob or two. Maybe I'll be in with a chance. Toy-boys like you, Georgie, are all very well but you never have any dosh. I need a bloke who is handsome, fit, sexy, generous, cheerful, understanding, considerate and rich, but when it comes down to absolute necessities, I'll just settle for rich. You can forget the rest.'

As usual, George listened to his boss's flight of fancy in silence. He stood meekly by the car while she checked for exploding booby traps. This was another of her strange habits. 'There'll be someone out there who's out to get me,' she'd explained to George once. 'No idea who, or even why, but I'm not giving him the chance.' George had lost count of the times he'd stood in the rain while his sergeant had inspected under the car and in the wheel arches, checking for unexpected lumpy objects with blinking lights and a dial counting down to zero. Too many James Bond movies was George's conclusion.

They finally clambered into the car and left the car park, heading west. During the short drive, Rose gave George the rest of the details. They pulled up outside one of the houses in a neat terrace. The properties all had small front gardens, and this one still had flowers in bloom, despite showing signs of recent neglect. They made their way along the short path from the gate of Yardley Cottage. The front door opened before they reached it. George looked at the tall man in the doorway and tried to visualise his boss's imaginary love interest. *Not very likely*, he thought. This tall, slim, well-dressed, good-looking man and his dishevelled, slightly crumpled-looking boss?

As if she could read his thoughts, she turned and whispered in his ear, 'I'll win him over with my personality and charm.'

Rose gave a broad smile and extended her arm. 'Mr Davis. It's good to see you again. And on such a beautiful day.'

The man attempted a smile in return. George thought he looked drained. Still, his handshake was firm when Rose introduced George.

'Come in,' Tom Davis said. 'I've got the notebook handy for you. I've typed out all the relevant extracts on my laptop and printed it out.'

George smiled. 'That's efficient of you. Do you usually bring your laptop with you when you visit?'

'Not always, and certainly not when I'm on holiday, but I needed to do some work while I was here. I used an old printer of Eddie's. I don't carry one of those around with me. Another couple of days and it would have been gone. I'm getting the house cleared at the end of the week. All the proceeds will go to charity.'

'That's thoughtful of you, Mr Davis,' Rose said. 'Some people in your place would grab as much money as they could for themselves and to hell with anyone else. Any particular charity?'

'Mental health. Maybe the Samaritans. I'm not entirely sure yet.'

'Okay. I can understand your reasons. You'll need to delay the sale though. CID may want a look at the house contents again, judging by what you told me on the phone. You said last time we met that you and your sister were extremely close. You still look a bit pale, if you don't mind me saying.'

They were now in the sitting room. Tom picked up a small jotter from the table top.

'I was beginning to get over it. Then I found this just an hour or so ago. It's really shaken me. Here's what I think are all the important entries, copied out and pasted together. They're the ones that mention someone referred to as H. When you see them all together like this, it paints a pretty dramatic picture. Have a look.'

He handed a couple of printed pages to Rose. She read the contents with a furrowed brow, then flicked through the diary, cross-checking the extracts. She handed the pages to George.

Rose turned to Tom. 'Did your sister ever mention anyone whose name starts with the letter H?'

'No, never. And you can see all this happened quickly and was over within a few weeks. I didn't even know she'd been abroad. It all seems so unlike her.'

'Other relationships?'

Tom paused. 'Look, I always knew that she was probably gay or maybe bi, but we didn't really talk about it. She kept quiet about her private life. I did meet one of her girlfriends, but that was years ago, before she came to Dorset. It's all a total shock.'

'These will go to CID. Can you email me the file with the extracts? It'll save us the bother of retyping and speed things up a wee bit. George will check that you haven't missed any out. I think you're right to be concerned, Mr Davis. It needs looking into, and I'll make sure someone follows it up. But please don't assume there was some kind of criminal conspiracy at work. Relationships break up all the time, well mine do anyway. I sometimes feel like topping the nutter who dumps me, but I don't let it get to me.'

'But it's that last entry, Sergeant. You can see that she was in total despair. She obviously thought she might lose her job.'

Rose nodded. 'It does look that way. As I say, CID will look into it. How can they contact you?'

'I'll be going back to London late afternoon. My wife is going out for the evening, so it'll be a child-minding night for me. Here's my card. It's got my work, home and mobile numbers on it. I can leave a set of keys with you, if you want.'

* * *

Tom Davis continued sorting and tidying after the two officers left, but discovered nothing more that gave any indication of his sister's mental state in the days before her death. With time to spare before he needed to set off back to London, he decided to visit the neighbours. He'd talked to them before but that had been before his discovery of the small diary and its references to a relationship.

The conversations got him nowhere. Neither neighbour was aware of any visits from a young woman, but then, they might easily have missed such calls. One couple had been away for several weeks at about the same time as the relevant diary entries, and the other neighbour was an elderly man with poor sight and hearing difficulties.

He sighed. This short visit had been intended as the final act of his farewell to Eddie, an opportunity for closure, allowing him to move on. Instead it had opened up a whole new raft of questions. He sat in the car for a moment before starting the engine. It looked as though his plans to put the house on the market would have to go on hold.

CHAPTER 2: EXTRACTS FROM
THE DIARY OF EDWINA DAVIS

12 March. I've been asked if H can lodge with me for a couple of weeks. She's recovering from an illness and her mother doesn't want her left alone when the rest of the family are away on holiday in April. I've agreed as a favour, but I'm not sure I like H very much. Before she went off to university, I thought she was sometimes a bit immature for an eighteen-year-old. Still, I realise how vulnerable some teenagers can be, and how they need to be gently supervised during those first few months of recovery after mental illness. I agree it would be dangerous to leave her alone. Why don't they take her with them? It's in the university vacation after all. In the end I said I'd take her in.

8 April. H is a bit irritating. She seems to follow me around and suddenly pops into view when I least expect it. It can be embarrassing. Today she caught me coming out of the shower with no clothes on. I thought she was still out in the garden. I was a bit worried because the incident could have been taken the wrong way, but H assured me she knew it was her fault. I pointed out how vulnerable my work as a senior midwife and ethics committee member made me, with her

being identified as at risk, even though she's nineteen now. She was so apologetic that I gave her a hug. Her smile was heart-warming.

10 April. H has started dressing differently. More mature clothes. Slightly sultry. She's wearing make-up more often as well. I wonder if she has her eyes on a young man?

12 April. We had some wine with dinner this evening. H probably had too much because she was being a bit provocative. What she said didn't seem to make much sense. Unless she's guessed about me being a lesbian.

15 April. H has been coming on to me again. I don't know what to make of it. I wondered if I was mistaken the other night, but she made it pretty clear this evening.

16 April. H and I were talking, late in the evening. She sat beside me on the sofa while we watched TV and started caressing me. I'm confused. I feel as if I want her to continue, yet don't, both at the same time. It's dangerous and thrilling. It's made me realise how lonely I really am.

18 April. This is ridiculous! She put her arms around me and kissed me. I'm so mixed up about it. She's so much younger than me. She just giggles when I tell her.

19 April. I think I might be falling in love with H. She kissed me again and I couldn't help but respond. I refused to go any further than kissing though. It's just too dangerous. She's awoken feelings that I never thought I'd have again.

20 April. Oh God. We kissed again, and one thing led to another. She spent the night in my bed. It was wonderful.

21 April. What future is there for us? The situation is just ridiculous!

22 April. There's a huge age difference but what does it really mean? Is it that important? H doesn't think so. I love her for saying it so clearly, so unequivocally. She's back at home with her family who returned from holiday this morning.

26 April. What a glory her hair is! I pulled some leaves out of it today, they'd got tangled in her long, red locks when she pushed through a hedgerow on a walk near the coast.

27 April. Oh, we've just had such glorious sex. I can't quite believe it.

3 May. Under the apple tree in the garden at the old pub — another kiss. We'd had too much cider! Is there such a thing as too much cider? And did I say kiss? I meant a long, sultry snog!

6 May. H gave me a present. It was a book on ancient history with a really lovely message on the inside. It was wrapped in pink paper with a pattern of lots of lips about to kiss. Really sweet. She still only signs everything H though. She never uses her full name.

11 May. I'm deliriously happy. I never knew happiness such as this existed in the world. Happiness has always been for other people, not for me.

12 May. H wants us to go on holiday together. We're thinking of a few days in Majorca. I'm free the second half of next week. She has a reading week before her exams start and claims that a weekend break will be exactly the right tonic for her. Dare I?

27 May. It's been a month of heaven. I must have pleased the gods to get a reward like this. Our break in Majorca was everything I hoped it would be and life has been amazing since we got back. I wonder. Will there be a payback later?

6 June. Have I sold my soul to the devil? H is being petty. Really petty.

14 June. This is pure torture. She says she's found someone else. My sanity is hanging by a thread.

15 June. Why is H doing this to me? Weren't we happy? Why does she refuse to answer when I phone?

17 June. I've eaten nothing for two days. I can't face the future without her.

18 June. Oh God. She's turned on me. She says I'm a pathetic old crone and that she never loved me. She's told her new partner about me, and she (the new partner) says I'm disgusting.

20 June. I can't believe this is happening. She's hinted that she will tell my boss. What if she does? It's just unimaginable.

What have I done? I've broken every rule in the book, I know I have. They'll go to town on me. I'll lose everything. She's told her mother and her new partner that it was all down to me, that I deliberately seduced her, that I assaulted her. They think it's been going on for nearly two years, from when she was still seventeen. She even says I manipulated her original request to stay with me. I can't see a way out. I'm finished.

CHAPTER 3: DOUBLE CHECKING

Detective Sergeant Barry Marsh pulled into the police station at Dorchester and slid out of his car. What was this visit all about? Why had they called on the violent crimes unit — of which Barry was second in command? One of the local CID men, Stu Blackman, had phoned him earlier but had been vague, merely saying that he needed advice on something unusual. Normally Barry would have tried to sort out the problem over the phone, but it was a quiet morning and his junior, Rae Gregson, could handle the current task. The boss, DCI Sophie Allen, was in Oxford for the day, attending an academic criminology seminar. Barry smiled. Blackman wasn't the most astute detective in the county, far from it. But he was trying to mend his ways, now he was no longer under the influence of his long-time sidekick, Phil McCluskie, who had been steered into taking early retirement. Barry had even heard that the seriously overweight Blackman had joined a diet and fitness group since his transfer from Blandford. Whatever had happened, it had come just in time for Blackman. With staffing cuts biting deep across the board, there was no longer any room for passengers.

Barry climbed the stairs two at a time. His fiancée, Gwen, had warned him that she expected him to stay fit after they were married. 'It's better for you, and it's certainly better for our relationship,' she'd said in no uncertain terms. Since their first date two years earlier, Barry had lost a stone in weight and he intended to keep it that way. No more pizza, fewer chips and regular exercise. That was the key.

Blackman came out from his office to greet him and the two men shook hands.

Barry looked at his colleague. 'You look a lot fitter, Stu.'

'Thanks. I feel better. Maybe I can start dating again soon.' Blackman chuckled.

Barry didn't know how to respond to this, so he decided not to comment. 'What's the problem? You were very cagey on the phone.'

He followed Blackman into the office.

'Some months ago we dealt with a case that was clearly suicide. It was a middle-aged woman, a senior midwife. The reason was never clear, not even to her family. She left a short note, addressed to her brother, saying only that she'd had enough and was taking the only way out. We all thought it was over and done with, but then her brother was here a few days ago to clear the house ready for sale. He came across a diary that she'd hidden. It seems to throw a different light on things. It'll still be suicide, mind. I'm not saying she was murdered or anything. But it makes the background a lot more questionable. It's a bit beyond me, to be honest. I need some advice, and your name sprang to mind.'

'Okay. Show me what you've got.'

Blackman handed over the diary and a single sheet containing the relevant extracts. Barry read it carefully.

'I can see why the brother was troubled.'

'So you think there might be something to it? Have you come across anything like it before?'

'Not really. But if someone was intimidated to the extent that they felt driven to suicide, it has to be investigated. This isn't as obvious as that, though. There's no mention of direct threats being made, is there? What does your boss say?'

'I haven't told him yet. The thing is, Barry, I don't want to make a fool of myself. I'm trying to make a fresh start and I can't afford to make too many misjudgements if I want people to take me seriously.'

'And that's where I come in, is it? I'm a kind of filter. Where did this come from by the way? How did it get to you?'

'It was Rose Simons who saw the brother. He phoned her when he found the diary. But you know what she's like. She's not going to go out of her way for me, is she? She might even be trying to trip me up — that's what I'm worried about.'

Barry scanned through the diary. 'It looks genuine enough on the face of it. My gut feeling is that the house might need another look, just to check that the brother didn't miss anything else.' He looked straight at Blackman. 'And I don't believe for one moment that Rose Simons would try to trick you. She may have an odd sense of humour but she's totally honest, and a first-rate cop. So did she get transferred here as well, during the staffing reorganisation?'

Blackman nodded. 'So you think it's worth following up?'

'I think so, but keep it short. And you'd better check with your boss. There might be other more pressing priorities.' Barry looked again at the paper in his hand. 'The thing is, it doesn't alter the fact that she took her own life. It just gives a reason for it where there wasn't one before. What you have to ask yourself is what would you have done if this had been found at the time? You'd have probably dug around trying to find out who this H was, and then tried to speak to her. Does it make much of a difference now we're a few months down the line? If there's time available, do it. If there isn't, report it and leave it to your boss to decide.'

Barry had a cup of coffee with Blackman, and then drove back to police headquarters at Winfrith.

* * *

Blackman's boss gave him the go-ahead to investigate further, so he visited the dead woman's place, spoke to the neighbours

18

and carried out another search of the house. He discovered nothing suspicious. He also visited the local hospital's maternity unit, where she used to work, but made no progress there either. No one had heard of a young woman whose name started with the letter H. Edwina had been a very conscientious, hardworking team leader, and respected by all, but she had kept her private life exactly that. Private. Her work colleagues knew nothing about her personal relationships. One colleague did say that he'd once spotted Edwina walking on the coast path with a much younger woman, but they hadn't stopped to chat. He seemed to remember that the young woman had long red hair, but he couldn't be totally sure.

Blackman contacted Edwina's brother to let him know that the enquiries had drawn a blank, and that no further investigation time could be justified. He asked if anything else had come to light in the meantime, but the answer was negative. Copies of the diary and documents were filed and the originals returned to Tom Davis, who was told that the house clearance and sale could go ahead.

And so the exact nature of the tragic circumstances surrounding the suicide of Edwina Davis remained obscure. At least, nothing came to light at the time. Then, several months later, something happened that gave Detective Sergeant Barry Marsh cause to remember the odd entries in Edwina's diary.

CHAPTER 4: DANCING LEDGE

By mid-morning the stormy weather had moderated, just as the forecast had predicted. Even so, some members of the Chatty Ramblers walking group struggled against the stronger gusts of wind that still whistled across the coast path every few minutes. Flick had wondered whether to cancel November's walk, but in the end she'd stuck to her guns.

'Let's have some faith in the forecasters, shall we?' she said. 'If you want to pull out, then that's fine. But I like being out when the weather's a bit breezy, and so do a lot of the others. It's bracing. You get a wholly different feel for the coast path in these conditions. Just make sure you're wearing suitable waterproofs and boots, and bring your walking poles. You'll be fine.'

True, the group was only half its normal size, but enough ramblers had turned up for the walk to go ahead. Flick was walking beside Pauline Stopley, now a regular in their ranks. Pauline's cheeks were pink and her eyes alive under her maroon bobble hat.

'Have you gone blonde, Pauline?' Flick asked, trying not to peer too obviously. Maybe she needed an eye test. Pauline had been a brunette during the year she'd been a member of the group and had never mentioned wanting to change her hair colour.

'Ah, you noticed. I'm not convinced yet but I'll give it another week or two before I finally decide if it's for me. Tony seems keen anyway. He's not been able to keep his hands off me since I got it done. It's just incredible how something as simple as going blonde can fire up a man's libido, don't you think?'

Flick nodded warily. That was the trouble with Pauline. You started a simple conversation and you just couldn't tell where it would end up. 'So you're saying it's true? Blondes really do have more fun?' Flick's own hair had always been a mousy brown. Maybe it was time for a change.

'Well, I wouldn't go that far. I had plenty of fun as a brunette. But some men prefer blondes, and Tony seems to be one of them. I would never have guessed.'

'He's a vicar, isn't he?' Flick tried to sound nonchalant.

'Makes no difference, though.' Pauline smiled. 'When it comes to sex, men are men. That's what I've decided. Well, most of them anyway. Long may it continue.' She walked a little closer to Flick. 'We're talking about getting married, but keep that to yourself at the moment. I shouldn't really tell anyone, but I'm so excited that it just bubbles over. It's been twenty years since I lost my first husband and this is just the best thing that's happened to me since. I know people think I've been a bit of a merry widow, but that's not entirely true. A lot of it was just down to desperation on my part. It's clear to me now, but that's hindsight for you. You never see things at the time, do you?'

Flick wasn't absolutely sure what Pauline was referring to, so she merely smiled back. 'That's great. I'm happy for you.'

The small group had reached the fence overlooking Dancing Ledge, so Flick made to turn east.

'Can't we get a closer look?' one of the men asked.

Flick looked at her watch. 'We're ten minutes ahead of schedule, so I suppose we could. The path down is quite steep once we cross the stile, so use your poles. If you'd prefer to stay back here, please do.'

All eight ramblers decided to have a closer look at the famous ledge, so they scrambled across the stile and followed the narrow twisting track down to the flat shelf. The sound of breaking waves became louder as they approached the base of the cliff, but at least the wind was less strong here. Now that they were in the lee of the tall limestone cliff face there was no longer a need to shout. The sea was still rough but Flick guessed it was much calmer than earlier that morning. A blue shape, bobbing in the waves caught her eye. She pointed.

'What's that?' she asked no one in particular. 'Can I borrow your binoculars, Jim?'

She focussed on the floating object.

'My God. I think it's a body.'

The chattering suddenly stopped and everyone craned forward to get a better look. Flick was right — the bobbing blue shape, half submerged in the grey water, was undoubtedly a body. The wind had changed direction during the previous hour and the shape was slowly moving eastwards towards the far end of the rocky shelf. Flick took her phone out and dialled 999.

* * *

A uniformed police unit from Swanage was first on the scene, closely followed by a coastguard team and the local police doctor, Mark Benson. But the body was continuing its drift further east, pushed by the wind and tidal currents, and was in danger of being carried beyond the eastern edge of the rocky shelf. Recovery from Dancing Ledge itself would be relatively straightforward but if the body drifted too far away the task would be much harder. The ramblers watched the coastguard volunteers hurry to the far end of the ledge. Two of the team donned wetsuits, attached themselves to ropes and slid into the choppy water. The bobbing blue-clad object was now beyond the end of the ledge and heading for the dangerous-looking rocks under the cliff. The onlookers watched, mesmerised by the drama of the scene.

It took only a couple of minutes for the two swimmers to reach the body and affix a sling. The tragic shape was pulled in. The body, that of a man apparently in his late twenties, was lifted onto a lightweight stretcher so that Mark Benson and the police officers could carry out a cursory examination.

'He hasn't been in the water long,' said Benson. 'At least I don't think so. What's your opinion?' The coastguard officers agreed. 'You can usually tell by the condition of the skin and the stiffness of the body. Maybe a couple of hours at most?'

Benson turned the body over and continued his swift examination, ensuring the watching ramblers had their view obstructed. 'Pretty well confirmed by the rectal temperature. That's all I can do at the moment.'

One of the police officers said, 'Any signs of suspicious injuries, Doctor? Or are they all consistent with hitting the rocks?'

'Nothing unexpected as far as I can see,' Mark replied. 'But I can't predict what may show up at the post-mortem. I suggest we get him out of sight as quickly as possible. There are too many onlookers. The place will be heaving with walkers by mid-afternoon, especially if we see a bit of sunshine.'

The police had already taken details from the rambling group members, but, of course, none of them had seen how the man had ended up in the water.

'He's wearing walking boots,' observed one officer. 'And a windproof jacket. Looks like a walker to me. Could he have gone too close to the edge?'

'Don't let's speculate, laddie,' answered the sergeant. 'Let's wait for any forensic clues. And let's get these ramblers on their way. They're clogging up the area. The forensic team should be here soon and we need to make sure they can use the path without a problem. I want everyone cleared back behind the fence, out of harm's way.'

* * *

The Chatty Ramblers began the final leg of their walk, heading back to Swanage via the Priest's Way footpath. They now had the wind at their backs and the going was much easier than the westward walk of mid-morning. Even so, they didn't talk much. Flick was relieved when they reached the car park at Durlston Castle. With much shaking of heads, they all headed home.

As she drove northwards, Flick cast her mind back to a question one of the police officers had asked her. Had the group passed anyone on their way to the ledge? She'd replied in the negative, but now she remembered that at one point there might have been a figure hurrying east on the upper coast path. Her group had used the lower path, closer to the cliff edge and a little more sheltered from the wind. Had she imagined it? She couldn't be sure. That was one of the problems of reaching your mid-sixties. Flick was beginning to realise that her memory was less reliable than a decade earlier. Maybe she'd phone the other walkers later in the afternoon. One of them may have spotted that lone figure.

* * *

Pauline Stopley was worried. She too had spotted the person on the upper path. Pauline was sure it had been a young woman, striding out eastwards, wisps of long hair peeping out from under a woolly hat. Could there have been a dog? Pauline hadn't noticed one, but why else would a woman be out alone in such forbidding weather? It had only been a brief glimpse anyway. But the real reason she hadn't spoken up to the police was the thought of another set of interviews, statements and meetings. Would they believe her anyway, with her history? And the possibility of coming up against that blonde detective again, that Sophie Allen woman, filled her with a mixture of fear and anxiety. And what other feelings? Pauline shivered. She was with Tony now, and planning a future as a vicar's wife. Those tempting thoughts had to stop.

By the time she arrived home, Pauline was beginning to feel ashamed of these thoughts. She made herself a cup of tea, phoned Flick and asked her about the woman she'd so briefly seen that morning. To Pauline's relief, they decided that as the group's leader, Flick should be the one to phone the police with the information. Pauline finished her tea, and then poured herself a gin and tonic to help settle her troubled thoughts. Maybe she wouldn't have to meet that blonde detective, not if Flick dealt with it all. Maybe.

CHAPTER 5: INVESTIGATIONS

'Hello, Benny. I don't know why I keep coming back. Most other DCIs send a junior along for something like this. Must be your natural magnetism.'

Sophie Allen smiled sweetly at Dorset's senior pathologist and took the proffered cup of coffee.

'What a relief. I was beginning to think I'd lost my touch. I poured that coffee with my own fair hand, O Golden Haired One. Everyone else gets one from the machine. You get the Goodall personal treatment. I hope you appreciate it. It's all in gratitude for those meals you cooked when we were students. You kept me alive, you know. Spaghetti Bolognese has never tasted the same since.'

'Probably a good thing. I dread to think what I used to put in it. Anyway, down to business. It's about that body that was found in the sea at the weekend. Find anything unusual?' Sophie sipped at her coffee. Not bad, she thought. But then anything was better than the machine-generated sludge that was usually on offer here.

'No, not really. No marks or injuries that aren't consistent with being flung hard against the rocks by the surf. No traces of drugs. A small amount of residual alcohol, consistent with a couple of glasses of wine the night before. He was a fit and healthy man. For his age, anyway. What was he? Early thirties?'

'Twenty-eight. Nothing else of note?'

'Not a thing. Every sign points to the fact that he died from drowning, and only an hour or so before he was pulled out of the water. So does that make it a puzzle?'

'Not really. It was very windy, and it swirls around a bit down on that ledge. He could have gone too close to the edge, and then lost his balance in a particularly strong gust. The ledge would still have been wet from the waves breaking over it earlier, at high tide. Easy mistake to make.'

'Or he could have deliberately jumped,' Benny added.

'Of course. But so far there's no evidence for thinking that.'

'What have you found out about him? Am I allowed to know?'

'I put Rae onto it, so you can imagine how quickly the picture built up. His name's Mark Paterson. He was single as far as we know and he was a researcher at Bournemouth University, looking into computer animation techniques.'

Benny snorted. 'Not another one! Computer people seem to be two a penny at the moment.'

'Don't snarl at me like that, Benny, please. Bournemouth's one of the top universities in the field, so what do you expect? He was midway through a two-year contract.'

'Do you think there might be some kind of conspiracy behind his death? Was he secretly hacking into government databases?'

This time it was Sophie's turn to snort. 'No, I am most certainly not saying that. His work was in animation, not security. Good job you became a doctor, Benny, and it was me that took up police work. You're as bad as Jade. At one time her head was full of conspiracy theories. She's better now, thank goodness. When she was young she was always telling me to arrest someone because they looked a bit shifty or their hair was greasy.'

'I can understand her point of view. Who wants our streets clogged up with shifty-looking, greasy-haired people? Put them behind bars where they belong. I'm with your daughter on that.'

'I'll ignore that. Anyway, while I'm here I need to ask if you and Roger want to come to a BSO concert next month. It's Beethoven's triple concerto. Martin wants to get tickets in the next couple of days and he knows you're a fan. We can have a meal beforehand, maybe?'

'Yes, please, but I'll have to check the date with Roger first. Maybe we can shock a few more of Dorset's concert-going public by holding hands.'

'Anything short of a full-blown snog is fine by me. I do draw the line at that, though. Maybe I should get Jade to extend her suggested list of arrestable offences to include middle-aged people snogging at public events. It lacks dignity, don't you think?'

'Who am I to disagree? You're the one who can lock people in the clink and drop the key down the drain.'

* * *

While Sophie was visiting the hospital, Barry Marsh drove to Basingstoke to visit the dead man's family. Mark Paterson's parents still lived in the house where Mark had grown up, and a local Hampshire officer who was also a family friend had brought the news of their son's death. The elderly couple were devastated. The dead man's older sister, Elaine Jenkins, admitted Barry to the house. She had driven down overnight from Stoke-on-Trent. Barry could see her resemblance to the dead man, though Mark had been darker. When Barry asked how her parents were, Elaine shook her head.

'They're taking it hard,' she replied. 'We all are. We still can't believe it. Why would he do this? Mark was such a positive person. It just doesn't make sense. If he was depressed, he kept it very well hidden. No one had a clue. What does his doctor say?'

'As far as we can tell, he had no record of depression or extreme anxiety, Mrs Jenkins,' Barry replied. 'Nothing in his medical history suggests the possibility of suicide. But we're always aware that medical records may not give the whole picture. There are plenty of cases every year, people who slip through the net and don't raise any alarms. So far we've only spoken to his GP by phone, but one of my colleagues will be visiting her this morning.'

'So why are you here?'

'We take all suspicious deaths seriously. We don't jump to quick conclusions, not unless the evidence is absolutely clear. So I'm here to meet you and your parents, to reassure you all that we are investigating his death, and to have a quick look in his old room, if I may.'

Elaine led the way into a lounge where Mark's parents were sitting in silence. He repeated what he'd told their daughter, but they seemed not to take it in. Totally shocked, thought Barry. He asked if he might see their son's room and Elaine took him upstairs.

'He hasn't lived here for many years, so you probably won't find much of use. His more personal stuff will be in his flat in Bournemouth.'

Elaine waited outside as Barry carried out his search. He guessed that the room reflected the personality of the mother rather than the son. She'd want to keep it as a room to put guests in when required. Barry found nothing of interest.

'Was he in a relationship?' Barry asked.

'Not that we were aware of,' said Elaine. 'He's had a few girlfriends, one that was very serious. But since that failed a couple of years ago, he's not said much about any others. There must have been some though. He was a really nice bloke, and I'm not just saying that because he was my brother. Good-looking too, in his way. Women liked him.'

Barry spoke to the parents again before he left. He wished his boss were here. She always knew exactly the right things to say in situations like this.

* * *

Detective Constable Rae Gregson was in Bournemouth, searching through the dead man's flat. It was a small apartment in a large Edwardian house that had been converted to flats, a ten-minute walk away from the university. The place was quite untidy, and Rae wrinkled her nose in distaste as she sorted through the unwashed socks. *Men*, she thought. How could anyone live like this?

The flat was not much larger than a bedsit. The front door opened into a general purpose room furnished with a couch, an armchair, and a small dining table. A waist-high counter separated the kitchen area from the rest of the room. A second doorway led to a tiny lobby, with entrances to a bathroom and a bedroom. The latter was just large enough for the double bed that took up most of the floor space, along with a narrow wardrobe that occupied the far corner. Rae had to squeeze herself around the furnishings.

It didn't take her long to search the bedroom. Most of Mark Paterson's clothes were informal. Loose T-shirts, jumpers, chino trousers. He seemed to own only a single suit and Rae only found two ties, both rather dull. Shame. She liked men who wore colourful ties. In her earlier life as a man, Rae had prided herself on her tie collection. It had been one of the few ways she could reveal her hidden femininity and, boy, had she made the most of it. Standing in front of this open wardrobe, secure in her current life, she could look back on those times with equanimity. She smiled at herself, shook her head, and walked through to the main room to continue her search.

A bookshelf unit stood in the corner, filled with texts on computer animation, programming, graphics and other tech-related topics. Rae scanned the contents of the bottom shelf — ring-binders and folders containing notes on similar topics. A powerful laptop lay on a small desk, another sat propped sideways against the wall. Rae bagged them for further examination. She opened the desk drawers and went through the contents, but nothing untoward caught her eye.

Everything in the flat was pretty well what she'd expect from a computer person. Except? She walked back to the bedroom and picked up a paperback book from the bedside shelf, a slim volume on ancient history, with two similar volumes beneath it. Why was this here? She glanced at the handwritten message on the inside cover: 'To Mark from H.' Rae took the books to the lounge and added them to the two laptops. She took a last look round, picked up the small pile and left.

* * *

Sophie listened to the accounts of her two juniors over coffee.

'How did he get to Dancing Ledge?' she asked. 'That's the obvious puzzle. There aren't any cars left abandoned in the local car parks, nor in any of the lanes close to Dancing Ledge. We've had people out checking them all, from Swanage and Durlston across to Worth Matravers, and all spots in between. There's an activity centre at Spyway and they've been out doing some of the searching. They've drawn a blank everywhere. So what does that leave?'

'Could he have come by bus?' Rae asked.

Barry shook his head. 'Apparently not. The local bobbies have spoken to most of the drivers who were on both routes to Swanage yesterday and no one remembers him. There's still a couple to see, but they're the ones who were on duty later in the day. The only other option is that he came in on the steam railway, but the times don't fit.'

'Could he have biked it?' Rae asked. 'Don't loads of cyclists come across from Poole on the ferry, then spend the day cycling around Purbeck on the trails?'

'But why haven't we found a bike?' Barry responded. 'We've had teams out on that bit of the coast path, and there's no abandoned bike there.'

Sophie shrugged. 'Well, we can't consider the case closed until we've covered all the angles, and there are still a few grey areas. Anything else of interest? Rae?'

'I've sent his two laptops for forensic analysis. I didn't want to look myself in case I put stuff at risk. I wanted to speak to his colleagues this morning but there was some kind of faculty meeting going on, so I'm visiting this afternoon. There was one other thing. I found these books beside his bed.' She handed the volumes to Sophie.

'Do we know who this H is?' Sophie asked.

Rae shook her head.

Barry blinked. 'What was that?'

'It's the inscription. It says, "To Mark from H."'

Why did that seem familiar? Barry shook his head slightly, as if to clear it, but the memory didn't surface. Sophie flicked through the book, and a slip of paper fell out. She held it up to the light. It was a till receipt from a bookshop in Exeter. She slid it back into the book.

'Barry, can you go with Rae this afternoon? There could be a lot of people to talk to and there's not much else on at the moment. I'll talk to the walking group leader who spotted the body.'

* * *

Bournemouth is one of the newer universities, and boasts a world renowned department of computer graphics and visual design. Rae, with her engineering background, was fascinated by the whole thing. Barry, a career cop from a farming background, was less enthused. The two detectives interviewed the dead man's closest colleagues, who gave a picture of a rather private and introspective person. Mark appeared to have got on with his work without seeking much contact with the others there. He was well liked, but his colleagues weren't overenthusiastic. One fellow researcher, a woman of about the same age as Mark, was able to provide a bit more insight.

'I dated him a few times,' Leigh Giminez told them. 'I was newly across from the States and felt a bit lonely so I kept pestering him until he relented and came out with me. He was kinda hard to get to know, but then so many British men are, aren't they? Doesn't it go with the territory?'

'When was this?' Barry asked.

'About a year ago,' she replied. 'But we didn't have much in common, apart from our work. I like a bit of liveliness, and he was kinda withdrawn. At least that's what I thought.'

'You don't know if he made any new friends recently? Any relationships?'

She shook her head. 'He wasn't one for small talk. That was one of the problems when we went out together. Maybe he was the archetypal computer geek. Most of us aren't like that, despite what people think. We can party with the best of them. Well, I sure can!' She took a swig of coffee. 'I did see him on campus recently, arm in arm with a woman. He looked quite animated which was unusual for him.'

'Was this very recent?'

'Probably about a month ago? I couldn't tell you much about her except that she was quite young, pretty striking and had long red hair. Probably a student. If so, he was on dangerous ground. That kinda thing is pretty much a no-no these days. I'll tell you one thing though, she wasn't from this department. I'd have recognised her.'

* * *

The two detectives returned to the station having gained little further information.

'Apart from his American colleague, no one had much to say about him,' Barry reported to Sophie. 'He was a bit of a solitary individual and didn't chat much but they all thought he was a nice guy. I'd guess it was a tragic accident, ma'am. No one seemed to think that he was depressed or suicidal.'

'He was registered with a doctor on campus, ma'am,' Rae added. 'No record of any depression or anxiety issues. His only appointments were about treating his asthma, and even that wasn't too serious.'

'And no one knew of a young woman with long hair? That report we got from some of that ramblers' group? A coincidence?'

'There was one report, from his ex-girlfriend, the American woman he went out with a couple of times last year. She was pretty clear about it. And it was fairly recent.'

'I'd say she was reliable,' Rae added. 'The woman had long red hair and was fairly young, and the two of them were very engrossed in each other. We checked around, but no one could identify her. It would be needles and haystacks in a place like that. There's thousands of students and many of them change their hair colour every month. It's the latest thing to do, isn't it?'

'Okay, Barry. Out with it.' Sophie had been watching Barry Marsh. He'd been running his fingers through his ginger hair, a sure sign that something was troubling him.

'I've got this uneasy feeling that I've heard something like it before somewhere. It's probably just me being paranoid as usual, but something's ringing a bell. It happened earlier as well, when Rae brought that book from his flat. Something a bit familiar, but I couldn't put my finger on it. I still can't. This time it was the hair colour.'

'Well, if it helps, two of the ramblers might have had a brief glimpse of a young woman on the coast path, about half an hour before they spotted the body. They didn't get a good look because she was a few hundred yards above them on a different path. The trouble is, one of them is our old friend, Pauline Stopley. I didn't speak to her, just to the group leader. Maybe it won't be necessary to see her, but I may have to steel myself.'

'Do you want one of us to do it?' Barry suggested.

'We'll cross that bridge when we come to it,' Sophie replied. 'Thanks for the offer, Barry, but it will probably have to be me. I'd already decided that I needed to update her about Polly Nelson's enquiry in Bristol. I bumped into Polly in Oxford, and she told me that they've found no evidence to implicate Pauline in the death of her husband's first wife. In fact they've discovered no evidence at all. It was all too long ago. It might have been him acting alone. It might have been the two of them acting together. But it's all too circumstantial, and they'll probably end up putting the case back into cold storage.'

'She'll be pleased,' Rae said. 'It must have been playing on her mind. Isn't she planning to marry that vicar?'

'Tony Younger? The mind boggles. I can't get my head round it. I keep imagining possible headlines in a gossip magazine. Seductress extraordinaire marries respectable vicar.'

'I actually liked her, ma'am,' Rae added.

'Well the thing is, Rae, so did I.'

35

CHAPTER 6: EXETER

'You're sure you don't mind me taking you to Exeter, Jade? I've got to go anyway so it seemed sensible to do it today when you've got your interview.'

'Of course not, Mum. Stop worrying about it. It's a heck of a lot easier getting a lift from you than trying to get there by train. I'd have needed two changes and it takes well over three hours. You're saving me hours of sitting in cold and draughty stations, so why would I mind?' Jade was almost eighteen and in the midst of interviews for university.

Sophie was in the hallway of the family house in Wareham, putting on her coat. Jade, now a good two inches taller than her mother, was waiting by the front door, already in her jacket and pink woollen hat.

'That spirit of independence you possess in such abundance, maybe?'

'It does sometimes have its drawbacks, Mum. I'm quite happy to give up the stroppy-teenager attitude when it suits me. Like now.'

'Well, let's be off. I'll only need an hour or so to find out what I need, so maybe we can find somewhere nice for lunch once you're finished. There'll be plenty of buses from the campus into the city centre. You can text me when you're done. Pub? Café? What would you prefer?'

'Let's make it a café. I don't want you anywhere near a beer pump, not if you've got to drive me back home safely.'

'If you're going to get cheeky, I might just change my mind about that lift.'

'Sorry, Mum. Won't upset you again. Anyway, the medical school isn't on the main campus. It's at St Luke's, which is closer to the city centre, so I can walk to wherever we're meeting for lunch. How about the cathedral refectory? It's meant to be good.' She paused. 'Oh, by the way, I've got an interview at Oxford next month, at Keble.'

Halfway through the front door, Sophie stopped dead. 'What? You never told me. Why didn't you let us know you were applying there? You are just so infuriating, Jade.' She dropped her bag, turned and hugged her daughter. 'But I love you, and I'm so proud of you. We both are. You have no idea what that bit of news means to me.'

'Well, if I didn't before, I do now,' Jade replied. 'And I didn't tell you because you seemed happy for me to have Bristol as my first choice, because of Granddad. I've always secretly wanted to go to Oxford, but I never told you. The thing is, Mum, I've always wanted to copy you, even more than the Granddad thing. I've got my role models but none of them can ever match you.' Jade was watching her mother's startled face. 'Now, hadn't we better be off? I don't want you breaking the speed limit and getting pulled over by the traffic cops. That would be so embarrassing.'

* * *

Sophie pulled the book out of her bag, extracted the till receipt and handed it over to the bookshop manager.

'I wondered why the receipt was for ten per cent less than the price on the book's sticker, and that was already a good bit less than the official cover price.'

The manager examined the slip for a moment. 'It's our standard student discount. Any book that's on a university set book list gets discounted to students who produce a current card.'

'So this is a set book?'

'It's not one of the main texts but it's on the supplementary reading list for the ancient history degree. The date's a bit strange, though. Late June's an odd time to buy a reader like this, just after exams are over. Autumn, January, even mid-spring are the usual times, well before the end of the exam season.'

'I think I know the reason for that. It was probably a birthday present. The guy who had it, his birthday was in early July. These other two books are also of interest but they weren't on that till receipt. Could they have come from here?'

The manager picked the books up. 'Quite possibly, though they look older and more used. They're also standard readers for the course.'

'Your staff member who sold the first one, would he or she still be here?'

The manager examined the slip again. 'No. Daisy was a student herself and only worked here on Saturdays. That's her code at the top. She graduated in the summer and left. She went to London, I think. She wouldn't remember one sale, anyway. Student sales would have dropped off by then but it's the height of the tourist season. We swap one type of customer for another. Look, it was late morning. We'd have been swamped.'

Sophie thought for moment. 'What degree was Daisy doing?'

'Economics, I think. I can check if you want. My assistant manager was often on the same desk as her.'

* * *

Sophie sat in the cathedral refectory looking at the artwork on the walls. This place was an oasis of peace, like the cathedral close itself, set on the fringe of the busy shopping and commercial centre.

Jade came in and sat down.

'How did it go?' asked Sophie.

'Fine. I liked it. It's meant to be the most forward-looking medical school in the country, and that really appeals to me.'

'The main campus is gorgeous, Jade. I came down a few times to visit a friend who was here when I was at Oxford.'

'Jamie's putting it down as his first choice, for computing,' Jade added, with no further explanation.

Sophie wondered where this was leading. Better to be non-committal. 'So, does that make it a more likely choice for you?'

'Not sure. The thing is, Mum, I really like Jamie. He's been my first serious boyfriend. But he can be a bit shallow and I'm starting to have doubts about us in the long term. Trying to talk about serious issues with him and his pals is just impossible. It's all football and computer games. We don't really have much in common and that worries me a bit. What do you think?'

'Let's get some lunch and talk it over. My brain works better with food.'

They were both well into their quiche and salad when the conversation resumed.

'It might be just a phase he's going through, Jade. You're both the same age, and isn't it a well-known fact that girls mature quicker than boys? And at about your age? Maybe in a few months' time he'll have caught up with you.'

Jade made a face. 'It'd be nice to think so, but I doubt it. It isn't just an age thing. I never told you, but he poked fun at my involvement in the anti-FGM campaign. Some of the other boys could see the importance and even got involved themselves, but Jamie refused. He told me I was wasting too much time on it. But I wasn't. I was still spending loads of time with him. Last Friday night he wanted me to go to a party at the football club with him, but I'd agreed to be on the discussion panel at the FGM exhibition in town. He'd known about it for ages, but he still thought I should pull out. I told him I could come along later but he got into a strop about it.'

'So are you still together?'

Jade shrugged. 'I don't know. The thing is, Mum, if he was the one for me, shouldn't I be feeling all weepy? Well, I'm not. I feel a bit betrayed and angry at his attitude but I don't feel upset, not deep down. So maybe it was coming to an end anyway. And in that case, do I really want to be at the same university as him? That's if he gets in anyway. They've given him an offer of an A and two Bs, but I don't think he's going to get the grades. He just doesn't take his work seriously enough, and I worry about that too.'

'Well, Jade, you know your own mind. Neither your dad nor I would want you to settle for second best, but we'll support you whatever decision you make.'

***

By late afternoon Sophie was back at Dorset police headquarters, talking to Barry and Rae.

'I didn't learn much, and I'm not sure we should spend any more time on it. Apparently the book is a standard background reader for ancient history courses. I'd imagine it's available from most academic bookshops, certainly those in university towns. By the way, Stu Blackman phoned. Apparently Phil McCluskie has had a relapse and is back in hospital. He started boozing again and his liver's packed up.'

Barry frowned. Then he slapped his hand on the table. 'That's it! Stu Blackman. I knew something rang a bell. It was back in September, ma'am. You were away at a conference and Blackman phoned asking for advice. I drove up to Dorchester to see him. There'd been a suicide, a middle-aged woman if I remember right. She'd left a diary with a lot of references to someone called H.'

'There are lots of people whose names start with the letter H, Barry.'

'Yes, but this H might have driven her to suicide, that's the implication of what she wrote in her diary. That's why Blackman contacted me. He wanted advice about it. But the

40

other thing was, ma'am, there was a small collection of books on history in the house. And one of them had a similar message in it. "Love from H," or something like that.'

'What was her job? The dead woman, I mean?'

'I think she was a senior midwife. In fact I'm sure that's what Blackman said.'

Sophie sat thinking for several moments. 'I think this needs a bit more time on it. Barry, you contact Blackman again and get all the facts. Rae, you can try and trace this Daisy person who sold the book in Exeter. I managed to find out from the assistant manager where she's working in London. The chances are pretty remote that we'll get anything useful from her but it's worth a try. It's possible that this H, whoever she is, was or still is an Exeter student, so one of us may need to pay another visit. It's probably nothing more than a huge coincidence, but we need to check.'

41

CHAPTER 7: LIAR! CHEAT!

Harriet Imber suddenly pulled free from her partner's arm and turned into the newsagents. She bought copies of a national newspaper and a local one that covered the southwest region, and walked back outside, scanning the contents.

'What's come over you, Hattie?' Maria asked. 'It's not like you to take an interest in what's going on in the world.'

Maria's skin was olive and her cropped hair was jet black, betraying her Greek origins and contrasting strongly with her partner's long, chestnut-red locks. She tried to slip her arm back into Harriet's, but Hattie was too engrossed in the local news. Nothing of note. What a relief. What was that saying of her mother's? No news is good news? Well, it certainly applied to her own current worries. Maybe a celebration was in order. She slipped the papers into her bag and grabbed Maria's arm.

'Wine. I feel like having a toasted sandwich for lunch and a large red wine. Make that two large red wines. At least two. Come on, let's get pissed.'

Maria shook her head. 'I can't. I've got a key tutorial this afternoon. You know that.'

'Why aren't you any fun these days? Talk about a fucking wet blanket. Life's for the here and now. We might see a couple of guys we can tease.'

Maria looked worried. 'I don't like your games, Hattie. We're together. Aren't you happy with that? Why do you have to come on to these young men, when you only plan to run out on them once they get interested? Aren't I enough for you?'

Harriet laughed. She flung her head back so that her long hair rippled in the breeze. 'Because it's fun. Because I like to see them get hot and bothered when I talk dirty to them. Because I like to imagine their faces after I leave them high and dry. They're men, Maria. They deserve it. Why should I worry about how disappointed they might feel? They're all animals, just interested in one thing.'

'You wouldn't treat a woman like that.'

'Wouldn't I? How do you know? I can act the way I like with anyone I choose. I'm a free spirit. No one owns me. I'm not answerable to anyone. I'm as free as a bird.' She pirouetted as she spoke.

Maria was clearly upset. 'But me, Hattie. You love me, don't you? Please say you do. I couldn't bear it if you ran off with someone else.'

'Don't be such a wimp, Maria. Of course I do. Tell you what, go to your tutorial and come to my room afterwards. I'll have a special treat for you, then we can go out celebrating tonight. We can postpone getting pissed until then. Okay?' She gave Maria a long, slow kiss on the lips and ran her hand over her buttocks, then slapped her hard. 'Time to go, Miss Goody Two Shoes. Run along.'

Harriet watched her partner hurry away and wondered about strolling back to the campus herself, but she still felt like a bit of excitement and novelty. It was Friday. Almost a week had slipped by after the events of the previous weekend, and the newspapers had gone quiet. Now the thrill was fading she felt a little flat, and she needed a quick shot of excitement. She glanced into the open doorway of a pub, her attention drawn by the clamour of voices, some of them young. She went in, blinking her eyes in the dim light. Good. Several groups of students at the far end, beyond the business types clustered at the bar. Who should she target? She went up to the bar and there he was. The youngest of the businessmen, all suited and tied and about her own age. He had moved aside to make space for her at the bar and, as she ordered a glass of beer, he turned and gave her a shy smile.

Ooh, easy pickings, she thought. She moved closer and pretended to be having problems opening the zip on her bag, giving her an opportunity to jab an elbow into his abdomen.

'God, sorry,' she spluttered. 'I'm so clumsy. I haven't spilled your drink, have I?'

'No, no,' came the reply. 'It was my fault as much as yours.'

She finally unzipped her bag and extracted some cash. 'I haven't been in here before,' she lied. 'It's nice, isn't it?'

'Here, let me get that for you,' he said. 'I've just had a bonus at work. Not sure what else I'll spend it on.'

'I'm sure you'll think of plenty of things,' Hattie replied, tossing her hair back and laughing. 'And thanks. I don't have a lot of ready cash at the moment.' She bent forward to zip up her bag, making sure he had a good view of her cleavage. 'So, I'm Hattie. Who are you?'

'Matt,' he replied, holding out his hand.

She ignored the hand, and instead leaned forward to plant a quick kiss on his cheek. Oh my, she thought. Is he really blushing again?

'That's for being so nice to me.' She sipped her lager. 'Friday afternoons are times for celebrating, don't you think? The weekend is coming, Christmas is on its way. I'm feeling happy. How about you? Why are you in here by the way? Business lunch with your office mates?'

'Yes. Well, I mean, sort of. It's a bit complicated really.' He took a sip from his glass of fruit juice.

'I'm a good listener. Tell me.'

'They're all from the local office. I'm a trainee at the Plymouth branch and I've been with them this week to pick up some extra commercial experience. I've finished now.'

'What, today?' she replied.

44

'This morning. I'm getting a train back this afternoon.'

'Have you been staying here all week?'

He shook his head. 'No. I come in each day. It was all a bit last minute.'

Thank you, God, Hattie thought. She exhaled gently. 'Any particular train? This afternoon, I mean.'

'Not really,' Matt replied. 'Why?'

'Well, I could show you the sights, since I'm an experienced Exeter resident.'

'Oh, okay.' He looked at her shyly. 'That sounds fun.'

His hand was still around the nearly empty glass. She gently traced her finger over his knuckles.

'We could make a start in my bedroom, if you like.'

* * *

Matt Brindle found an empty seat on the Plymouth train and sat down in a daze, only half aware of what was going on around him. His mind was still reeling from the afternoon's experiences in Hattie's small student flat. His body felt as though it had been through a gym routine, his groin ached and his anus felt sore from Hattie's probing. He had never experienced anything like it before, and was confused and bewildered, exhilarated and shocked, excited and muddled. Matt had continued to live with his parents after leaving school, and was still with them now, even though he was approaching his twentieth birthday. He was an only child, cushioned and cosseted, and had never in his life experienced such torrid sex. In fact, he'd never had sex before, his only erotic encounters being a few unsatisfactory fumblings with young women who, like him, were committed members of the local church, and who refused to go beyond some passionate snogging.

The train started to move, heading south along the Exe estuary before turning west to follow Brunel's magical route along the Devon coast. Normally Matt would have been gazing through the window, admiring the view and trying to spot seabirds scudding low above the waves. Today, there were too many thoughts and images swirling around in his brain. Finally he closed his eyes and dozed, waking up with a start when the train drew into Plymouth.

His elderly parents were both in the house when he opened the front door. He heard his mother call out a greeting. He muttered something in reply and climbed the stairs to his room, where he dumped his bag on the floor and flung his jacket on the bed. He grabbed a change of clothes and made a dash for the bathroom, where he stripped off and examined himself in the mirror. A few teeth marks around his nipples, a love bite on his left shoulder, and a definite redness to his penis. He needed to shower. He could smell sex on the skin of his torso, and it wouldn't do to leave it there.

Ten minutes later he entered the lounge where his parents were watching TV. His mother looked up and smiled. 'Alright, dear?'

'Yes, Mum. The train seemed a bit grubby so I thought I'd shower.'

'Cleanliness is next to godliness, dear,' his mother replied. 'Dinner will be ready in about half an hour. I've just put a lasagne in the oven. Is that okay?'

Matt nodded.

'Sally Pullman will be back from university for the weekend, so I expect she'll be at church on Sunday. Her mum told me at choir practice last night. Maybe you could wear that new tie I bought you for your birthday. She's a lovely girl, Sally. Clever too.'

Matt didn't know what to say. It was if the afternoon's experiences with Hattie had transported him to a parallel universe. Everything seemed the same, but it felt unreal. Finally he spoke.

'I met someone in Exeter this afternoon, Mum. We had a chat. She's really nice. I might see her again.'

His mother frowned. 'Exeter? Is she local?'

He shook his head. 'No. She's at university there. She's studying ancient history. She wants to be a museum curator.'

'So she's clever too? Must be if she's at the university. That's good, Matthew.' She appeared to be waiting, but Matt didn't add anything. Finally she spoke again. 'What's she like?'

'Really nice. I liked her.'

He felt his parents' eyes on him. Had he said too much? Could they somehow guess what had happened just from looking at him?

'What's her name, dear?'

'Hattie. Hattie Imber.'

'Well, it's early days yet, dear. Remember that Sally is a lovely girl, and she's someone we know and trust.'

Matt walked into the kitchen and poured himself a glass of water. He gulped down the first few mouthfuls and then sipped more slowly. His mother was so naïve. Hadn't she spotted the change in Sally since she'd been away from home? The glossy skin? The self-assurance? That new smile, with its hint of worldliness? He'd noticed it right away and guessed what it meant. His old Sunday school chum was now an experienced young woman. Maybe she was into the same type of adventures as Hattie, although he somehow doubted it. Sally's more restrained character and background wouldn't allow her quite the same free-wheeling approach to self-fulfilment.

* * *

Maria tapped on the door of Harriet's room in the student block, and pushed it open. The occupant was peering into a small mirror on the wall, touching up her make-up. She waved Maria in.

'Did you do anything interesting, Hattie?' Maria asked.

'Not really. It was pretty boring, so I'm ready to go out on the town with you. I feel like getting rat-arsed so if you're up for it, let's get started. Food first? I'm ravenous.'

Maria turned to follow her partner out of the small room and sniffed the air. Hattie was hiding something. The smell of sex was unmistakeable. Could she just detect the scent of a man? Oh, Hattie, you liar. You cheat! Saying nothing, Maria followed Hattie out of the room.

CHAPTER 8: YUM-YUM

Hattie's arm snaked out from under the duvet and fumbled for her mobile phone. The ringtone was meant to be the *Ride of the Valkyries*, but at this time in the morning it sounded like nothing on earth. She picked up the phone and gazed vacantly at the display. Ten in the morning? On a Saturday? Who dared to phone her at this time? The display read *unknown number*. She swiped receive and grunted.

'Hello, Hattie? It's Matt. From yesterday. You gave me your number.'

A short silence followed while Hattie tried to gather her thoughts.

She coughed, and tried to sit up, but Maria's arm and shoulder across her stomach pinned her in place. With some difficulty she took a swig of water from the tumbler beside the bed. Finally she could speak.

'Hi.' This time the words came out as she intended. 'This is not the best of times for me. Can I phone you back in an hour or two?'

She closed the call, put the phone back onto the shelf and attempted to slide back under the duvet and gain a few more minutes of precious sleep. No such luck. Maria had started snoring. Only gently, but with her mouth just a few inches below Hattie's ear it was loud enough to prevent her from slipping back into dreamland. Harriet sighed and lay still for a few more minutes, trying to come to terms with the new day. After a while the pressure on her bladder had become insistent, so she slid out of Maria's embrace and staggered to the tiny en-suite where she sat holding her head in her hands. Finally she stood up again, swaying slightly, ran some warm water into the basin and sank her face into it for a few seconds. Coffee: that was what was needed. Or tea. Whichever was closer to hand. She switched on the kettle and looked in the mirror. Christ, she looked awful. Not surprising, considering the night before. Two bars and a dance-club, before they meandered back to their accommodation block in the early hours. She ran her fingers through her tangled locks. Why had she given that innocent young man her phone number? Had it just been a moment of weakness or did he have some potential that she'd spotted at the time but which she had now forgotten? She yawned again. She made two mugs of coffee and carefully carried them back to the bed.

She poked Maria hard in the ribs. 'Oi, you. Time for coffee. Shove over.'

Hattie sipped her coffee and tried to think things through. Matt was another young innocent, just like Maria. No challenge, so not worth too much effort. Anyway, was she really ready for something new? Shouldn't she let sleeping dogs lie for a couple of months and just play around gently with Maria or Matt? No point stirring up muddy waters until she knew exactly how safe she was. On the other hand having fun with Maria, or even Matt, might be entertaining but didn't bring much in the way of thrills or excitement. God, why was her life always so full of these dilemmas? Too many choices! She finished her coffee, leaned over and began to nibble at Maria's nipple.

* * *

It wasn't till early afternoon that Hattie remembered to phone Matt back. He sounded both excited that she'd bothered to reply and a little disappointed.

'I was free today and could have got a train up to Exeter like you suggested yesterday,' he said. 'It's a bit late now.'

'God, sorry. I had an extra tutorial,' she lied. 'And I overslept. Things are so hectic, you know. It's a really hard course, ancient history, and I have to work like stink. But I'm doing quite well. How about tomorrow? I'll be free for most of the day.'

'It's Sunday,' Matt replied, as if this fact was self-explanatory.

'Um, yes?' Hattie replied, mystified.

'I always go to church.'

'God, yes, so do I usually. Why don't you get a train up here straight after breakfast? We could go together. There's a special service on the campus, I think. Or we could go to the cathedral. Then maybe do some more *exploring* afterwards?' Hattie slyly smiled to herself and listened. Yep. Matt's breathing had quickened.

'Okay, I'll let you know. I usually go with my parents, you see. And my friends.' He added the final words quickly, as if he were trying to assure her that he did have some.

'Sure, yeah,' Hattie replied. By now she was smiling broadly to herself. This was all so entertaining, so strange, even intriguing. It was as if Matt came from a previous age, one where people still lived by strict religious principles. And she'd hooked him. She had him in her grasp, a beautiful, innocent male virgin. Well, not a virgin, not after her exuberant efforts of the previous afternoon. And his body was all hers. Yum-yum.

'Did you just say yum-yum?' Matt asked.

Hattie spluttered. Had she really said that aloud? 'Oh, yeah. I was just looking at a photo of beef stroganoff in a magazine. It's making me feel hungry.'

'I thought you said you were a vegetarian,' Matt replied.

Sod it, she thought. Why did I tell him that? 'Yeah, I am. But mushroom strog is my all-time favourite and that's what I was thinking of. Listen, I have to go. I've got hockey practice. Will you text me later to let me know about tomorrow? I could meet you at the station. St David's is only just down the road from here. I love trains. I always think they're so romantic. Don't you?'

Hattie quickly closed the call before her lies got her in any deeper. Hockey? What on earth had been going through her mind? Running about on a cold, wet day with a crowd of Hooray-Henrietta types waving sticks in the air? Fuck that for a game of soldiers!

CHAPTER 9: WEDDING PLANS

'Mum, can you remember how you felt when I got my Oxford acceptance letter? It would have been just before Christmas when I was coming up to eighteen.'

It was Saturday morning and Sophie, along with her husband Martin, had spent the previous evening at the theatre in Bristol with her mother, then stayed over in her Clifton flat. Martin had gone out after breakfast to buy some newspapers and had not yet returned. Susan Carswell stopped reading her book and peered above her reading glasses at her daughter.

'Don't you remember?' she asked.

Sophie shook her head. 'Not really.'

'I was thrilled for you. I think it was one of the proudest moments of my life. Things had been so hard for so long, and I remember thinking that maybe, at long last, those times were coming to an end. Anyway, you deserved it. You'd worked so hard for it.' She paused. 'What's brought this on?'

'Jade just told us a few days ago that she's included Oxford in her university applications. She's got an interview at Keble later in the week. She never told us when she was completing her applications a couple of months ago. We both thought she'd stick to the newer universities, knowing her personality and her anti-elitist attitude. It took me by surprise, I can tell you.'

'Like you, then? That's exactly what I thought all those years ago.'

'But I did talk it over with you in advance, Mum.'

'So did Jade.'

'What?'

'Jade talked it over with me. If you must know, she asked me about those very same concerns, about elitism, and whether you felt them at the same age. I told her that of course you did. We had a long chat about it, then she swore me to silence. She didn't want you and Martin to know until you had to. I still remember hugging you for what seemed like a very long time. I didn't want you to see me crying, so I kept my arms around you for longer than I should have. If you must know, I wasn't just crying for me, it was for your father as well. Graham would have been so proud of you if he'd lived, I just knew he would.'

'I don't know what to say.'

'There's no need to say anything. Don't say anything to Jade, either. She's always felt the weight of expectation pressing down on her. The two of us have often talked about it. It wasn't the same with Hannah, because of what she's always wanted to be, an actress. But Jade has lived with it for a long time.'

Sophie was upset. 'But we've never put any pressure on her. God knows, Martin knows exactly what that kind of parental pressure is like. So we always made it clear that everything was her own choice.'

'I didn't say that the expectation came from you or Martin. It came from within Jade herself, just the same as you, all those years ago when you were the same age. It's fine, Sophie. Jade can handle it, so there's no need to worry. I think one of the key turning points for Jade was around the time of the funeral a couple of years ago. She got a lot more mature very quickly after that. My guess is that she's also been talking to Florence and James. I don't need to say how thrilled they'll be if she gets in.'

Sophie was too choked up to reply immediately. She recalled that Jade had spent a long weekend with her great-grandparents in Gloucester late in the summer. That's when she must have spoken with them. And she, Sophie, had been too bound up in her own concerns to notice.

She shook her head. 'What a failure I am. I didn't realise.'

Her mother laughed. 'You're no failure. You're the foundation on which this whole family structure is built. We all know it, apart from you. Give yourself a break, Sophie. You can't be everything to everyone, nor do we expect you to be. You do a fantastic job with all of us and you need to go a bit easier on yourself. Even Hannah says that. She's a keen observer of human nature and she ought to know, having watched you on and off since she was tiny.'

Sophie sighed loudly. 'They keep taking me by surprise, particularly Jade. We've always known that she's academically gifted but the insight she occasionally shows is staggering. I don't remember being anything like that when I was a teenager.'

'That's because it was you. We are rarely aware that our own personalities are exceptional. It all seems so normal to us. Yet you've always had great empathy, even when you were young. Lots of the other children hung around you. They used to ask your opinion about lots of things. Linda Fleming was devastated when you chose Oxford. She really thought you'd opt for Exeter, like her. I remember her mum telling me.'

'I kept in touch with her though. I used to go down and see her. I still keep in touch. I think it's so important to keep up old friendships.'

'You see what I mean? You still have that sense of responsibility. You think it's normal, but it really isn't, not at the level you show. And Jade's the same. So's Hannah, for that matter. You make a great trio, the three of you. The Allen women, out to save the world.'

'That sounds cynical, Mum.'

'Well, I'm entitled to be. Look at me, nearly at retirement age and still unable to make my mind up about what I want from the rest of my life. The neighbours still treat me warily, you know. They wonder if I'm a woman of ill-repute because I have boyfriends rather than a proper husband. To be honest,

Sophie, I sometimes wonder if I'm happier that way. I just couldn't bear the thought of getting married to some nice man and then coming to realise that he isn't really as nice as he seemed. He leaves his dirty socks on the floor, refuses to shower before bed, wears frayed cuffs, belittles me in front of his mates. I couldn't cope with it.'

Sophie was indignant. 'But Bill isn't like that at all. He's such a thoughtful bloke. And in our house, Martin is tidier than me. Aren't you exaggerating?'

'Probably.' Susan paused. 'He's asked me to marry him. Again.'

'And?'

'I'm thinking of accepting. But how will I measure up to his first wife? I'm scared stiff, Sophie.'

'You know, one of the great things about you having me so young is that there's only seventeen years between us. I'm so much closer in age to you than I am to Hannah and Jade, and when it comes to married life, I've got rather more experience than you. None of us can ever be certain, Mum, but I think it's worth a try. You'll be giving up your independence, sure, but you'll gain in other ways. Look, Jade really likes Bill. What more can I say?'

Susan looked pensive. 'Do you think she'd like to be a bridesmaid? Along with Hannah?'

Sophie looked at her mother through narrowed eyes. 'You sneaky individual. You'd already decided to say yes, hadn't you? And I'm sure both of them will say yes. They'd love it.' She paused. 'When are we talking about?'

'At the New Year? Maybe?'

'For pity's sake. When were you going to tell me? I need a special outfit for this. There can't be many forty-four-year-old women who get to attend their own mother's first-ever wedding ceremony. Should I go muted or bright? What are you wearing?'

'For goodness' sake, Sophie. Does it matter? It's not as though it's going to be a big church wedding or anything remotely like it. It'll be here in Bristol, in one of the quiet hotels and without any fuss. I've told Bill my terms and he seems to accept them. He knows I don't want too much of a palaver if I do decide to go ahead.'

'Who do you want to give you away?' Sophie asked, then realised what she'd said.

'You must be joking. Do you really think I'll have anything to do with some outdated concept of male ownership? You know me better than that. I was thinking that James might be happy to walk me down the aisle or, if not him, Martin. What do you think?'

Sophie smiled at her mother. 'Martin would do it like a shot, you know what he thinks of you. But James is the ideal choice if he'll agree, which I'm sure he will. It'll be so meaningful for him.' She paused. 'You know this is going to cause a few tears, don't you?'

Susan sighed loudly. 'Yes, I know. To be honest, that's why I've been putting it off. But then I finally came round to your way of thinking and thought why should I spend all this time wondering what to do? Just get on with it. So I did. Bill doesn't know yet, though. I'm telling him tonight.'

'The champagne moment? Would the two of you like to come across to Wareham for Sunday lunch tomorrow? You can break the news to the others then. Hannah will be with us. She'll be arriving late this afternoon and bringing Russell, her boyfriend, with her. The timing will be perfect, Mum.' She heard the sound of the front door opening. Martin was back. Sophie looked at her watch. 'Talking about timing, we'd better be off. I told Jade we'd try to get home for lunch. Thanks for putting us up last night.'

CHAPTER 10: FAMILY LUNCH

Sophie poured Bill a pint of beer from the small keg that was sitting on a rather too rickety table on the rear veranda. Bill was a tall, slightly stooped man with a head of pale, sandy-coloured hair. He looked slightly uncomfortable in his buttoned up collar and brightly coloured tie.

'Dorset beer,' she said, as if he'd challenged her. 'Can't be bettered.'

'I won't argue with that, Sophie,' he answered diplomatically. 'Where's Martin?'

'In the kitchen. Up to his armpits in potatoes, leeks, beef and lots of other stuff. You know him and his cooking. We'll take him a beer.'

'Are the girls up and about?'

'Not yet.' She looked at her watch. 'I'd maybe better rouse them. They were all out clubbing last night in Poole and I have no idea what time they got back. Hannah's boyfriend, Russell, is here. He's been up over an hour now, but popped out for the newspapers. He said he needed the fresh air. I'm guessing he was the only one who stayed sober last night. It was his turn to organise the taxis and shepherd them from place to place. He's a lovely young man. I'm so relieved that

Hannah's ended up with someone like him. It's a minefield, Bill. I worry constantly, but I try not to let it show.'

'What about Jade's boyfriend?'

Sophie frowned. 'Even Jade is beginning to have her doubts. Anyway, today isn't about them. It's about you and Mum. There's champagne for later. You are free to have as many beers as you like, but I would tactfully suggest that you don't, particularly with my mum watching.'

Bill laughed. 'Your mum and my soon-to-be wife. I still can't quite believe she's changed her mind about marrying me.'

'Just go with the flow, Bill. Don't start analysing her 'cause it'll be like entering a labyrinth. But you'll have to stay on top of things, you know. The first dirty sock on the floor and your marriage will be over, trust me. The way to her heart will be a cup of tea in bed every morning.'

'Oh, right. How do you know that?'

'Like mother, like daughter. I couldn't cope without it. I'd be a wreck.' She poured a little sherry into a glass and handed it to him. 'This is for Mum, her favourite. Just one glass, mind. We don't want her up on a table singing, not with her voice.'

They delivered a glass of beer to a slightly flustered look-ing Martin in the kitchen. Hannah had just joined him and had volunteered to help with vegetable preparation. She was sipping at a mug of coffee.

'A good night?' Sophie asked.

Hannah pursed her lips. 'So-so. Jade's chucked Jamie.'

'Really?' Sophie tried to sound more concerned than she felt. 'What happened?'

'He was being a complete arsehole. He was niggling her all night, and then he got drunk and pushed her so she fell against a wall and bruised her arm.'

'Is she alright?'

'She's fine, Mum. Don't know about him though. Jade kicked him on the shin then socked him in the nose. Russ and I grabbed hold of her and we scarpered. I think he probably had a nosebleed.'

Sophie put a hand to her brow. 'I can't believe this. Here I am, a senior officer in the county police force and my daughter is out brawling in a nightclub.'

'We weren't in a nightclub, Mum. We'd just left one. Anyway, he deserved it. He was being a right prick, picking on her all the time. She was really upset before it all blew up. If it had been me, I'd have walked out on him ages ago. If anything, she's been too kind-hearted.'

'Russell didn't tell us any of this when we had breakfast. He said you had a good night out.'

'Of course he didn't tell you. He's very diplomatic, as you well know. And we did have a good time before Jamie started having a go at Jade. We came home right after.' They heard the sound of running water in the shower. 'That'll be Jade. Don't mention it, Mum. She's fine. I went in to see her before I came downstairs. She'll tell you when she's ready.'

Sophie turned to Bill. 'And you thought I had a carefree family life, didn't you? I need beer.' She swallowed the remains of her glass in one mouthful. 'Let's take this sherry through to your future wife. At least she doesn't get involved in punch-ups on Saturday evenings out. At least, I don't think so.'

* * *

Sophie poured the champagne. She had asked Martin to propose a short, informal toast.

'I love it when romance is in the air,' he said. 'Although I have to say, Bill, that you probably need your head examined. Why give up your freedom for someone like Susan? Granted, she's warm-hearted, reliable, very attractive, has a wonderful personality, a great sense of humour and money in the bank, but why give up your freedom for such . . . unimportant things as these?' He waited for the laughter to subside. 'Seriously, you lucky sod, you've landed the best woman on the planet other than my own better half. So here's to Susan and Bill, and their very happy future together.'

They all clapped, cheered, and sipped at their glasses of bubbly. Martin added, 'Lunch will be ready in about half an hour. Jade, can you help with the starter?'

Sophie watched as her slightly pale younger daughter followed her father through to the kitchen. She then turned to her own mother and gave her a hug. 'Love you, Mum. I guess I can stop worrying about you now. One down and two to go.'

* * *

Sophie finally had a moment with Jade that evening, after Susan and Bill had set off for Bristol, taking Hannah and Russell with them as far as the local railway station.

'I know Hannah's told you about last night, Mum.'

'It's not wise to react like that, Jade. I know you were provoked but any police officer chancing by would have seen you as the guilty party and reacted accordingly. A night in the cells is not a very pleasant experience.'

'I know it was stupid, but I'd been bottling it up all night, and it really hurt when he pushed me against the wall. I just kind of erupted before I knew it.'

'It's a good job he didn't hit back. He might have really hurt you.'

'I don't think he could have done. Hannah and Russell moved in between us pretty quick.' Jade rubbed her arm. 'I'm a bit ashamed, Mum. I know I shouldn't have reacted like that, but it just seemed to happen. I'll be more aware next time. I've got a huge bruise. It really hurt at the time.'

'Do you want me to have a look?'

Jade nodded. There were tears in her eyes. 'I shouldn't have let it get this far. I should have finished with him weeks ago. That was part of the problem, keeping on trying to patch things up. It didn't work and it made him think he could say what he liked to me.'

'Will you be okay at school tomorrow? He'll be there, after all.'

'I'll be fine. He texted me earlier with an apology.'

'I always knew he had some decency in him, Jade. You wouldn't have gone out with him otherwise. It would be good if you could stay friends.'

Jade gave her mum a slightly tearful smile. 'And, Mum, I wasn't boozed up. I know you think I was, but I hadn't been drinking much. I wouldn't do that, not with you in the job you're in, and when I'm not eighteen yet.'

'Jade, you're one of the good guys. I've always known that. I see no reason to change my opinion of you, sweetheart.'

CHAPTER 11: TROMPETTE MILITAIRE

Hattie Imber sat in the cathedral, listening attentively to the sonorous notes of the organ. This was her quiet place, the only thing that could take her back to the inner calm she had lost so long ago. For her, there was no other route to peace. She knew why. Church organ music took her back to the time before all this madness started. She could appreciate the complex harmonies, being a talented organist herself. She'd been well taught, at the hands of an expert, and in more ways than one.

The music faded and died away. Hattie had forgotten where she was and who she was with. She clasped her hands tight, tears in her eyes.

'That was so beautiful,' she murmured. 'He's a magician.'

They got out of their seats and made their way towards the exit. She grabbed Matt's hand. 'That organ is pure history. In the whole country there's only three with a trompette militaire stop, and Exeter cathedral has one of them. I feel as if I'm walking on air.'

Matt didn't know what to say to this. To him, organ music sounded somewhat pompous and much too noisy, but Hattie clearly felt differently. In the few hours they'd had together she had never seemed so animated. He basked in the joy that poured out of her, and when she grabbed his arm as they emerged into the bright sunshine outside the door, he felt he was in heaven too.

'Oh, Matt, this has worked out so well. I wouldn't have gone to that service if it hadn't been for you, and I'd have missed that music. I'm in raptures.'

'It's so great being with you, Hattie. You're not like anyone I've ever met before. I can't believe I met you on Friday and this is only the second time we've been together. I'm kind of confused by it all. I couldn't follow that music like you could, but I love it when you're happy.'

She turned to face him, and kissed him hard on the lips. 'Let's get a quick lunch and something to drink. Then we can go back to my room. Okay?'

Matt's heart leapt. 'Where shall we go?' he asked.

'How about the bar where we met on Friday? It's the place that brought us together so we ought to give it a toast. Two lost souls, wandering the universe, and finally finding each other. I'm so happy, Matt.'

* * *

This time when Matt returned home late that evening, his mother looked at him with more suspicion. He felt her gaze flicker over him and saw the distant look in her eyes.

'Sally was asking about you, Matthew. She was surprised that you weren't in church with us. I told her you'd gone to Exeter to meet a friend. I think she was disappointed.'

Hardly likely, Matt thought. His mother was undoubtedly exaggerating.

'I was at church, Mum. Hattie took me to the morning service at the cathedral, and then afterwards she explained all about church organ music. She says that she can play really well and has had lessons since she was small.'

His mother's attitude seemed to soften. 'That's nice. What did you do in the afternoon, dear?'

'She took me round the campus. It's all landscaped.'

'That's what Sally said. She tried to get into Exeter but her grades weren't good enough. She said she's happy enough at Reading, though. She said it has a lovely campus too.' His mother's eyes hardened again. 'I still don't understand why you couldn't have got back here in time for tea. It just doesn't seem right, you staying out late on a Sunday. I dished up a plate of salad for you. It's in the fridge.'

'Thanks, Mum. I'll have it now, then maybe I'll have a shower and go to bed. I'm quite tired.'

* * *

Back in Exeter, Hattie was lying on her bed, staring at the ceiling and turning things over in her mind. Her blissful earlier mood had gone, to be replaced by one much darker. She rose, changed her clothes, slipped into her coat, pulled on a pair of high-heeled boots, put a few odds and ends into her largest bag and walked out into the late autumn darkness. Some things couldn't wait, and a special appointment with one of the university's most senior professors was one of them. He was so naïve. He didn't even realise she was a student here. But she knew very well who he was. She had photos from their weekend away together in the early autumn and was ready to use them when the time was right. She walked away from the campus towards the city centre and one of the more down-market hotels. This one had a back entrance, usually kept locked. Ten pounds in the right hands and the door would be left on the latch for an hour or two.

A short while later, Hattie was in her element. She finished tying his naked limbs to the bedposts, using a soft cord she'd extracted from her bag. This time she wasn't quite so gentle with the knots and he gasped. A slight smile played around her lips although he wouldn't be able to see it, not blindfolded. She took out the riding crop and sliced it through the air, listening to the swishing noise it made. She aimed a couple of experimental blows at his buttocks. He emitted a soft moan, whether of pain or pleasure it was hard to tell. Time to find the rhythm. She struck faster, harder and he groaned. He muttered something indistinct.

'Did I hear you say something?' she asked. Her voice was as sharp as a barb. 'Did I say you could speak?'

She reached forward, low over his back, grabbed his hair and pulled his head back so that his body arched. She couldn't see his face but guessed that he was grimacing. She struck him again, this time with more force. Her long red hair swung to and fro, in time with her movements.

'Fucking wimp,' she taunted.

She slapped him hard across his buttocks then slid her hand up between his thighs. She squeezed, hard. He moaned again, louder now. She laughed but there was no humour in it.

'What's wrong? Cat got your tongue?' Several more hard blows. 'So, is this more like it? Is this what you're looking for? You'd better be enjoying it because I've only just got into my stride. There's plenty more to come. You'll get your money's worth from me, I can assure you of that, you worthless piece of shit.'

CHAPTER 12: THE GAME'S AFOOT

Sophie was outside an upmarket apartment block in Dorchester. She rang the doorbell, and stood back. A crackly voice said, 'Yes?'

'DCI Sophie Allen,' she replied. Early on a Monday morning probably wasn't the usual time for detectives to visit witnesses, but it would help to keep this particular conversation on safe ground.

'Come on up and straight in,' said the voice. 'The door will be unlocked and coffee's on. I remember you like a good cup of coffee.'

Sophie listened for the buzz and pushed the door open. Pauline Stopley lived on the first floor, so Sophie mounted the stairs rather than taking the lift. She entered the flat and followed the sound of a radio through to a spacious kitchen, where Pauline was setting out cups and saucers. Sophie stopped dead in the doorway and Pauline looked up, eyebrows raised. Then she smiled.

'Ah, it's the hair colour, isn't it? I went blonde last month just to try it out. What do you think?'

Sophie smiled back. 'You look great, but then you looked equally good as a brunette. I heard that congratulations are in order. Is the new look marking your engagement to Tony?'

'Partly, I suppose. And thanks for the card. It was thoughtful of you.' Pauline poured the coffee and pushed a cup across the table. 'I've got about twenty minutes before I need to be off, so what do you want to know?'

'I saw Flick Cochrane, your walking group leader, on Friday and she thought that you might remember this woman more clearly than her. So tell me what you saw.'

Pauline gave a deep and rather exaggerated frown. Ever the actress, Sophie thought.

'We met up in the car park at Durlston at eleven. You know, the country park. It probably took us an hour to get to Dancing Ledge, what with the stiff wind blowing in our faces. I think we were almost halfway there when I saw her. We were on the coast path proper, just above the cliff top but she was on a path further up the slope. She was by herself and hurrying the other way, back to Durlston. I thought it was a bit odd that there didn't seem to be a dog around. I suppose it's possible that she had one, but I didn't see it.'

'Can you remember what she was wearing?'

'I don't think she was in normal walking clothes. She had a woolly hat pulled down over her head with strands of hair peeping out and blowing in the wind but she was wearing a coat rather than an outdoor jacket. You know, a normal knee-length coat like you'd wear in town. I think it was a reddish colour.'

'Does that path head to anywhere other than Durlston?'

'I'm not really the person to ask,' Pauline replied. 'Flick would know a lot more than me, but I think there are smaller paths branching off and heading down into Swanage.'

Sophie took another sip of her coffee. 'When you arrived, did you notice any other cars in the car park?'

'We all parked as close as we could to the castle 'cause we knew we'd need the loo when we got back. There may've been a small, blue car up at the top end but I can't be sure. Maybe Flick will remember. She was there first, being the organiser. Wouldn't she have looked around when she arrived?'

Sophie shrugged. 'Apparently not.'

'And that's it, Chief Inspector. I've been trying to think through what I saw in case I forgot something, but I think that's everything.'

'It's all very helpful, Pauline. By the way, what were your first thoughts when you spotted the body in the sea?'

'I was shocked, like everyone else, I suppose. Then when the police and rescue squad arrived and got the poor man out of the water I thought, "Shit. I wonder if that Sophie Allen will be round, asking me questions." So my first thought was to keep quiet about what I'd seen.'

Sophie laughed. 'Well it's nice to know I still have some effect on people. I don't know why you were worried though. I thought we parted on good terms.'

'It's the other thing still hanging over me. The Bristol stuff.'

'Well in that case, I have good news for you. They haven't been able to find any new evidence, so you can rest easy. The investigation has gone back into cold storage.'

Pauline closed her eyes momentarily. 'Oh God. Thank you. That means Tony and I can start planning properly. For our wedding, I mean. Will you come? Please?'

'I'll try. That's two weddings I've been invited to in one weekend. It must be in the air.'

'Who's the other?' Pauline asked.

'My mother. Like you, she's carrying a terrible sense of loss around with her. There'll be tears of sadness as well as joy.'

Pauline looked at her. 'I can't thank you enough for what you did. I know I don't deserve it. You must have thought I was some strange kind of she-devil.'

'The thought did cross my mind. But it's all in the past now.'

* * *

DC Rae Gregson was working her way through a list of possible places in west London where the erstwhile Exeter bookshop worker, Daisy Lancaster, might now be employed. This really was a shot in the dark, so much so that her immediate boss, Barry Marsh, had expressed serious doubts when Sophie had allocated the task.

'DCS Dunnett would have had a fit if he'd still been in charge, ma'am. We're treating this as if it's a murder enquiry, yet it's not. Not officially, anyway. Can we justify the cost?'

'Well, our good friend Dunnett is no longer in charge, thank God, so that particular problem isn't about to arise. And with a tentative link between two suspicious deaths, we have a duty to find out if that link is real or just a coincidence.'

So here Rae was, crossing out the name of the seventh company on a list of eleven, all financial businesses that had major branches in Uxbridge. She dialled the next number on the list and explained the purpose of the call.

'Yes,' came the reply. 'Daisy Lancaster is with us. Would you like me to put you through?'

Rae sat up with a start. Another voice came on the line and she again explained about the bookshop, the till receipt and the book in question.

'You're asking a lot, aren't you? Have you any idea how many customers we used to serve on a Saturday?'

'Oh, I can well imagine. But this wasn't a Saturday. According to the till receipt it was a Tuesday morning at nine thirty.'

There was a long silence.

Finally Daisy spoke. 'Yes, I do remember now. There was a Tuesday when I covered for one of the other girls. She had an emergency clinic appointment and I had no lectures then, so I did the first part of her shift.'

'So it would have been quieter than normal?' Rae suggested.

Another silence. 'It was so long ago. But one person does stick in my mind from that morning. I think she was a student,' Daisy replied. 'She was sneezing and spluttering. I wondered if she suffered from hay fever or just had a summer cold. She had long, red hair. Don't know her name though. I think I'd seen her before on campus a couple of times. Maybe a bit of an arty type? But I can't be sure that the book on the receipt you've got was hers. That's just asking too much of me. She might have bought something completely different.'

Rae scribbled down a few details and thanked Daisy. Was this enough to go on? Rae doubted it. At least it hadn't been a complete waste of time, but there was still no definite link between the red-haired young woman and that particular book. This meant that it couldn't be used as evidence. What had the boss called it? Intelligence gathering, rather than evidence gathering. All it did was help build up the background picture. Rae hoped that Barry was making better progress. He was looking into the female suicide victim. If her house had already been cleared and sold by the brother, they would have to rely entirely on the evidence Stu Blackman had already found there. That would mean they were really up shit creek.

***

'So the house has been sold, boss?' Rae Gregson was chatting to Barry in the office they shared.

Barry frowned. 'I suppose it was too much to hope that everything would still be there, untouched and waiting for us. We're talking months rather than weeks since Stu Blackman first contacted me and from what I can tell, it's a very attractive cottage on the fringes of Dorchester. Apparently it was snapped up immediately and the new owners moved in as soon as they could.'

'Is it really a problem? I mean, the place was searched pretty thoroughly, wasn't it?' She was puzzled by the time being spent on a suicide and an accidental death.

'Yes, I don't have a problem with that. I expect the family went through the place with a fine toothcomb, along with Stu Blackman. I think Rose Simons and George Warrander were involved as well. But the boss and I always like to visit to get a feel for a place.'

'Can't you still do that? Ask the new owners?'

'Not easily. We wouldn't want to let on that a body had been found dangling from one of the ceiling beams in their lovely new home, and that we were still investigating it almost six months later. What kind of message would that send out about us? Anyway, that's what the boss thinks. She said that we need to keep it very low key. How did she put it? "We live in an age of political policing and we can't afford to go trampling on the sensitive toes of Joe Public."'

'She has a way with words, doesn't she?'

Barry nodded glumly. 'But what we can do is chat quietly with the neighbours and friends. And all her workmates. My guess is they hardly touched on that before. Anyway, the boss seems to be treating this almost like a murder enquiry. So we have to give it the full works.'

'Does she know something we don't?'

'No, but I think she's convinced herself that there might be something wrong, and she wants to nip it in the bud before we have another death on our hands. If it is the same woman behind these two deaths, then she's right to push hard. Killers can soon get addicted to what they do. The boss is worried that she might have already chosen another victim. If that's the case, it's a race and we're handicapped because there's so much we don't yet know.'

* * *

Rose Simons and George Warrander walked out of Dorchester police station and made their way towards the car pool. The rain had just stopped falling. By the time Rose had scanned the underside of their vehicle and George had started the engine, the sun was beginning to peep out from behind the previously dark clouds.

He steered the squad car towards the exit gate. 'Where to, boss?'

'Winfrith,' she said. 'Our holy county headquarters. Your favourite detective in the whole wide world wants to pick our brains about that peculiar suicide at the old cottage. Remember? The one where we did a follow up search a couple of months after it happened. Peculiar or what? The game's afoot, as her probable ancestor was wont to say back in good old Baker Street. I wonder what's tickled her interest.'

George shrugged. 'Apparently there was a death down on the coast last weekend. Someone was found in the water after a storm. The talk was that it could have been a suicide, though the guys involved thought that it was more likely that he ended up in the sea by accident. The rocks were very slippery from all the rain and surf.'

'So what's the connection to the suicide we were involved with? You're a clever laddie. Anything there?'

George shook his head. 'No, nothing I can think of. But I did hear that there was a lot of searching going on in the Swanage area, interviewing bus drivers and taxicab people and the like.'

'Beats me, then. But that's what's in those files on the back seat. All the stuff from the suicide. And she wants a few minutes picking my brains. That's what she said. Fat lot of use that's gonna be. Where most people have brains, I have pickled walnuts. Ask me a hard question and my eyes glaze over. You were there when we did the second search of the cottage. Did anything seem out of place to you?'

George shrugged. 'No. How was she found? The dead woman, I mean.'

'Hanging from a beam. She'd also taken an overdose of sleeping pills and paracetamol. She wanted to make doubly sure, I suppose.'

'Isn't that unusual for a woman? The hanging, I mean? The overdose fits, but usually it's men who hang themselves, isn't it?'

'You're the one with the brain, Georgie boy. I don't know these things. Too morbid for a gorgeous, vibrant creature like me. Now let's get a move on. We don't want to be late. We've still got our routine work to do once we get out of Colditz.'

CHAPTER 13: HISTORY BOOKS AND
SKETCHBOOK

'There's nothing that links them. Apart from those history books, and the possible sightings of a young woman with curly red hair. What else have we got?' said Rae. She stepped back from the incident board to inspect the results of her work — the information about the two apparent suicide victims, Edwina Davis on the left side and Mark Paterson on the right. A middle column contained a few sparse details about the mysterious H.

Sophie came and joined Rae at the incident board. 'Rose Simons and George Warrander had nothing to add, though we've now got the case file to go through. Rose was there when her body was cut down, so that was useful. I've just been on the phone to Tom Davis, Edwina's brother. He got the house cleared as we guessed he would, but he hung on to those history books. He said they puzzled him. He's driving down today and bringing them, along with the diaries he found. This will be key, Rae. We need to compare the two messages and look for similarities in the handwriting.'

'It's still all very thin, isn't it, ma'am? What makes you so sure that they're connected? Aren't you staking an awful lot on what might just be a coincidence?'

Sophie shook her head. 'It could be the same book, Rae. That's why I phoned Tom Davis. To check. And the message seems to be written in the same place, on the first page inside, in the top right-hand corner with almost the same wording. What are the chances of that? I know it sounds unlikely, but I think we may have stumbled on something here. Look, I really don't know what to make of it. And Rose Simons just admitted to me that she felt uneasy about Edwina's suicide, but it wasn't anything she could put her finger on. Meanwhile, there's something you can do. Her brother said he took other books and stuff from his sister's house to a charity shop in Dorchester. Can you get up there with Barry, once he's finished what he's doing, and go through the place?'

Rae frowned. 'But how will we identify what was hers?'

'Tom completed a Gift-Aid form. That means his sister's stuff is all recorded as it sells, so the charity can claim the tax back on the sales. He told me his number and gave me a rough list of what he'd donated. Have a chat with the house clearance people. Come on, Rae, cheer up. You once told me you enjoyed rummaging about in charity shops and the like. While you're doing that, I'll be traipsing around the vicinity of her cottage and chatting to the locals, then paying a visit to her workplace. I need to get a feel for what she was like, and the only way I can do that is by talking to people she knew. I'll need to be back here by mid-afternoon when the brother is due to arrive. If you find anything that could have a bearing, call me. Okay?'

* * *

Sophie strolled around the area surrounding Edwina Davis's cottage, talking to anyone she met. She called at the local corner shop, the pub, the petrol station. Some people remembered the reserved, middle-aged woman who'd lived in Yardley Cottage, some didn't. A few commented on how helpful and supportive Edwina had been when they'd told her about their problems. A picture was already beginning to emerge.

Her final stop was a small hair salon next to the local store.

'Eddie Davis? Yes, she was one of my customers,' the manageress said. 'It's only me here so I get to know all the regulars. She was one of the best. A lovely person. Quiet when you first met her, but she was really bubbly underneath. I miss her. What a tragedy. I'm surprised to see you back again. It was months and months ago. I thought everything was all tied up, neat like.'

Sophie nodded. 'Yes, it was. But there are one or two loose ends. Did Edwina have any appointments in the months just before she died?'

'Yeah, a couple. She was in every fortnight, on a Saturday morning.'

'How did she seem?' asked Sophie.

'It was a bit odd, to be honest. There was a spell when she seemed almost high, as if she was on drugs or something. Really chatty, laughing, smiling. It's not that she was a miserable sod before, but this was *seriously* upbeat. Then everything suddenly changed. She looked ten years older, really worried, you know? But she wouldn't talk about it. In a way, I wasn't surprised when I heard the news that she'd taken her own life. I was shocked at the time but it kind of made sense when I remembered her last appointment, you know?'

'The time when she was so "up," did she ever say what was making her so happy?'

'It was bound to be a relationship, wasn't it? What else could cause something like that? A new man maybe? That's what I wondered at the time. She had someone staying with her but I didn't see who it was, nor did anyone else. He must have been a bit special to have that effect.'

'Did you ever catch sight of a young woman?'

'Yeah, once. I thought maybe she was a niece or something. Tall and slim with long red hair, a bit wild. The hair, I mean. Eddie mentioned a name once but I can't remember it now.'

'Please try.' Sophie crossed her fingers inside her jacket pocket.

The hairstylist screwed up her face. 'No, it's just not coming.'

'Could it have begun with the letter H?'

'Ah, yes, maybe.' She closed an eye. 'Hettie? Hattie? Yes, I think it was something like that. Not common names, are they?'

Sophie returned to her car and drove into the town centre to visit the maternity unit. She spoke to Edwina's bosses and work colleagues, none of whom had a bad word to say about their erstwhile colleague. Their picture of her was similar to the hairdresser's — a short period of intense happiness followed by a sudden dip into depression that she wouldn't talk about. One colleague had overheard Edwina muttering to herself, 'Why was I so stupid?' She also thought Edwina might have had someone staying with her during some of the happy period, but couldn't supply any details. Edwina had clammed up when asked about it.

'That was curious in itself,' she said. 'Eddie had always been happy to chat about her personal life before. I never got to the bottom of why she wouldn't do so on this occasion. It wasn't like her. It was almost as if she was being extra-cautious about it for some reason. You are aware that she was a member of the local board's ethics committee?'

'Yes. What exactly does that entail?' Sophie asked.

'They consider things related to professional conduct. They try to sort out problems before they get referred on to a higher authority.'

Sophie drove back to police headquarters in time to meet the brother, Tom Davis. She met him at reception.

'Why the sudden interest?' he asked at once.

'I'll be absolutely open with you, Mr Davis,' Sophie replied on their way up the stairs. 'We had another apparent suicide ten days ago, and there are some possible similarities. That's why I asked for that history book, but as I said on the phone, there was no need to bring it all this way yourself. I'd have been quite happy if you'd posted it.'

'Except that then I'd have been in the dark. I really wanted to meet you and find out what's going on. Look, Chief

Inspector, she was my big sister. She looked after me when I was young, after our parents died. I owe it to her to find out why she died, even if it was suicide. I want to know what drove her to it. I couldn't live with myself if there was stuff to find out and I wasn't involved. Can you understand that?'

Sophie nodded.

Inside the Violent Crime Unit's office, she introduced him to Rae and Barry. Tom took the slim book out of his shoulder bag and held it out to her, but Sophie told him to place it on the desktop.

'Has anyone else touched it apart from you?'

He shook his head. 'It's been in a box in our loft since I brought it home.'

Sophie used a pen to raise the front cover and stared at the message written in the top right-hand corner of the title page. Marsh leaned over to look, and Rae peered over his shoulder. Sophie put on a pair of latex gloves and took out the book from Mark Paterson's bedside table.

Tom gasped. 'It's the same one!'

Sophie flipped open the cover, exposing the message inside. Was the handwriting the same? It was difficult to tell.

'Where did this one come from?' Tom asked, looking shocked.

'The flat of the man who we think committed suicide ten days ago,' Sophie replied.

'So was he in some kind of liaison with Eddie? Was it him who gave her the book?'

'We don't think so, although we can't rule it out at this stage.' She looked at Tom. 'Did you ever discuss your sister's relationships with her?'

Tom narrowed his eyes. 'What do you mean?'

'Look, Mr Davis, we can't pussyfoot around if we want to get to the bottom of this. Was she gay? If so, you must tell us because it will save so much time. We don't want to be looking for possible boyfriends if you know she never had any. Come on, we need help here.'

Tom remained silent for some time. Finally he sighed. 'Yes, she was. We never really talked about it though. She just wasn't interested in men. I picked up on that a long time ago.'

'Thanks. And rest assured that bit of information stays in this office for the time being.'

'So is this H person a woman, do you think?'

Sophie nodded. 'It seems likely. As yet we know nothing about her. But don't worry, we'll get to the bottom of it.'

Tom Davis left, shaking his head.

Sophie took Barry aside. 'Anything of interest at the charity shop? The house clearance people?'

'Sort of, but I'm not sure how useful. Most of her clothes had already been sold, but we went through the stuff that was still there. We found this entry ticket in a jacket pocket, tucked right down at the bottom. It was no wonder her brother missed it.'

Sophie took the plastic evidence bag he held out to her and peered at the contents.

'It's for the Abbotsbury Swannery,' Barry said. 'Down on the coast past Weymouth. The till receipt with it is for two adults and it's dated April the twenty-sixth. Rae thinks that's one of the dates mentioned in her diary.'

Sophie thought hard. 'Yes. I've been looking at the case notes that Rose Simons brought across. Edwina mentions in her diary that she pulled some leaves out of H's hair on a walk near the coast. That's good, Barry. Definitely worthwhile. Anything else?'

Barry nodded. 'Yes. We visited the place that did the house clearance. Apparently the brother had missed a drawer in the base of the bed. Maybe he thought it just contained spare sheets and pillowcases, but there was this as well.'

He pushed a sketchpad towards Sophie. Using a pen, she turned the pages. Only the first five had sketches, and all were of Edwina Davis, in a variety of poses and mostly outdoors. Three were done in pencil and two in charcoal. All were beautifully drawn and all bore the single letter H in the bottom left-hand corner.

Barry still looked puzzled. 'Something else has been bothering me, ma'am. Those diary extracts. Why would Edwina have only referred to the young woman as H? Why didn't she use her full name?'

'My guess is that she was worried about the trouble she might be in if the relationship ever came to light and the diaries were found. In fact, that's possibly what drove her to suicide — the threat of exposure for having a relationship with someone who was vulnerable and young. Given her position as a responsible senior healthcare worker on the ethics committee, it would have had to be investigated. Maybe she'd have been suspended for a while. Edwina was hiding it because she knew the problems. Of course she never expected that the threat would come from the young woman herself.'

CHAPTER 14: SLUGS AND SNAILS

Barry Marsh had spent the morning phoning various travel agents and airline offices, looking for two women who had gone on holiday to Majorca in the early summer, seven months previously. Finally he found the bookings at a local Dorchester travel agency.

'Who was the other person travelling?' Barry asked.

'The name we have is Harriet Imber.'

At last, thought Barry. Here was their H. 'Is there an age recorded for her?' he asked.

'Nineteen.'

'What type of room did they book at the hotel?' Marsh was scribbling furiously.

'A double room. For four nights. According to our records, all the travel arrangements went to plan and they enjoyed their holiday. They completed a short online review when they returned. Is there anything else I can help you with today?'

Barry thanked the travel agent and ended the call. They now had a name. He went to Sophie's office and told her the news.

'That's great,' she said. 'Now we have to get back to Exeter University and see if they have a student with that name.'

Sophie had the sketch book open at one of the drawings of Edwina. 'Look at this, Barry. What do you think?'

'I'm no art expert, ma'am, but it looks good to me. It's skilfully done, I would've thought.'

'What are these down here?' Sophie pointed to the bottom of the sketch which showed the ground at Edwina's feet.

Barry looked closely. 'Good heavens. Slugs and snails. And is that a tiny spider about to run across her foot? I hadn't spotted them before. They're a bit faint and blend into the general shading if you don't look closely.'

Sophie turned a page. 'And this one?'

Again nothing stood out at first, but then Barry saw it in the fine detail of the grass at Edwina's feet. 'Is that a scorpion? Next to her toe?'

'Exactly what I thought.'

Sophie turned to the next page. Barry spotted it sooner this time. The innocent-looking birds in the background looked a lot like vultures.

'That's a bit sick, isn't it?' he said.

Sophie handed him a magnifying glass. 'Have another look. Take your time.'

Marsh squinted through the magnifying glass and examined a heavily shaded area of undergrowth. 'Is that what I think it is?'

The faces of several tiny devils could be made out, peering from behind the blades of grass, and looking up at Edwina Davis.

'Now the last sketch,' Sophie instructed.

Marsh turned the page and again inspected the shaded areas of undergrowth and foliage. Were those tiny figures there, hidden in the grass? He moved the magnifying glass around and then he saw it. Tiny imps, copulating in a threesome. He looked up at his boss with an expression of distaste.

'Look at that tree on the extreme left,' Sophie said.

Barry went over it again, trying to spot what was hidden amid the leaves. And there it was. Two tiny forms suspended in the tangled foliage. The first seemed to be a man, and the second was undoubtedly a woman.

Barry looked up. 'Did you say that Edwina Davis was found hanging from a beam?'

Sophie nodded. Barry returned his attention to the sketchbook. 'What about the first two drawings? I can't see anything unusual in them.'

'I didn't spot anything either, but the whole thing will have to go for forensic analysis. It looks to me, Barry, as if the artist added these figures after the sketches were finished. I can't be sure about it though. An expert may be able to confirm it one way or the other.'

'What would that mean?'

'That the artist, possibly this H person, made the drawings of Edwina and maybe even showed her the sketchbook. But later, when the relationship ended, she drew these nasty little extras before handing the book over. That's not definite, of course, but possible. They might even have been added by someone else.'

'How was it done? We needed a magnifying glass to make out the detail. How could someone draw something so tiny?'

'With a large magnifying glass, a very sharp pencil and a lot of patience. Whoever it was has a lot of talent. I'll tell you one thing, Barry, whoever did this is sick. What normal person would even think of such a thing?'

Barry shook his head slowly and returned to his desk. Time to phone Exeter University and trace this Harriet Imber person. For once, he didn't have long to wait. Yes, the university did have a Harriet Imber on their books. She was an undergraduate student on the ancient history course. Would he like to be put through to the Dean of that particular department? Barry soon found himself talking to a Professor Wendy Kominski, who sounded increasingly concerned as the conversation progressed.

'Can you come down?' she asked. 'Something as sensitive as this would be better done face to face. I'm uneasy about releasing personal information over the phone unless it's of immediate importance. I hope you don't think I'm being obstructive, but I have a duty of care towards my students.'

Barry sighed. Did he really want to make this trip? The boss seemed to like Exeter. Maybe if he put it the right way she might step in. He made an appointment with the Dean for the following morning and explained that one of the other team members might appear for the interview.

'What? You've never been to Exeter, Barry? This is your opportunity. And tomorrow would suit us really well.' Sophie subjected him to a short lecture on the history of the town and the university, then returned to studying the case file on Edwina Davis.

Barry left her office, and sighed again. He'd obviously given her the wrong impression entirely, and now he was landed with this bloody trip. Sophie and Rae were both graduates with degrees. Didn't they understand how he felt about that? Visiting a university always seemed to reinforce his feelings of inferiority. Maybe he should consider getting sponsorship for some kind of further qualifications. But what would happen if he failed? It would end up as a blemish on his record, always there. It'd be better not to start something like that, just in case. After all, he had justifiable cause for pride in his career so far. It wasn't bad for a Dorset farmer's son with a pretty ordinary school record. 'He excels at games and team events,' had been the most positive statement from his school years, along with 'a reliable and trustworthy young man.' His fiancée, Gwen, had a similar school background. Reliable and solid application, but distinctly lacking in any sign of academic brilliance. Maybe they were two of a kind, perfectly suited to each other.

CHAPTER 15: NEW HAIR

Dusk was falling as Hattie made her way to her residential block. She walked around the corner and stopped dead. A police squad car was parked in front of the main doors.

'Shit, I've forgotten something,' she said to the student she'd been talking to. 'I think I've left a notebook back in the seminar room. You go on. It'll only take me ten minutes to go back and get it. I'll maybe catch up with you later.'

She turned and hurried away. Maybe the police visit was nothing to do with her, but it was better not to take any chances. She looked at her watch, and made a quick decision. There might just about be time. She took a path that led towards the shops and pubs clustered around St David's station, past a small minimarket and a café until she reached a small hair salon. No customers. Maybe she was in luck. She opened the door and spotted the manageress sitting in the corner reading a magazine. Hattie forced a smile.

'Hi, Jen. Listen, do you have time to cut my hair? It's finally got too much for me, and I want to get rid of it.'

The stylist looked at her in surprise. 'What? Now?'

'Sure. Take it to a mid-bob length? And listen, can you get rid of this red colour? Make it light brown with a few blonde streaks? I know this is a bit sudden but I'll pay whatever you want. Cash.'

The hairdresser shrugged. 'Okay, but it won't be perfect, not at this time of day and in the time I've got available. I don't want you complaining afterwards.'

'Absolutely not. Just do the best you can, okay? I've ditched my boyfriend and I want to get a new look,' she added as an afterthought.

The new-look Hattie Imber returned to the student block some ninety minutes later to find the panda car gone. Even her closest friends wouldn't have recognised her. The slightly wild-haired, gypsy look had been replaced by something altogether more sophisticated and sultry. Her curls had been tamed and the chestnut-red colour was now a muted golden brown, with a few blonde streaks to brighten it up. Maria's jaw dropped when she realised who had pushed herself into the seat she'd been keeping free for Hattie.

'Better close your mouth, Maria. It's not pretty hanging open like that.'

'What have you done?' Maria gasped. 'You look . . . wow! I don't know what to say!'

'Jen did it, down at the salon by the station. I let her choose the look. It's great, isn't it? The new me!'

'But that must have cost a lot of money, Hattie. I thought you didn't have any.'

'God looks after the righteous, Maria. That's what my gran always said. Money seems to appear when I really need it. Maybe it's my fairy godmother. I always used to think I had one. I'm going to get a couple of photos done right now, and get my university card updated first thing tomorrow. I love this new look so much that it's going to be me from now on. I really fancy looking efficient and business-like. Maybe it'll get me a better degree. By the way, does anyone know why there was a police car here earlier?'

'Someone had their laptop stolen. I heard it was that Christopher Ealing on the second floor. You know, the one

who's always drunk. He probably left his room unlocked
again.'

* * *

True to her word, the following morning Hattie appeared at
the door of the university administration offices soon after
they opened, photos in hand. She even offered to save time
by helping with the laminating, an offer that was gratefully
accepted by the over-stretched staff. Hattie also helped them
exchange the photo on her official student record.

'That's so helpful,' the administration clerk said. 'We're
understaffed today because of the flu epidemic that's just
started. Your name rings a bell, by the way. I'm sure it cropped
up yesterday. Just wait a minute, will you?'

The secretary went and spoke to a colleague. 'Yes, there's
a message from your Dean's secretary. Someone's coming
down from Dorset to see you later this morning, so you need
to be back in your faculty building by then.'

'Who is it?' Hattie asked.

'Don't know. We only heard because Louise over there
was helping out in your department yesterday afternoon. She's
temping because of the staff shortage.'

Hattie's cheerful smile vanished. She turned on her heel
and hurried from the office, confused and anxious. What
should she do? She hadn't checked her message box or emails
yet, so maybe she should do it now. When she finally saw
the message, her stomach turned to water. Someone from the
police wanted to speak to her. He was travelling from Dorset
and would be arriving at eleven. The message slip suggested
that she should meet the officer, a DS Marsh, in the reception
area and take him to the interview lounge. Oh, Christ. Oh,
Jesus. Oh, God. What did he want? She frantically thought
back over the events of recent weeks. Had she made a mistake somewhere? She didn't think so. Fuck. If only she'd got
her hair restyled the previous week rather than waiting till

yesterday. Wouldn't such a recent change of appearance be too obvious? Had she left it too late? But she couldn't have got it done before yesterday. She'd had no money, for Christ's sake. Why was the world so much against her?

* * *

Hattie sensed a possible victory soon after she took the detectives into the interview lounge and sat down with them. The bloke had been wary at first, as if weighing her up, but now he seemed quite open and relaxed. The woman hadn't said anything. Round one to me, thought Hattie.

'Sorry, my memory's like a sieve,' Hattie said. 'Who did you say you were again?'

'Detective Sergeant Barry Marsh. I'm with Dorset police. And you're Harriet Imber, a student on the ancient history course, is that right?'

'Yes.' Hattie nodded eagerly. It felt strange not having her long, curly locks brushing her shoulders. This shorter hairstyle would take some getting used to. 'It's a great subject. I love it.'

'We were looking at your file just now with the Dean. I see your home is in Bridgeford St Paul, just outside Dorchester. I've driven through it a couple of times. It's a beautiful village, isn't it?' He smiled.

Hattie gave him her brightest smile in return. 'It's perfect. I can't imagine living anywhere else in the whole world.'

'Do you get into Dorchester very much? When you're at home, I mean?'

'Oh, yes. It's lovely as well. I went to school there.'

'That was at Corfedale, the private school?'

'Yes. But I've got loads of friends from all types of backgrounds. That's what's great about being here. I've made lots more friends.'

He nodded. 'The reason we're here, Harriet, is that we're investigating the death of a man on the Dorset coast two weeks ago. Mark Paterson. Did you know him?'

Harriet opened her eyes wide and shook her head. Her bobbed hair swayed gently. 'No. I don't know anyone of that name.' She put her hand to her mouth, looking shocked. 'How did he die?'

'His body was found in the sea. He'd drowned, but we're not sure how he ended up in the water. A young woman was spotted on the coast path nearby.'

'It wasn't me,' Hattie replied quickly. 'Why did you think it was me?'

'Your name cropped up on a list of possible contacts. Can you tell us where you were on Sunday morning, just over two weeks ago?'

She said nothing for a few moments. 'I was here. I didn't leave the campus. The weather was really bad, and anyway I had an essay to finish. It was due in the next day.'

'Can anyone vouch for you?'

This was proving tougher than she'd expected. Maybe this bloke wasn't quite such a pushover after all. She furrowed her brow.

'Not really. Oh, wait, I remember now. Later that morning I was with one of the engineering lecturers. He's keen on church organ music, like me, so I took him to the cathedral to hear the organ playing.'

'Right. What's his name?'

'Doctor George Markham. He's Canadian, just here for a year. The organ at the cathedral has got a trompette militaire stop which is very rare. I got to play it once. Anyway, he wanted to hear it so I took him that morning. Then he bought me lunch.'

'Isn't that a bit unusual? You and an engineering lecturer?'

She looked shocked. 'Oh no, not at all. Not in the world of church organ music. You quickly get to know all the enthusiasts. There aren't many of us, you see. You mustn't think there's anything between us. I've got a boyfriend, though he lives in Plymouth. Anyway,' she giggled, 'Doctor Markham is much too old for me, and he's really senior on the staff. He might be married for all I know.'

'And does your boyfriend like church organ music?'

She laughed. 'A bit, but I think he says so just to please me. He gets more nookie that way.'

Careful, Hattie. Don't get carried away. Hattie heard a slight movement and turned to see the woman pulling a book out of her shoulder bag.

'Have you seen this book before, Harriet?' she asked.

Hattie looked at the book and then at the woman's face. She was middle-aged, with short blonde hair, and dressed in a mottled grey skirt suit. She looked very business-like. Her expression was impossible to read and she had green eyes, like a witch.

Beware! thought Hattie.

'It's one of my favourite books on ancient history,' Hattie replied cautiously. 'Who did you say you were?'

'I'm Detective Chief Inspector Sophie Allen. I'm the senior investigating officer, and I deal with all suspicious deaths in Dorset. Tell me about the book, please.'

'I'm not sure what you want to know.'

'It has a message from someone with the initial H written on the inside.'

Hattie lowered her eyes and spoke quietly. 'I gave it to a friend as a present.'

'To Mark Paterson?'

She looked up again, seeming puzzled. 'No. I said I didn't know him. I gave it to someone else. A woman friend. For her birthday.'

'What's her name?'

'Why should I tell you? What's it got to do with this investigation you're doing?'

'Let's just say that it would be helpful to us. It would save us a lot of time and effort. The police are always grateful when that happens.' The woman didn't smile.

Hattie nodded as if she understood. 'I gave it to Eddie Davis. She was a family friend and she helped me a lot. I've been having a difficult time recently, and had a problem with depression. She was a really good adviser on health issues, and she got me through a bad time.'

'You say was rather than is. Why's that?'

Hattie paused. This woman was sharp. 'She died in June. Well, actually she committed suicide. It was a shock to us all. I really liked her.'

The woman pulled another book from her bag. God! It was the same book! Where had she got that from?

'What about this one? It's the same book.'

Hattie looked astonished. 'I don't understand. Is this some kind of trick?'

The woman shook her head. 'It puzzles us as well. Two copies of the same book. Can you explain it?'

'No, no,' Hattie protested. 'I bought a copy and gave it to Eddie in May, like I said. Why would there be two? This is crazy.'

'So you gave a copy to this family friend, Eddie Davis. Did you often give her presents?'

'No, but she took me away for a short break in Majorca because she said I was too pale and needed a trip to the sun. I didn't have much money so I got her that as a thank you present just before we set out. She took it with her and I used it to explain bits of ancient history to her while we were away.'

'Was it a family trip? Did anyone else go?'

Hattie looked indignant. 'No. I'm nineteen years old, for God's sake. She was forty-four! What are you suggesting?'

'I'm not suggesting anything. But the fact is, there are two copies of the same book, both from H. It's a big coincidence, isn't it?'

Hattie shrugged. 'Spooky things happen all the time. To me, anyway. The one to that man, whoever he is, must be from someone else.'

'Was, not is. He's dead, remember.'

'Well, I'm sorry for that, but I don't see why you're having a go at me. I didn't know him. I hope you find out how he ended up in the sea, but I can't help you.' Hattie put her hand up to her hair in her usual gesture, ready to pull her fingers through her long curls. But of course, there were no curls there. She frowned in exasperation.

The woman looked at her. 'You're a very attractive young woman, Harriet.'

'Thank you.' Hattie was flattered, but wary.

'The photo of you in your student file is a perfect likeness. You're very photogenic.'

What did the witch mean by this? She meant something, that was for sure. Did she know about the change of hairstyle? Was that what she was getting at? 'Thanks,' she muttered weakly.

'Do you know of anyone else who committed suicide, Hattie? From when you were younger?'

Trap, trap, trap! Don't say anything, Hattie told herself. The voices were starting to whisper in her head and she tried to ignore them. Concentrate on what this witch is saying. Listen and think! She shook her head, unable to speak. She felt cold, as if an icicle was resting against her spine.

'If anything else does occur to you, if you remember anything that might help us, please contact one of us. Here's my card.'

Hattie cautiously stretched out her hand and took the card, careful not to touch the woman's fingers. Her touch might be infectious. Oh God. How much longer could she keep this up? She hoped her loose jumper would hide the tremors running through her body.

Still looking at Hattie, the woman stood up, her lips compressed. 'Thanks for your help. We'll probably be back in touch.'

Hattie almost fled from the room. She walked quickly out of the administration block into the bright sunshine, and then ran towards the shrubbery. She stopped to check that she was out of sight, then grasped the railings, shaking all over.

'Fuck, fuck, fuck!' she moaned. 'Jesus, help me.'

CHAPTER 16: ORGAN MUSIC

Barry Marsh led the way out of the small office and back to the reception desk. 'We're looking for the engineering block,' he said. 'Could you direct us please?'

They walked in silence for a while. 'Well, that was useful,' Barry said. 'What do you think, ma'am? She seemed open enough, though a bit dramatic.'

Sophie didn't reply. He glanced at her but she seemed lost in thought, so he said nothing further. They walked on through trees and hedges, all in their autumnal colours. How beautiful was this?

'Here we are — engineering,' Barry announced.

They entered and were told to go up to the second floor. They took the stairs and soon found the door they were looking for. Sophie still hadn't spoken.

'You're quiet, ma'am,' Barry said.

'Mmmm.'

Sophie tugged at a lock of loose hair. They waited for the department secretary to finish a phone call, and then Barry explained who they were. He asked to see Dr Markham. The receptionist spoke quietly into the phone, and then pointed to an inner door.

'You or me, ma'am?' Barry asked.

'You.'

Doctor Markham was a fairly young, fit-looking man with fair hair, slightly taller than Barry, and dressed in denim trousers and an open-necked shirt. He stood up to greet them, and then sat down behind his desk.

He picked up a pen and began twirling it in his fingers. 'How can I help you?'

'This shouldn't take long. We just need to check the whereabouts of a student here on Sunday morning two weeks ago. Harriet Imber said she spent the second half of the morning with you. Can you confirm that, please?'

Markham frowned. 'Yes, yes. That's right.'

Barry waited but Markham said nothing further.

'So can you give me the details, please?'

'Oh, I see. Of course. We were in the cathedral for the late morning service. We're both keen on organ music.'

'And then?'

'I bought us some lunch.'

'Whereabouts was that, sir?'

'In the White Hart, if my memory serves me right. Then I came back here to get on with some work. I've no idea where Harriet went.'

'Have you known her long?'

'Not really. About six months.'

'And it was through church organ music that you met her?'

'That's right. I'm from Toronto, as you might be able to tell by my accent, but my family originally comes from Devon. My great-grandfather was a parish vicar and amateur organist. I wanted to find out more while I'm here. There's a small group of church organ enthusiasts in the university, and Harriet is a prominent member.' He paused. 'What's all this about?'

'We're not really at liberty to say, sir. But we're glad we can strike Harriet off our list.'

'Well, if that's everything, I need to get back to work.'

The two detectives left the building and walked back to the car park.

'What do you think, ma'am?' Barry asked.

'He was tense. That pen never left his hand. He twirled it around his fingers all the time we were speaking.' Sophie stopped suddenly. 'Let's go back. There's a staff chart on the wall near reception. I'll distract whoever's on the desk while you use your phone to take a photo of his mugshot. Totally unethical, I know, but I'm rather uneasy.'

* * *

Sophie and Barry drove to the cathedral and, after a frustrating hour, managed to track down the stewards at the Sunday morning service Harriet and Markham claimed to have attended. No one could remember them but equally, no one could be sure that they hadn't been there.

'Those stewards are quite elderly, ma'am, and, to be honest, I'd be hard pushed to recall something like that,' Barry said at the door. 'Should we head back to the car now?'

'No,' Sophie replied. 'Lunch first. I know the very place.'

She led him through the narrow lanes on the west side of the cathedral close until they emerged onto the busy thoroughfare of South Street. Barry glanced across the road at the old building opposite.

'I should have known,' he said. 'There's always a method in your madness.'

Sophie laughed. 'The beer's meant to be really good here. And you're driving.' They crossed the road and entered the narrow coaching courtyard of the White Hart. The lounge bar was dimly lit, with low-beamed ceilings.

'Lunch is my treat,' she said. 'Let's talk to the bar staff, and I'll see what ales they have.'

They were in luck. The duty manager, a middle-aged woman in a smart black skirt suit, had also been on duty for part of the Sunday in question. She looked at the photo Barry had taken.

'Yes, I remember him. He was with a young woman. But you're wrong about it being after the morning service at the cathedral. It was in the evening and they'd just attended evensong because I remember them talking about the organ music that had been playing. I'm pretty certain he wasn't in during the lunchtime session. We were fairly quiet and I would have noticed them. They both had venison casserole and I'm sure that wasn't on the menu at lunchtime. That's why I remember it.' She looked back through a pile of menus on her desk. 'No. It was definitely the evening.'

'And the young woman had a short bob hairstyle? Fair with blonde streaks?'

The manager looked puzzled. 'No. She had long, curly red hair. Really striking.'

'Right,' Sophie replied. She turned to face Barry. 'I thought as much. It was all too perfect this morning. A celebration pint is called for. Just a half for you, though.'

After their lunch, they returned to the cathedral. This time, they found someone who remembered the young woman and her companion, but at the evening service. So why had they lied?

'Can we lift them, ma'am?' Barry asked.

'No. It's too circumstantial. And what would we charge them with? We don't even know for sure that a crime has been committed. We need to tread carefully, Barry. More digging, I'm afraid. It may be time to cut Rae loose. She'll fit in like a natural down here on the campus.' Sophie looked at her watch. 'We'd better call in at the local cop-shop before we head back and let them know what we're up to. I don't want to alienate the locals. I like Exeter too much for that.'

* * *

They were back in their office by late afternoon. Sophie told Rae that she was sending her to Exeter for a few days.

'I need to know more about both of them,' she told the two junior detectives. 'Something's going on there and I want

95

to know what it is. But keep it low profile, Rae. Don't show yourself. The local squad know you'll be there but you only need to call on them in an emergency. We'll talk every day on the phone. Okay?'

'Of course.' She paused. 'Ma'am, there's something you need to know. After you phoned earlier with the information, I did a bit of digging on that village where she said she lived, Bridgeford St Paul. I didn't really expect anything.'

'But?'

Rae took a deep breath. 'There was an unexpected suicide there five years ago. The local church organist. Very talented. Apparently he was very well known in church organ circles. He taught some of the local youngsters. He was found hanging from a beam in his house.'

CHAPTER 17: UNEASE

The following morning, Rae paid a quick visit to the Exeter CID unit to let them know she was here, and checked in to her guest house. She made her way to the city centre and sat sipping a coffee in a small café. She wanted to get a feel for the place, particularly the university campus and the area around St David's, where so many of the students spent their time.

This university had a rather different feel to the one she'd attended at Portsmouth, with its city-centre location. Rae listened to the accents of the students in the café, and noted that a higher proportion came from wealthy backgrounds. A decade earlier when Rae had been looking at university courses, Exeter had been described as one of the favourite landing grounds for Oxford and Cambridge rejects. She wondered why Hattie Imber had chosen to come here. Was it because it was fairly close to her home, or had she been turned down by one of the top places? Rae finished her coffee, paid her bill and left the café. Time to start work.

First, she would visit the university security offices to see the director and pick up a pass. She walked north from the city centre towards the main Streatham campus and the administration offices. Soon she was in possession of her security pass and a copy of Hattie Imber's timetable. She made her way around the landscaped gardens, heading towards the large building that housed the ancient history faculty. Hattie was due to attend a seminar with her tutor at eleven. Rae sat on a nearby wall, watching the students come and go. She thought she recognised a tall, slim young woman who seemed to fit Hattie's description. If this was indeed her, she didn't look like the self-confident, bubbly character that Barry had described. Maybe it wasn't her. Rae followed her into the building.

A young man approached the young woman and spoke to her. 'Hi, Hattie. Into the lion's den. Did you get the essay done?'

Hattie gave an exaggerated scowl. 'Yeah, but it's crap. I had too much personal stuff to deal with. Left it too late. It'll be my worst mark of the year so far, I know it.'

'It'll still be better than mine.'

Rae followed the pair up the stairs, pretending to flick through the pages of a notebook. They turned in to the seminar room, while Rae walked on along the corridor to the far end. She had an hour's leeway, plenty of time to find the engineering block. She wondered where Markham lived. She hadn't mentioned him to the security director, guessing that the security staff would take a dim view of the police doing surveillance on a senior staff member.

She entered the block under the suspicious gaze of a porter. He asked to see her identification, and looked surprised. 'Security?' he said. 'You're new, aren't you?'

She gave him a vague wave and went over to the staff availability board. Markham was available for student consultations for an hour, late in the afternoon, in his office. Good. She would come back then. She walked up the stairs, turned a corner and there he was, standing in the corridor talking to a couple of other staff members. She walked past, aware of at least one pair of eyes on her. Normal enough, she guessed. She was wearing tight black jeans and knee boots, after all. But it was confusing to have men watching her. Part of her welcomed it. It proved that her transition had worked extremely well. But now she understood what it was like to be objectified in this way. Was it really all down to that bloody testosterone? Did the stuff itself cause some men to have an over-masculinised, self-centred, predatory approach to life? Or was it 'cultural' in origin? A societal norm? Whatever the cause, it was a relief to feel that particular cast of mind slip away during her treatment.

Rae left the building and strolled around the campus, matching buildings, paths and roads with the map on her phone. She returned to the history block in time to see Hattie coming out of the seminar room, chatting to a small group of fellow students. Rae followed at a distance. The group meandered slowly away, its members heading off in different directions until Hattie was alone with a young woman with cropped black hair and olive skin. She'd been waiting outside the seminar room, apparently for Hattie. A close friend? Rae was too far back to hear their conversation. The pair in front of her reached the student accommodation and went inside a three-storey block of flats. Rae seated herself on a low wall and enjoyed the sunshine. She already had a note of the room number and floor of Hattie's flat. Would the two of them appear again, or would they have their lunch inside? Rae waited, and it was more than an hour before Hattie and her friend re-emerged and went back to the history block. Rae followed at a safe distance, and then visited a café, where she asked some of the students about local hair salons. She was told of three that offered discounts to students.

Rae had decided to visit all three salons to ask the staff for suggestions about restyling her hair, mentioning that Hattie had recommended the salon. The staff in the first two didn't know who Hattie was, so Rae trudged round to the third, a much smaller salon near St David's station. The stylist happily described the drastic change Hattie had asked for just a few days earlier, and said how pleased she'd been with the result.

'I think she looks great,' Rae said. 'It's such a change, isn't it?'

She chatted for a further few minutes and made an appointment for herself the next morning. Why not get a new look while she was here? Maybe Craig, her boyfriend, would be pleased.

Rae arrived back on campus just as Hattie emerged from her final lecture of the day. It all seemed to be going well.

* * *

Back at police HQ in Dorset, Barry was searching for details of the suicide in the village of Bridgeford St Paul some five years earlier. Lawrence Jackson had been a well-respected organist at the local parish church for nearly eleven years, having taken over the role soon after moving to the village with his young wife, shortly after their marriage. He was forty-seven years old when he died, leaving a widow and two young children — a daughter of nine and a son aged six. The press reports concentrated on the plight of the family, and his wife, Rachel's, sense of devastation. Apparently she'd discovered her husband's body hanging from a beam in their cottage. Lawrence was a civil engineer, and had masterminded several large-scale bridge-building projects in the region. Church organ music had been his passion ever since his boyhood. According to the press reports, he'd won several awards for his engineering work, but even more for his organ playing. One press story stated that he would be especially missed by some of the teenagers in the area in whom he'd instilled a love for church organ music.

Rachel Jackson worked as a legal secretary in nearby Wareham. Barry searched for her name, but it appeared she no longer lived in Bridgeford. Where had she gone? And would it be fair to attempt to find her? She might not want to reopen old wounds. Barry managed to find a photo of her in one of the press reports. It looked as though she was much younger than Lawrence. He'd need to check on her age. If the report was correct, she'd have married at the age of nineteen. He continued to read through the reports, a slight sense of unease forming in his mind. It had been Lawrence Jackson's second marriage. Was there a hint in one of the obituaries that his first had ended acrimoniously? From the possible timeframe and the age of his second wife, it was possible that an affair with Rachel had sealed the fate of his first marriage. Maybe he would need to look for the first wife.

Meanwhile, Sophie studied the coroner's report on the death and examined the police log of the incident. The suicide had been totally unexpected. Jackson had no recorded history of mental health issues of any kind. His wife had discovered his body when she returned home after collecting the two children from school. Sophie imagined the horror she must have felt, seeing his body dangling from a noose attached to a ceiling beam. Apparently she had run out into the small front garden, dragging the children with her, all of them screaming.

Dreadful, dreadful, dreadful. Sophie shook her head. What would drive a loving husband and father to such an act? There were no serious money worries. The neighbours all said they were a perfect couple, and always seemed happy together. The two children were well behaved. No explanation for the tragedy had ever been found.

She walked across to Barry. 'I wonder if we should visit his widow, Barry? We need more information, and she's the only person who can supply it.'

'My thoughts exactly, ma'am. And maybe the same for his first wife?'

Sophie looked startled. 'I didn't realise. I'd only just noticed that he was a good bit older than Rachel. Where did you find out about that?'

'One of the obituaries. Rachel married him when she was about nineteen. Meaning that she was at least a couple of years younger than that when their relationship started.'

'So you're saying that she might have been underage when they first met? It ties in with what we suspect about Harriet Imber, if there was something going on between them.'

'Exactly.'

'And if there were something going on, and Harriet threatened to spill the beans, then that would explain the suicide?' Sophie looked at him.

'It fits, doesn't it? From what we know about the relationship she had with Eddie Davis? Eddie's diary entries suggest that Hattie was about to inform on her, and we think that's what drove her to suicide. A relationship between her and this guy Jackson would be far more damaging if she was underage at the time. He'd face criminal charges that would ruin his reputation and put him in gaol. No way out.'

Sophie looked at the photo of the mourning widow at the funeral. 'I think I know where she works. If I've got her right, she's a legal secretary at the solicitors Martin and I use. I'll phone my contact there and ask. If she's agreeable, maybe we can meet this afternoon.'

CHAPTER 18: SLEEPING DOGS

Rachel Jackson sat in the small sitting room of her home with her hands folded in her lap, looking pale and nervous. She was an attractive woman of medium height with fair skin and blonde hair, wearing slim-fit jeans and a mohair jumper, but she had chosen to sit in the shadow created by the curtains that draped the edges of the window, making it difficult to observe her expression.

'I have about an hour before I need to pick Bobby up from school,' she said. 'He's old enough to come home by himself now, but he just won't. I think he's terrified of walking in the door and finding me like his dad. He'll never come into the house from the front unless he's with someone.'

'Poor soul,' Sophie said. 'I feel for all three of you. It must have been a nightmare. An hour is plenty of time, Rachel. I don't want to put you under any stress.'

'Tell me again why you need to see me,' Rachel said. 'It was five years ago, and I've been trying to forget, to build a new life for us. To have to remember it all again is just so hard.'

'We wouldn't put you through this unless we had to, Rachel. It's just that there have been two other more recent suicides in the county, and we're looking for a pattern.'

Rachel looked puzzled. 'I'm not sure I understand. How can there be a pattern to suicides? They're all down to the victim's personal circumstances, aren't they? Why would there be a link?'

'That's what we're trying to discover. Please bear with me. I want to ask you some questions about the death of your husband. I'll try and be as gentle as possible. I've looked at the case details that we have on record and I've read the coroner's report. The facts aren't at issue here. I'd like to learn a little bit more about your late husband and his contacts in the village.'

Rachel sat forward and stared at Sophie. 'What do you mean?'

'Well, it seems obvious that his death was a total shock to everyone. He wasn't suffering from depression and there weren't any overwhelming money issues as far as I can see, so I think we can discount those as likely reasons. Am I right?'

Rachel nodded. She looked wary.

'What I want to do is to look for other possible causes. I need you to be honest with me, Rachel. Had Lawrence somehow got himself trapped in a corner, one from which he could see no way out?'

Rachel flushed. 'I don't know,' she snapped. 'Don't you think I haven't thought about that? Don't you think I haven't spent countless sleepless nights turning it over and over in my mind? I never got anywhere. All I could do was speculate. But it was poisoning my memory of him, so in the end I forced myself to stop.'

'Why did you move away from the village, Rachel? You must have had friends there who would have supported you? Why come into the town?'

Rachel looked away and played with the handle of her cup. 'It's more convenient for us. I don't have to drive everywhere. I can just walk to work and to the schools. Even the shops are only ten minutes on foot.'

'You didn't feel a need to escape?'

'Whatever gives you that idea?' Rachel's indignation sounded forced.

Sophie decided to change tack. 'You were nineteen when you married Lawrence. How did you meet?'

'I took lessons with him in church organ music.'

'Was that here in Dorset?'

Rachel shook her head slowly. She seemed tired. She placed her cup back on its saucer. 'In Somerset, a village near Taunton.'

'How old were you when you first started those lessons?'

'Sixteen, I guess?' She dropped her eyes. 'I can't remember exactly.'

'And how long until you realised that there was something more to the relationship?'

Rachel looked miserable. She spoke in a whisper. 'A year maybe.' She continued to look at the floor, her hands clasped together. The knuckles were white.

'He was married at the time. Was the split a messy one?'

Rachel nodded. 'I realise that now. I didn't pay much attention to it at the time. I just felt so alive and loved. Everything was rosy for me. I didn't want to spoil it by getting involved with his break-up from Caroline, his first wife. As time's gone by I've felt more and more guilty. Why did I do it? How much hurt did I cause her? I'm not a cruel person really. I was just swept along by it all.'

Sophie breathed out. She had to ask. 'Rachel, is it possible that the whole pattern might have been about to repeat itself? Could Lawrence have formed an attachment with someone else, someone young, much as you'd been when you first met him?'

Rachel burst into tears. Sophie waited. When her sobs had subsided Rachel began to talk in a low monotone. 'I thought it was me, that I was less attractive. The children wore me out when they were toddlers, and I was still trying to work part-time. I was always exhausted. I sensed that something was wrong, but I never thought it could be that. And before I could ask him about what was wrong, he was dead. I've never told a soul. I always thought it would spoil my memory of him. He was good to me. He showed me so much consideration and kindness, always. The children as well.'

'Did you suspect anyone? Any of the young women who were taking lessons from him?'

Rachel shook her head. 'I just didn't want to believe it. The whole village rallied round and supported the three of us. I felt guilty when we moved away, but it had to be done. I needed to break with the past and start afresh. It was the right thing to do.' She gazed at Sophie, almost pleadingly.

'I'm not disputing that, Rachel. I'd probably have done the same thing in your position. You haven't answered my question, though.'

'No, I know I haven't.' She paused, and then continued in a whisper. 'It was curious. In the days that followed, I kept seeing a girl sitting on a wall across the village green from where we lived. I'd never seen her there before. She seemed to be watching our cottage. I put it down to my over-active imagination. It only happened a few times and I never saw her again.'

'Can you remember anything about her?'

'It was five years ago, for God's sake!' Rachel's voice was stronger now, and more abrupt. 'What do you expect from me? She may have had long hair, but I really can't be sure.' She fixed her eyes on Sophie again. 'Look, what is this all about? You must be raking over all of this for a reason. What's this pattern that you mentioned earlier?'

'I can't tell you that, Rachel. Not yet, anyway. I promise to keep you informed, though, if we do find anything relevant to Lawrence's death. If anything else crops up, would you be willing to speak to us again?'

Rachel sighed, and slowly nodded.

The two detectives let themselves out.

* * *

Outside the door, Barry ran a hand over his head. 'Phew. That was definitely worthwhile. What are your thoughts, ma'am?'

'Same as yours, I expect. It sounds as though Lawrence Jackson had a penchant for teenage girls. He may or may not have been a paedophile, it depends on how young they were. She was a bit cagey about precisely when they started having sex, and I didn't want to push it on this occasion, but we may need to see her again and turn the screw a bit more. By the way, his first wife was eighteen when they married, even younger than Rachel. We'll need to track her down and speak to her as well. I wonder if she still lives in Somerset?'

'Do you think the girl on the wall could have been Harriet Imber?'

Sophie shrugged. 'Possibly. If it was her, then our man Lawrence Jackson suddenly found out that he'd bitten off more than he could chew. It must have all seemed so smooth to him while he was in control. But with her? Eventually she turned the tables on him. Where would that have left him? With nowhere to hide and his whole social status at risk, plus a young wife and family who, it seems, he really did love. Maybe he killed himself to protect them. My guess is that Rachel began to suspect what had happened after he died. Maybe she even had an idea who it was. I don't think she was telling the truth about her reason for moving into Wareham, not the whole truth anyway. She was very cagey about some things. What if she herself was underage when they started having sex? She'd want to keep that under wraps. She's got two children by him, for goodness' sake. She wouldn't want to mess with their futures. Better to let sleeping dogs lie.'

CHAPTER 19: HIGH HEELS

There was Hattie, disappearing from view as she turned into the stairwell in the geography block. Why was she here, in geography? Looking for a friend? Rae walked up the stairs and pretended to inspect the noticeboard. The lists of tutorial groups, seminars and lectures reminded her of her own days as a university student, back in her previous life as a man. Thank goodness that was all over.

She saw Hattie stop for a moment outside an office door. Rae stopped too, and rummaged inside her bag as if she was looking for something. She pulled out her phone and thumbed an imaginary text. She could see Hattie hesitate and glance around. Then she bent down and slid an envelope under the door. She hurried away from the office, looking back over her shoulder, almost colliding with Rae.

'Watch it,' said Rae.

'Fuck off,' Hattie replied, and walked quickly away.

Rae wasn't sure what to do. Should she follow Hattie, who seemed to be keyed up and in a hurry, or try to identify the occupant of that office? Maybe she could manage both. She approached the door. Its nameplate read 'Professor Paul Murey.' She couldn't see the envelope. Rae listened and heard movement inside, so she backed away and stood looking at the noticeboard. The door opened and a man peered out. He was around forty, thickset with dark hair greying at the temples and was wearing a loose shirt and chino trousers.

'Was there someone here?' he asked brusquely. His voice had a trace of a Scottish accent.

'Someone pushed past me on the stairs,' Rae replied truthfully. 'Why?'

The man opened his mouth to speak, then shrugged, stepped back inside his office and closed the door. Rae sped towards the stairs and made for the exit. She caught sight of her quarry in the distance. Where would Hattie go now? Back to her room, or off to somewhere else where she could let off steam? She saw Hattie come to a stop in front of her, a mobile phone to her ear. Who might she be calling? If it comes to it, thought Rae, we can always examine her call log. Rae checked the time on her watch. This idea triggered another chain of thought. If Hattie needed to get a message to this Professor Murey, why hadn't she just called him or sent a text message? It was a bit odd, in this technological age, to slide envelopes under doors, messages that might be accidentally picked up by someone else.

Hattie started walking again, back to her accommodation block. Had she arranged to meet someone? Rae followed, keeping well back from the hurrying figure. Hattie entered the block, and Rae followed, falling in behind a small cluster of students entering the building. She climbed the stairs to Hattie's floor, taking care as she rounded the corner that Hattie wasn't still in view. The corridor was almost deserted so Rae slid into a recess and pretended to check her phone. Almost immediately the spiky-haired young woman she'd seen earlier appeared and hurried to Hattie's room. Maybe she was Hattie's closest friend. If so, it might be worth finding out a little more about her, in addition to Markham and Professor Murey.

* * *

The weather was taking a turn for the worse, with squally showers forecast overnight. Rae wore a dark coloured parka, ready for an evening stake out of Markham's home. She had asked Barry to find the address. Markham rented one of two first-floor flats in a converted Edwardian house situated in a quiet neighbourhood not far from the campus. Rae parked in a secluded spot on the opposite side of the road and got out. She put her hood up and slid her gloved hands into her pockets. At present the rain was little more than a drizzle but she could feel the breeze strengthening as she made her way across the deserted street.

She took a look around. The large detached Edwardian house was half-hidden behind tall hedges, and the garden was filled with shrubs. A short driveway opened into a parking area to the right, where four cars were neatly lined up against a wall. The only security light seemed to be a dim lamp above the front porch. The small front gate had been left partially open so Rae slipped inside and stood beneath the hedge while her eyes adjusted to the near darkness. She could hear the faint sound of music coming from one of the flats. Church organ music? Yes, that was it. She decided to stay where she was for a while longer, giving herself time to map out the probable location and direction of paths and grass verges. Once she started moving, she didn't want to stumble into flower beds or tread on any undergrowth that might give her away. She was just about to take the first step when she heard the squeak of a gate opening, over to her right. A tall, slim figure appeared and Rae heard heels tapping up the path. Then Hattie appeared, silhouetted against the faint light from the lamp above the door. She pushed a button and turned her back to the door. Rae held her breath. Surely she'd be seen? At the faint sound of a buzzer, Hattie stepped inside. The door closed behind her with a gentle click.

Rae breathed deeply. Interesting. Hattie had changed her clothes and was presumably wearing a skirt or dress under her coat, but it was the shiny, high-heeled boots that had caught

Rae's attention. Those four inch heels couldn't be easy to walk in. Rae made her way along a narrow path that ran along the side of the house, past the open window. A vent was fitted to the wall just beyond the window and Rae could detect the faint smell of food cooking. She suddenly felt hungry. Maybe she should have eaten before setting out on this scouting expedition. There was the sound of voices, discernible above the organ music, but it was impossible to identify what was being said. A low, male voice and a higher one, probably Hattie's. Suddenly the music was switched off, mid-passage. A man's voice, close to the window, said, 'That's everything in. I'll turn it down and it'll be ready in an hour. Shall we go and play?'

That's got to be Markham, Rae thought. She continued around the rear of the property. A low, pink light glowed out from behind a curtained window, but Rae could neither hear nor see anything. She waited for a while, and then gave up. She was almost at the gate when she ran up against something soft and heard a young woman's voice uttering an exclamation. It sounded Greek. She saw a dark figure turn and hurry away. The scared face glancing back at her was that of Hattie's spiky-haired friend. She must have followed Hattie and stayed by the gate, watching and waiting. Was she spying on Hattie? What was going on? Rae watched her until she was out of sight, then crossed the road and slid into the driver's seat of her car. She might be in for a long wait. Better to be out of the wind and rain.

An hour passed, and then another. A nearby church bell struck ten o'clock, its sound muffled slightly by the dampness in the air. How much longer should she wait? Maybe Hattie would stay the night. Rae needed to find something to eat before returning to her bed and breakfast hotel. Then she became aware of movement at Markham's flat. A familiar tall figure emerged through the door. What was she doing? Illuminated by the overhead light, Hattie bent down. Of course. She was removing her high-heeled boots. She took a pair of shoes from her capacious shoulder bag, put them on and continued on her way, silent now in her new footwear. Thank goodness for that. At last Rae could think about getting warm, getting some food and then getting into bed. Luxury. And then she realised that Hattie was heading directly away from the campus. Rae got out of the car and crossed the road. Luckily the wind had picked up, covering the sound of her footfalls.

Less than five minutes after she'd left Markham's flat, Hattie stopped outside a detached house in a secluded side street, her outline almost merging with that of a tall gatepost. She stood watching the house for a while, then opened the gate and slipped inside. Rae hurried the few yards to the entrance, moving silently and keeping to the shadows. She stood still, listening. Just above the sound of the breeze, she heard movement in the undergrowth. The clouds cleared momentarily and in the moonlight Rae made out the figure of Hattie in the act of flinging a handful of something towards one of the upstairs windows. She turned back towards the gate as the rattle of gravel hitting glass sounded across the small garden. Rae shrank back into the shadows as Hattie hurried out of the gate and walked quickly away, this time heading in the direction of the campus. Rae saw a light go on inside. A curtain was drawn back and two faces appeared at the window, peering out into the gloom. Could the one on the left be the professor she'd briefly spoken to in the late afternoon? The recipient of Hattie's envelope, Paul Murey? The other must be his wife. This was getting more and more intriguing.

Maybe Markham wasn't the target of Hattie's current campaign after all. Could it be Murey?

She walked back to her car and climbed in wearily. Tomorrow was Friday, which gave her the daytime hours before her boyfriend, Craig, joined her in Exeter for the evening. He would be staying over until Saturday afternoon, when they would both return to Dorset. She and Craig would be off clubbing on Friday night, if she could identify Hattie's favourite haunts in time. With Craig there, Rae wouldn't look out of place, and she wouldn't feel vulnerable, something that was still a problem for her when visiting a club alone, late at night.

'Your job is to stay out of trouble,' Rae had told Craig. 'Not that I'm expecting any.'

CHAPTER 20: PREDATOR

Caroline McLelland, Lawrence Jackson's first wife, was almost the exact opposite of Rachel, her successor. She was shorter than average, dark haired, olive skinned and more heavily built, almost matronly. She invited the two detectives into her small terraced house and showed them into a tiny lounge. She cleared a small table and asked them to sit down.

'You're about five years too late, aren't you? What's this all about?'

'It's a bit difficult to explain, Mrs McLelland. It's a new investigation but it might touch upon your ex-husband's death. We won't know until we find out more about him. What we do know is that he told no one that Rachel was his second wife.'

Caroline gave a sardonic laugh. 'Well, isn't that a surprise? When it came to relationships, he was a devious schemer. He had every reason for keeping quiet about his background, believe me. It's no wonder he reinvented himself when he moved to Bridgeford with her.'

'Do you feel animosity towards Rachel?' Sophie asked.

Caroline responded with a deep sigh. 'No, not for a long time now, if I ever did. When we all first met I thought she was a lovely girl, a young innocent. I realised afterwards that he'd planned it all from the moment he first set eyes on her, when she first turned up for organ lessons. She was a dream for someone like him. Slim, blonde, blue eyes. Really angelic.'

'When you say "someone like him," what do you mean exactly, Caroline?'

'He was a predator. He had a thing about teenage girls but he hid it so well that we, his victims, had no idea what was going on.'

'Did the same thing happen to you?'

'Pretty well. But we were a bit closer in age. I was fourteen when we first met, and he was twenty-two. Same method though, through church organ lessons. I hate the bloody things now. Never go near a church if I can help it, not if it's likely to have an organ playing.'

'What are your circumstances now? Are you single?'

'God, no. Though it took me a while to get over what happened. I've been with Graham for ten years and we got married three years ago. He's a really decent guy, with no airs or graces like you-know-who. And no twisted kinks either.'

'Did Lawrence's behaviour go deeper than just wanting to be with younger women?'

'Yeah, in a way. He liked me to dress up as a teenager. I didn't mind. In fact I quite enjoyed it and didn't see any harm in it. I still don't. The trouble was, he was also out looking for the real thing — chatting to young girls, suggesting things to them. I told him to stop but obviously he couldn't. I don't think anything happened with any of them until Rachel came along.'

'How old were you when you first had sex with him?'

Caroline didn't answer immediately. 'This was all long before Jimmy Savile. It wasn't the big thing it is today.' She sighed. 'It was on my fifteenth birthday. He invited me over to his flat. He cooked a meal for me. We drank some wine. I felt so mature, so grown up. I suppose I knew what might happen and I sort of wanted it. I dressed up in a sexy way and acted a bit provocative. It made me feel sort of in control. I didn't see at the time how he'd manipulated me into behaving like that. Anyway, the sex was really great. He wasn't a dirty old man in the traditional sense. He could be really romantic and he was good-looking. We had sex fairly regularly until we got married when I was eighteen.'

'What did your parents think? Didn't they realise what was going on?'

Caroline shook her head. 'My dad died when I was young and my mum really struggled. She had a new boyfriend about that time and I didn't like him. Meeting Lawrence gave me a way out, and getting married to him gave Mum the freedom to do whatever she wanted. It was win-win all round. Or so I thought.'

'Do you think the same kind of thing happened with Rachel? What was it, six years later?'

'I'm sure of it. He arranged a weekend break for me to go and visit my mum in Derby. I found out later that it coincided with Rachel's sixteenth birthday. This time he made sure she was legal. Whether they'd had sex before then I could never tell. It wouldn't surprise me. Anyway, what's to gain from knowing? He's long dead and good riddance. I breathed a sigh of relief when I heard, I can tell you.' She paused. 'Had he done it again? Is that why he killed himself? Was someone going to spill the beans on him? He couldn't have coped with that, particularly once he got a higher profile in his work. The thought of being humiliated terrified him. That became clear to me once we'd split up.'

'We don't know for sure. If it did happen that way, then he chose the wrong victim.' Sophie paused. 'Did he continue your maintenance payments right up to when he died?'

'It's funny you should mention that. They stopped a couple of months before his death. I briefly contacted Rachel about it after his funeral, but she didn't seem to know what I was talking about. I remember her saying that more money was going out of their account than ever, so how could my payments have stopped? I decided to let it drop. She was in a right state and I was worried for their children. Thank God I never had any by him.'

* * *

Sophie and Barry sat in the car. 'That was all very interesting, ma'am, but it doesn't really get us anywhere, does it?' Barry said.

'A couple of things, Barry. Technically, you're right. We're not even looking into Jackson's suicide, not directly. It was all over and done with years ago. But it is relevant to our investigation. I'm not convinced that the latest one, Mark Paterson, was a suicide. What hold did she have over him? None. That's how she would have manipulated the others, but him? Not possible. He had a two-year research post at Bournemouth University. She's a student at Exeter. He was under no threat, as far as I can tell. Maybe it was an accident but, if so, why didn't she report it if it was her the walking group spotted on the coast path? I wonder if she's crossed a line. Maybe she pushed him in. He wouldn't have stood a chance in those stormy waters that day. So we need all the information we can glean about the way she's manipulated past situations. Or been manipulated herself, in the case of this Jackson man.'

Barry looked at her. 'And? You said a couple of things.'

'The money, Barry. The payments to Caroline stopped but money was still going out of their account, according to Rachel. I wonder if Hattie was blackmailing him.'

CHAPTER 21: WEATHER REPORT

'That morning, the Sunday Paterson ended up in the sea, could you find out the exact wind direction, Barry? It's something I should have thought of sooner. I don't want a general forecast, just how the wind at Dancing Ledge would have changed direction during the course of that morning. You may need Met Office help.'

Sophie and Barry were having their usual early morning chat, discussing ideas that had occurred to them overnight.

Barry looked at Sophie in surprise. 'You think it might help?'

Sophie pursed her lips. 'I'm not sure. But I've a feeling the overnight storm moved away in a slightly unexpected direction that morning. It was something one of the rangers at Durlston said when we were chatting about cars in the car park. Maybe the wind direction veered about all over the place, or maybe it changed course more predictably. Anything that might have had a bearing on what happened on the ledge that morning is worth considering.'

'Leave it with me.'

Sophie picked up a report from her in-tray. It was from the local council, so late in arriving that she'd almost given up hope of it coming at all. It listed the ticket machine trans-actions for the car parks within walking distance of Dancing Ledge on that fateful morning. She scanned down the list, looking for early morning sales, and spotted one. It was from the machine at Durlston Country Park, where the walking group had assembled for their morning ramble, but it was a good hour or more before their cluster of ticket purchases. Eight forty-five. Pretty early for a Sunday morning. The ticket was for four hours, giving ample time to get to Dancing Ledge and back. Moreover the time of the return walk would fit with Pauline Stopley and Flick Cochrane's glimpse of the young woman heading back towards Durlston. What was it Pauline had said? That she thought she'd seen a small blue car parked in the top corner of the car park? Well, maybe that needed looking into.

She logged on to the DVLA database and searched to see if Harriet Imber owned a vehicle. No luck. But Imber was such an unusual name that it would be worth looking for other cars belonging to an Imber. She waited. Yes, there it was. A blue Ford, belonging to Mrs Mary Imber of Bridgeford St Paul. Bingo!

Sophie searched the insurance details for that vehicle and discovered two registered drivers, the owner and her daughter, a certain Harriet Imber. The picture was becoming clearer.

Sophie poured herself a coffee and sat pondering. Just how dangerous was this young woman? Sophie cast her mind back to their interview. Hattie had been very focussed on whoever she was talking to. Her gaze was like the beam of a searchlight. Sophie had observed the way she listened to Barry. It was almost as if she, Sophie, didn't exist. The concen-trated gaze was fixed entirely on Barry. Then, when she had interrupted, Hattie had seemed confused for a few seconds before refocussing on her. She had noticed something else too. Hattie had treated her much more warily than she had Barry, almost as if she'd been instantly identified as a threat, but Barry hadn't been. It had been a bit uncanny.

She looked up and saw Barry approaching.

'The Met Office'll get some charts emailed across later this morning, showing how the wind direction and speed changed during the course of that day. They reckoned hourly intervals would be enough. It'll be the readings for Durlston, but Dancing Ledge is only a mile or two away. I think I can see where you're going with this, ma'am. It's all a bit iffy though, isn't it?'

Sophie shrugged. 'The whole thing's a bit iffy. But it all helps.'

When the detailed weather report for the Durlston coastal strip arrived later in the morning it showed that Sophie had been right to be suspicious. The charts, attached to an email, showed precise wind directions, as Barry had requested. Sophie pointed out the details as they examined the printouts. 'See, Barry, about the time Paterson was at Dancing Ledge, the wind was coming in from the south. Look here at the figures. It was still blowing at about thirty miles an hour. That would have blown him *away* from the cliff edge, not over it. I know it doesn't prove anything, but it adds to the possibility that he either jumped, or he was pushed.'

'And if she was there,' said Barry, sounding excited, 'then she pushed him? It must lead that way, surely? If he fell in, she'd have phoned for help, in a panic. That's what anyone would have done. Come to mention it, even if he'd jumped, she'd have still phoned it in, surely? Wouldn't any normal person? Why would you watch someone jump from some rocks or fall in and not do anything about it? So if we can place her there, she's implicated.' He stood gazing at the map, frowning. 'I just don't get it. Why would a young woman like her do all this? What's her motive? She doesn't gain anything from these deaths, not moneywise. So what does she get out of it?'

'A kick? Maybe a kick like no other. Do you remember Andy Renshaw or whatever his name was? The man who killed Donna Goodenough? He was a psychopath. He liked hurting people. Well, if our suspicions are correct, Hattie is a bit like him. But inflicting pain doesn't interest her. It's just their deaths that do it. She has a morbid fascination with causing death, but indirectly. Have they all hurt her in some way? It's impossible to know, and in the case of Eddie Davis it's unlikely. Even Hattie herself spoke affectionately about her, if you remember, though she may well have been acting.'

Barry frowned. 'So she feels nothing?'

'Exactly. That whole interview was an act, a performance. She only became wary when I started probing about the two books. Then she looked scared. But it went deeper than that. Something changed in her. I could see it in her eyes. Did you notice that she was shaking when she left?'

Barry shook his head.

'It worries me a bit. I wonder if I should get Rae to change tack, and look at her medical background. I need to think about the best way to go about it though, because she's only a suspect at the moment. We can't just demand access to her medical records.' Sophie frowned.

'What are you driving at, ma'am?'

'I wonder if she's schizophrenic. We think she was abused as a teenager, but maybe it started earlier.'

'So?' Barry looked puzzled.

'Some of the latest research into schizophrenia has shown a link to early childhood abuse in some sufferers. The voices in the head are creations of the sufferer's own brain. It's their way of dealing with the mental pain and anguish they experienced as a child. While the abuse was ongoing, they'd mentally shut down but the experiences were still being logged and filed away in some dark recess. Over the years they fester and form the basis of new revenge-seeking personalities, all created by the subconscious. It's not their fault. They are being told what to do. The "voices" start to whisper violent instructions to the conscious mind, all linked to the suppressed memories. This may not be the case with all schizophrenics, but it's thought to be for some.'

'So we try to find out more about her childhood?'

Sophie nodded. 'Maybe it's time to see her parents. But it's a tricky one. We haven't yet charged her with anything and we don't have any concrete proof, as you keep reminding me so regularly.'

Barry looked anxious.

'Don't worry, Barry. You're just doing the job I always wanted you to do, keeping me on the straight and narrow. If you weren't here I'd be making a complete prat of myself all the time.'

* * *

The Imbers' house in the village of Bridgeford St Paul was a picture postcard thatched cottage, with a small front garden and what looked to be a much larger one at the rear. A gravelled driveway ran along the side of the property towards a rickety timber garage. The front lawn was bordered by flower beds, the blooms all faded at this time of year. Sophie pushed open the small wrought iron gate and led the way to the front door.

'I'll lead with the questions, Barry,' Sophie said.

Barry pressed the doorbell. Nothing happened. He rapped on the brass knocker. 'Why don't people get these things fixed?' he hissed. 'All it probably needs is a new battery—'

The door opened. An aloof-looking woman faced them. She was taller than average, slim, with cropped greying hair. She looked them both up and down.

Barry showed his warrant card. 'This is DCI Allen and I'm DS Marsh, from Dorset police. Are you Mrs Mary Imber? We'd like a few words if we may.'

Her lip curled. 'Police? What on earth do you want? Is this some kind of house to house?' She looked up and down the deserted village street.

'May we come in for a few minutes, Mrs Imber?' said Sophie. 'We have quite a few questions that we need to put to you, and it's a wee bit chilly out here.'

The woman gave an exaggerated frown but opened the door. 'The sitting room is through here. Follow me. And I hope your shoes aren't dirty. It costs a fortune to clean carpets nowadays and I can't afford it.'

Sophie smiled pleasantly at her. 'We can take them off, if you wish.'

'No need,' she replied grudgingly. 'You look presentable enough.'

She led them into a low-ceilinged room that was furnished just as a thatched cottage should be — old-fashioned chairs and sofas with floral covers, matching curtains and china ornaments on polished shelves.

Sophie looked around her. 'This is lovely. I live in a thatched cottage in Wareham.'

Mary Imber merely nodded, still looking irritated. Barry thought the cottage furnishings probably matched their owner's personality — cold and clinical. This place wasn't at all like his boss's slightly disorganised, homely cottage.

'May we sit?' Sophie asked, not waiting for an answer. She settled herself on a small sofa. Barry sat on a hard-backed chair to one side, while Mary Imber lowered herself into an armchair opposite.

'Now, what is this about?' she demanded. Barry thought there was now a trace of anxiety in her voice.

'Your car, Mrs Imber.' Sophie smoothed out her grey skirt. 'The small blue Ford. Are there any other drivers on the insurance apart from you?'

'Well, my husband has his own company car. He's away at the moment. I think he's on the insurance policy.'

Sophie waited, looking calmly at her.

'And my daughter.'

'So who would have been driving it on Sunday morning twelve days ago?'

'I don't know,' Mary Imber replied. 'How can I be expected to remember that?'

'It was a very windy day. You probably remember the previous night's storm. It was right above us here in Dorset. The worst was over by the next morning but it was still extremely gusty. The wind only died away late in the afternoon.'

Mary Imber did not respond. Barry watched in fascination.

'Where's the car at the moment?' Sophie asked.

A pause. 'My daughter has it.'

'Locally?'

'No. She's in Exeter. She's a student there.'

'Does she often take the car with her to Exeter?'

'Yes. It's difficult to get there by train from here. There's no direct service.'

'So while she's at university she has the car with her? All the time?'

Grudgingly, Mrs Imber nodded.

'What about that weekend? Was she in Exeter or here?'

'She came home that weekend. She had a great deal of laundry to do.'

'Did she go out in the car? That Sunday morning?'

Mary Imber looked angry. 'Look, what's all this about? Why are you interested in my car and its whereabouts? Why aren't you out catching criminals? God knows we pay enough in taxes. When there's a break-in around here nothing happens, and yet here you are asking bizarre questions about my car. I may well make a complaint about this waste of taxpayers' money. Who is it? The Police and Crime Commissioner? Probably some man who never leaves his comfortable office, all paid for at our expense. It's a shameful state of affairs.'

'A man died that morning. His body was found in the sea just off Dancing Ledge. Do you know the place, Mrs Imber?'

'I'm aware of it. We may have walked past it on the coast path a couple of times. But I don't see what this man's death has to do with my car.'

'We've accounted for every car parked in the vicinity. Apart from yours, that is. I just want to know what it was doing there, parked at Durlston Country Park. It was there for just over three hours that morning.'

Silence. Mary Imber grew pale. Her face seemed to sag.

'I'll just put the kettle on,' she whispered hoarsely.

'DS Marsh is a highly talented tea and coffee maker, Mrs Imber. Perhaps he can give you a hand.' Sophie smiled, but

Hattie's mother had already left the room. Barry followed her through the hall and into a small, well-fitted kitchen. She switched on a kettle. Barry took down three mugs from their hooks and placed them on the work surface. Mary Imber kept her back to him all the time. He could feel the tension, so intense the air almost crackled.

Finally she spoke, coldly. 'I don't need your help. Please go away. Go back to your colleague. I'm sure you have things to talk about, like all busybodies.'

'I can help carry the mugs,' Barry said.

'What makes you think I was going to make a drink for you? I may have just felt the need for a coffee myself. That was highly presumptive of you.'

'You seem anxious, Mrs Imber.'

'And you have a damned cheek in commenting upon how you think I feel. Did I ask for your opinion? Most definitely not. Kindly keep your thoughts to yourself.'

Angry pink spots had appeared on her cheeks. She poured water into one of the mugs. Barry saw that her hand was shaking.

'Coffee or tea?' she asked, reluctantly.

'That's kind of you. Coffee for both of us, please.'

He carried the three mugs back to the sitting room. Sophie was standing at the fireplace, looking at the framed photos arranged above it. She turned and smiled at Hattie's mother.

'This must be your daughter. Harriet, did you say? And is this your son?'

Mary Imber nodded curtly. 'Richard is younger. He's still away at school, doing his A levels. He doesn't drive yet.'

Sophie sat down again and took a sip of her coffee. 'So do you know what Harriet was doing that morning, parked at Durlston?'

Mary Imber shook her head. She said nothing.

'Did you know Edwina Davis, Mrs Imber?'

Mary Imber looked shocked. Her face paled again. 'What?'

'Edwina Davis. I understand she was a senior county midwife. She was very well respected for her knowledge of general health issues.'

'Why do you ask?'

'She died under curious circumstances. The name Imber cropped up in some of her paperwork. It's a very unusual name, so the chances are that it was you or someone from your family.'

'Yes, we did know her. She became a sort of family friend some years ago.'

Barry noticed that she was more wary now. Anxiety had again taken the place of belligerence in her demeanour. Her eyes flickered over the two detectives. She's seriously worried, he thought.

'So how did that come about?' Sophie asked.

'She lodged here with us for a short while when she first came to the area. Then she moved to Dorchester, but we stayed in touch. Christmas cards and that kind of thing.'

'So she wasn't involved with your family on a professional basis in any way?'

'Of course not. What are you suggesting?'

'I'm not suggesting anything, Mrs Imber. I'm just asking questions.'

'We're a happy and loving family, if you must know. I love my children and they love me. Why would I ever need to refer to someone for advice?'

'Someone outside the family was worrying you, maybe? Taking an interest in Harriet?'

There was no response. Mary Imber took another sip of coffee and sat staring at her hands.

'Now's the time to tell me, Mrs Imber. Did you ever feel the need to ask Edwina Davis for advice, either officially or unofficially?'

Mary Imber stood up abruptly, her face flushed. 'I must ask you to leave. You've caught me at a bad time and I'm feeling distinctly unwell. Please go.'

'Of course, if that's how you feel. I'll leave you my card, so that you can phone me. Please do so soon, because I need to see you again.'

The two detectives left, their coffees hardly touched, and made their way to the car.

'I hadn't guessed, ma'am,' Barry said.

'Nor did I, until I was inside the house. Then it struck me. If Hattie was involved with that creepy organist as a four-teen- or fifteen-year-old, and they only realised what had been going on after his suicide, maybe they'd consult someone who could offer advice about such things. And if Eddie Davis was a family friend, who better? That's why Eddie was so cagey about identifying Hattie in her diary. The whole thing had been hushed up, that's my guess. After all, what would be the point of bringing it all up after he was dead? Maybe Eddie's advice was to let sleeping dogs lie, although I would have thought that unlikely, given her background. Maybe that was the mother's decision.'

'So it kind of makes sense now? Is that what you're saying?'

Sophie shook her head. 'There might be more. It might go further back than that. I think Hattie is maybe more dam-aged than we suspected. And did you spot the other thing? Mary Imber said that her husband is insured to drive the car. But he isn't, not according to central records. It's just her and Hattie.'

'Could be a genuine mistake. It's easy enough to forget details like that.'

'Absolutely. But it's odd that none of the family photos in the lounge showed a man. They were all of the mother and the two youngsters.'

CHAPTER 22: DEMONS

Rae visited the campus security director's office first thing on Friday morning. She wanted to identify the spiky-haired student and find out more about her relationship with Hattie, then find out more about the staff members Hattie seemed to be embroiled with. But she'd need to tread carefully, as Sophie had warned her during their long telephone conversation at breakfast time. It was one thing to carry out a covert watch on a student, rather more sensitive if a visiting lecturer was involved, but one of the university's most senior professors was a wholly different story. Sophie didn't want to risk anything getting out, particularly since the nature and extent of Hattie Imber's network of shady relationships was unknown. So Rae merely asked about the unknown fellow student. She imagined she would be on a similar course to Hattie's, although that wasn't certain. The fact that this friend might be foreign would help. She searched for Spanish, Italian and finally Greek students but got nowhere. Then she noticed that there was a Greek Society and found from the website that the current secretary looked a lot like Hattie's friend. There she was. Maria Katsaros was studying economics and business, and had occupied the room next to Hattie during their first year. Maria's fresher photo showed her with long hair but with the same gentle smile that Rae had noticed the previous day. Rae noted the relevant details about Maria, thanked the security chief and left. Investigations into the two staff members would have to be done elsewhere, possibly using online data.

Rae called Barry, then returned to her hotel room, dug out her laptop, and set about finding out all she could about Maria, Markham and Professor Murey.

Maria was clearly a very committed student. Rae read through her profile, and the long list of societies and groups that she belonged to, some as a committee member. The Feminist Society, the Drama Society, the LGBT group and a social support group for foreign students. The Film Society, the Swimming Club and the Tae Kwon Do Group. She had taken lead roles in several student drama productions and had still found time to volunteer as a coach in a self-defence class for women students. She was open about her lesbianism, and proud of it. According to her profile, she'd achieved marks in the top ten per cent in her first year exams, and was on course for a first-class degree.

Doctor George Markham had a one-year placement as a visiting lecturer under a Commonwealth exchange scheme, specialising in tall structure engineering. He was to remain in Exeter until the end of August, advising research students. He had little contact with the undergraduates. He listed his interests as walking, climbing and church organ music. Rae wondered whether it was his profile post that had sparked Hattie's interest in him, though it was always possible that the university community hosted a group with that particular interest.

Professor Paul Murey was clearly very influential both within the university and beyond. He was in his early fifties, a graduate of Edinburgh and Cambridge and a specialist in the geography of landforms. In fact he was an international authority on the subject, judging from the list of conferences he was due to address during the current academic year. His interests included coastal walking, bird watching, photography and sketching. So where had he met Hattie? He claimed to be happily married, and his wife, Fiona, was a peripatetic music teacher. Now for Hattie herself . . .

> *Although my name is Harriet Imber, I prefer to be called Hattie. I think it reflects my personality better. I'm studying ancient history but I have many interests including church organ music, pencil sketching, clubbing and fashion. I can play church organ well enough for normal Sunday services, weddings and other services. I've set up a small society here at uni. It has six members. Contact me if you want to find out more. I love making friends so get in touch if you fancy meeting me, whether you're male or female, or even in between. I'm not picky!*

Rae noted that Hattie's photo showed her with her new hairstyle. She'd obviously been very thorough earlier in the week, erasing any trace of her previous look. That was suspicious in itself. Rae could understand why she might want some of her photos updated, but the speed and thoroughness with which it had been done was surely suspicious. Did she suspect that she'd been spotted on the coast path that stormy Sunday morning? And was she concerned that she might be identified as the young woman seen arm in arm with Paterson on the campus of Bournemouth University?

***

Her phone told her a text message had arrived. It was now late morning and Rae was sipping a coffee in one of the cafés on the campus. The message was from Barry, telling her that Hattie Imber probably had a small, blue Ford somewhere in Exeter, and giving her the registration number. She put the phone down and thought. Students weren't allowed to bring cars onto the campus, so anyone with a vehicle faced the problem of finding a long-term place to park. Parking wasn't cheap, so where would a hard up student leave their car? Residential streets were the most likely bet. If she was so friendly with this visiting engineering lecturer, George Markham, could she have cadged his parking space? She thought back to the previous evening. Four flats, four parking spaces, four cars. Was it worth a look? Rae finished her drink, slipped her jacket on and left the café. She was soon outside the house she'd been watching the previous evening. There were two cars left in the parking area, one of which matched Barry's description. She took out her phone and double checked the registration details. Yes, it was the Imber car. Judging from the dead leaves on the roof and bonnet, it must have been parked there for several days.

Rae then retraced her steps from the previous evening, returned to the house with the gravel driveway and made a note of the address. It wouldn't take long to confirm who the occupier was. More important was to get to the bottom of whatever relationship existed between him and Hattie. The gravel-throwing incident had clearly been intended to intimidate. Did she have some kind of hold over him? If so, what was its nature?

She returned to the campus and sat thinking. A quick look at the local phone book confirmed that it had indeed been Murey's house that Hattie had visited after leaving Markham the night before. Clearly there was now some kind of friction between them. Why else would she fling gravel at his bedroom window and then leave?

Rae looked again at the dates of the conferences Murey had attended during the past year. The most recent was a weekend event in Cambridge in early October. Those dates seemed somehow familiar. She looked at the data she had on Hattie's attendance record. She had missed all of that Friday's lectures, tutorials and seminars. Coincidence? The website indicated that a local upmarket hotel had been block-booked for the delegates to stay in. Surely he wouldn't have taken an unknown young woman to that hotel? So what would Murey have done? Book her into a different hotel? Another, more downmarket one? Rae decided to pay a visit to the county police headquarters.

'I thought you said we wouldn't see you again,' said DS Steve Gulliver. 'Not that I'm complaining. It's always good to see a fresh face.'

'I just need an official phone for a while, sir. Is that okay?'

'Use mine. I can't cope with modern technology anyway. Give me the pigeon post any day.'

Rae merely smiled politely, then spent the next twenty minutes tracking the room bookings for the weekend conference in October. Just as she had thought, there was no Imber. But she did discover that Professor Murey had stayed two nights, had a double room to himself and had left after the final conference lunch on Sunday afternoon. She asked the local Cambridge CID to help her identify nearby hotels. The manager of the Red Rose Hotel told her yes, a double room had been booked for Harriet Imber for the same two nights, and the reservation had been paid for in advance by a gentleman called Murey. So it looked as though the good professor had brought Hattie along as a night-time plaything during his conference. Well, well.

So what had been in that envelope, the one Hattie had slid under his office door the previous day, causing him obvious anxiety? Photographs, maybe? A demand for money? If so, was she putting herself at risk of harm?

Rae shook her head. Just what kind of person was Hattie Imber, and what drove her to act this way?

CHAPTER 23: DISTINCTLY QUEASY

'I saw a crossdresser earlier,' Craig said. 'In the café next to the station. I got here sooner than I'd expected and grabbed a coffee while I waited for you.'

'Why are you telling me this, Craig? Do you think I want to know?' Rae looked across the table at her boyfriend. They were in a busy Chinese restaurant near the cathedral, at a small table in a window enclosure. The light from a wall lamp shone down on his head, and his fair hair glinted with orange highlights. She liked him a lot. He was considerate and thoughtful, smart and very huggable. But that didn't give him the right to start a conversation that he must surely know she'd find irritating at best and upsetting at worst.

He looked embarrassed. 'I didn't mean it that way. I didn't mean to compare her to you. I know the difference.'

'Do you? There's an old, bitter joke about it. What's the difference between a transvestite and a transsexual? About five years.'

Craig looked puzzled. 'Not sure I understand.'

'I'm not a transgender purist, Craig. I've never split people into *this* and *that*. There are very subtle gradations in gender variance. It hits people in different ways, to different degrees and at different stages of life. If you must know, I admire people who manage to find a sort of part-time balance that keeps their relationships together, particularly if they're older and have family and relationship commitments. I was young when it all happened to me, so I wasn't in that situation. But I sometimes ask myself, what would I have done if it had all exploded on me a decade later than it did, when I could have been a married man with a family? How would I have handled it? Sometimes people just feel they have to stick with what they are for the sake of their families, and take opportunities to be their preferred selves when they can. I admire them for it. Those labels that people used a decade ago are way out of date.'

'Yeah, well, that makes sense. But I still don't understand the joke.'

'Because for a few years before I transitioned, I was only a woman part of the time. I went to support groups and other events, but at work I was a "normal" bloke as far as everyone knew. Those evenings out were my lifeline. So what was I then? In those outdated terms, I was a transvestite, a crossdresser. Then three years later, I officially became what I am now, a legal woman. It's an insult to still be using these demeaning labels for people struggling with gender identity issues. It makes me bloody angry.'

'Anything else make you angry?' said Craig. 'Do you want to get it all off your chest now?'

'Why not? This obsession the media has with male to female trans people, for instance. Do you ever hear anything about women who transition to men? The media is just not interested in them. But they're there all right, in nearly the same numbers.'

'Why's that? Why don't the press tell us that?' He looked genuinely puzzled.

'We could speculate for hours but I can't be bothered. Look, I don't want to waste time thinking about it. I just want to be me, Rae Gregson, person. I'm happy as I am, and people need to accept that.' She looked at her boyfriend. 'Are you having second thoughts about me? Is that what this is all about?'

Craig looked unsure. 'I don't know. I guess it's always there at the back of my mind.'

'Maybe I shouldn't have told you about my background. Some don't.'

'No, you did the right thing, and I admire you for it. It couldn't have been an easy decision.'

'So do you want to split? I don't want us to stay together if all you feel is pity for me.'

It was some time before Craig replied. 'It isn't anything like that. It's the dead opposite, in fact. I really like you a lot, I fancy you like mad and the sex is great. It's just when I visit my sister and her family. She's pregnant again.'

'And I can never be pregnant. I can never have your children. Is that it?'

Craig nodded. 'I never really thought about it much before, about kids and things. But recently . . . well.'

'There are ways round it, Craig. There's adoption or surrogacy.'

'It's all complicated, though, isn't it?'

'Yes, I guess it is. But if we're committed to each other, we'll get through it. And we'll need that commitment if we're to have a family.'

Craig reached across the table and put his hand on hers. 'I think I'm okay with that.'

Rae felt tears welling up. All she could think of to say was one of Sophie Allen's favourite phrases, 'Oh, you sweetheart.'

The waitress arrived with their food and they smiled at each other across the steaming plates.

* * *

The strobe lights flashed and the music pounded. Rae and Craig had managed to grab two vacant seats at a small table and were looking across the packed dance floor at the revellers. Rae had spotted Hattie and Maria a few minutes earlier when the two of them made their entrance. Maria was wearing silky, olive-coloured combat trousers with a matching vest and soft brown ankle boots, and blended in with the crowd. Hattie, though, was hard to miss. She was wearing a tight, strappy emerald blue dress that glittered in the disco lights, and her high heels made her even taller than usual. Were they also blue? Rae couldn't see for all the people crowded around the two young women. Hattie was simply gorgeous. It was a wonder she hadn't been picked up by a modelling agency. Her height and looks were near perfect for such a career. Tonight she seemed a far cry from the sullen, cursing figure that had bumped into Rae in the geography block corridor.

Hattie spent some time in her large group of friends, until a hungry-looking young man approached from the other side of the room. They moved away, Hattie laughing conspiratorially, her left hand on his elbow. She glanced at Maria, who was talking to another group of students. Hattie pulled the man towards a secluded corner near the toilet corridor. Maria stared at them and frowned. Rae rose from her seat, told Craig to stay put, and followed after them. Where had they gone? Rae edged towards the recess and discovered a narrow corridor off the dance floor that led to two office doors, both locked, and what appeared to be a storage area adjacent to a fire exit. Rae made her way quietly along the corridor and peered into the storeroom. There, against one wall, Hattie and the young man were having sex. After a while he groaned and shuddered, and Hattie pulled her dress down. Rae saw him pass her a small bundle of what could only be money.

One thing was for sure — Hattie Imber was no novice.

Rae backed away and hurried to the exit, where she leant against the wall and studied her phone. She watched them return, Hattie to the group of students. The young man left the club. Less than ten minutes had passed, and Hattie didn't seem to have been missed. Except by Maria. She stood at the edge of the group and stared venomously at her friend. With a flourish, Hattie extracted several banknotes from her bra and made her way to the bar.

Rae sat down beside Craig. 'I think I've seen enough. I'm beginning to feel distinctly queasy.'

Craig looked puzzled. 'I was thinking how well behaved they all seem to be. Was it the food? I'm always a bit cautious about stir-fried duck.'

'Nothing I've eaten, I promise you. It's what I've just seen. I need some fresh air and maybe a quiet drink in an ordinary pub. Let's go.'

CHAPTER 24: SWEARING AND SPITTING

Saturday morning dawned bright and sunny in Plymouth,
although a chilly wind was blowing in from the east. Matt
Brindle opened his bedroom curtains and looked out across
the railway line just beyond his parents' back garden. He'd
been looking forward to today all week, for he was due to
travel to Exeter to visit his girlfriend, Hattie. He wanted her
to know what she meant to him, and he was going to tell her
how much she'd changed his life in the week since he'd met
her. He was a different person, an adult at last with an adult's
view of the world. And he was deeply in love. He would tell
Hattie and then they would celebrate this love that they had
for each other. He was sure she felt it too. Her text messages of
the past couple of days had been full of the kind of things only
true lovers would send each other. They also hinted at what
she'd like to try with him when they were alone together in her
room. He looked at the clock on the wall. Enough daydream-
ing. He'd better get some breakfast and head off to the station.

On the train, Matt soon put his magazine aside and sat
looking out of the window at the Devon countryside flashing
by. He was wondering if he could transfer to the Exeter office
permanently. He knew that he'd impressed the local manager

during his week's secondment, his boss in Plymouth had told him so. The estate agent Matt worked for had branches in most of the county's major towns, and was opening new offices in Cornwall and Somerset. He could be looking at becoming an assistant manager within a few years and a branch manager by his mid-thirties. Would that impress Hattie? He wasn't sure. She'd see the benefits, though. Just think. If he was careful with his money, he might be able to afford a small house in a couple of years and then, if his career developed according to plan, a cottage in a small Devon village. He knew that Hattie would love such a home. Nevertheless he was worried that someone with a passion for ancient history, music and art might not rate such a career as highly as his own family members, with their very ordinary background. From the sound of it, Hattie's family were all very middle class, privately educated and with degrees and such things. Could she ever be satisfied with a man in his line of work? Even if she did seem to like him a lot at the moment, how long would it last? He'd already seen how very changeable her moods could be.

The familiar sense of inferiority crept over him, one that had been with him, on and off, since the later years of primary school. A sense of puzzled underachievement, despite all his best efforts. He sighed. Come on, Matt. Why be sad? He was on his way to visit the love of his short life. The sense of anticipation kicked in and he lost himself in the memories of the previous passionate weekend.

The train finally pulled into St David's and Matt slung his bag over his shoulder and strode towards the exit. He looked at the clock and a sudden doubt struck him. It was just before ten o'clock and he was due to meet Hattie at ten thirty. Or was he? He checked the text message she'd sent two days earlier, and discovered his mistake. It was eleven thirty that they were to meet for coffee. Stupid. It was his longing to see her, probably. What should he do with this spare hour? Maybe he'd just walk up to the campus now and give her a surprise.

* * *

139

Hattie Imber was angry. Why couldn't Maria see that she only went with these guys for fun and profit? Maria was being ridiculous demanding total loyalty. For God's sake, she was living in another era. Maybe it was her Greek Orthodox background. Hattie had told her often enough how she wanted to live her life. Hadn't she been tricked enough in the past — used, abused and tossed aside like a dirty plaything? Well, it wasn't going to happen again. She was going to stay in total control of all her relationships from now on. They would be on her terms or not at all.

It had all ended up in that row over breakfast this morning, with Maria in tears and she, Hattie, saying things that she now regretted. And it wasn't just Maria giving her grief. The fucking professor was refusing to play ball and turf up the extra money she was due. She'd show the bastard. The voices in her head were starting up again, whispering suggestions to her about how she could pay them back. She pushed them to the back of her mind, just as her therapist had instructed and walked quickly away from the campus, down to the leafy street where the professor lived. What would he be doing on a Saturday morning? Playing golf? Pruning the roses? Did it matter? She needed to vent her anger somehow. She reached his driveway and then just stood there in the middle of the pavement, staring at his house.

It was five minutes before a white-faced Paul Murey appeared. He strode out of his gate and grabbed Hattie by the arm.

'For Christ's sake, what do you think you're doing?' he hissed.

'Let go of my arm or I'll scream rape,' she hissed back. 'Loud enough for the neighbours to hear.'

He stepped back. 'My wife's seen you. What are you playing at? We have an agreement and you're not sticking to it.'

'Is she watching now?'

'No. She's just gone into the back garden. It's a good job she's never seen you before, because she's got a memory for faces. Don't ever come round here again, or there'll be hell to pay. For both of us. She's not stupid.'

'Unlike you, then,' Hattie retorted. 'You must be stupid to try to cheat me like this. I want another two hundred quid for last Sunday evening, and that's cheap considering the time you got out of me.'

'I paid you for the two hours. It's not my fault that we both fell asleep afterwards. Considering all the money you've already had out of me, I'd have thought you'd understand that.' He glanced back towards the house. 'She's getting suspicious, she's checking up on our bank accounts.'

Hattie's look was full of derision. 'Not my problem. You pay for the hours I give you and nothing less. Fair's fair.'

'Okay, I'll get you the money but it'll have to wait a while. And what were you doing sliding messages under my office door? Are you mental? Anyone could have seen it. I'd be finished if they found out.' He looked at her and the strain showed in his eyes. 'You're a student, aren't you? At the university? At my place? How else could you have got into the building to deliver that stupid note? Christ, I'd never have started with you if I'd known.'

Hattie laughed. 'Mistress Pandora. Mystery is my name, cruelty is my game. Did you think those were just empty words? You don't have a clue, do you?' She stepped back. 'You've got until this time next week, so get your fucking act together, you prick, or things will get much worse for you.'

He stared at her. 'That was you round here the other night, throwing gravel at the windows, wasn't it? You stupid bitch!'

She spat at the ground, turned on her heels and marched, still seething with anger, to George Markham's flat. It was a fortnight since she'd used the car, and she needed to check that it was ticking over okay before going home the next day. She might as well do it now, since she was in the vicinity. She climbed into the small car and turned the key. The engine coughed and died. She tried again but it still refused to start.

Fuck, fuck, fuck. Everything in her life seemed to be falling apart. She rested her forehead on the steering wheel, wanting to cry. After a few minutes she climbed out. Markham was standing by the car, watching her.

'You look upset, Hattie,' he said. 'It's only a cold, damp battery. An hour on charge and it'll be fine.'

She gripped the car door. 'I don't have a fucking hour,' she hissed. 'Christ, why is this all happening to me today?'

He put his hand on her arm, but she whirled round and knocked it away. 'Keep your fucking hands to yourself, you perv. Don't fucking touch me. I don't want any of you to touch me again. Ever. Fuck off.'

She spat on the ground at his feet, turned and hurried away.

* * *

Across the road, Matt Brindle watched the end of this scene with interest. You'd never see *his* girlfriend behave like that young blonde woman, swearing and spitting at people in public. He was looking forward to surprising her. He'd brought a selfie-stick with him, so that he could take a photo of the two of them together, to show his parents. He'd already described her to them, her slim figure and the way her long, curly, chestnut-red hair cascaded around her shoulders.

Should he text her first, and let her know that he would be arriving an hour early? No, let it be a surprise. Matt liked surprises. They were always good, in his experience.

CHAPTER 25: BRIDESMAIDS

Sophie Allen realised that she had just yawned, and her grandfather had spotted it.

'Sorry. That was rude of me. It's probably my age catching up on me.'

James Howard looked concerned. 'You're not in danger of burning yourself out again, are you? You should take more care of yourself, Sophie. Go on a holiday or something.'

Sophie laughed. 'No, I'm not overworked, not at the moment anyway. I'm busy making lists in my head, now that Mum has decided to get herself hitched in the New Year. Has she spoken to you, Grandad?'

He smiled. 'Yes. And what a wonderful gesture. I'd be delighted to accompany her down the aisle. We were both very amused by the way she described it. She refused to use the expression, *give me away*. I can see where you and the two girls get your independent spirit.'

'So you'll do it?'

'Yes, of course. We're not sure what two old fogeys like us will add to the occasion, but we're willing.'

Sophie, Martin and Jade had driven to Gloucester soon after Sophie finished work on Saturday afternoon. They planned to stay with the Howards until Sunday afternoon, partly to assess the wellbeing of the elderly couple. Florence's health was beginning to deteriorate, although mentally she was as bright as ever. 'It's the joints, I expect,' she said. 'They're giving out on me at last. But I can't complain, can I? My body's done well to get me this far.'

Now, sitting in the lounge of the Howards' home, Sophie recalled the conversation. Sophie looked at her grandfather. 'How is Florence really, Grandad? Is it just aches and pains or is there something more serious? I'm your next of kin, remember, and I'd take it really hard if you were keeping me in the dark.'

'Well, I'm a wee bit worried about her, if you must know. There's something not right, even if they can't pin it down yet. She's not sleeping well and gets up in the middle of the night for a cup of tea. And she was really upset last week, but won't tell me why.'

'It might be the wedding. It's probably brought up old memories. For my mum especially. She still bears the scars of what happened to Graham. It'll be the same for both of you, but you have each other. Florence will be reliving feelings she thought she'd left behind. While I was talking Mum into this marriage, I felt that somehow I was betraying both of you. It's not easy for any of us.'

They heard Jade and Florence's voices, and stopped talking.

'What are you working on at the moment, dear?' Florence came through to the lounge, followed by Jade, carrying a tray of coffee cups.

'It's a strange one. A death that might be a murder, but then again might not be. Several suicides that might or might not be down to coercion. All linked to a strange young woman, who I suspect to be schizophrenic. I haven't told you this, by the way. Let's get on to more pleasant things. What are you planning to wear, Gran? For the wedding, I mean.'

'Susan suggested green with flowers. What do you think?'

Sophie shrugged. 'Sounds fine. What are you wearing, Jade? The same sort of thing?'

Jade rolled her eyes. 'Not quite, no. Gran wants Hannah and me to be sort of bridesmaids but wear something edgy. Apparently Hannah spotted just the thing in a London store a couple of days ago, so next weekend I'm going to have a look with her. Hannah's up to something, Mum. She wouldn't give any details over the phone, and why didn't she take a photo and send it to me? I'm suspicious that it'll suit her colouring but not mine.'

'That's hardly likely, Jade. This is Hannah we're talking about, not some thoughtless person on an ego trip.'

'Point taken. But what does Gran mean by edgy? What's edgy to her isn't edgy at all to me. The two are entirely different.'

'Yes, I can see that. I expect she didn't have some barely decent clubbing outfit in mind, all lace and sequins.'

Jade was indignant. 'Mum! I don't own such a thing and I don't intend to. You know that.' She paused. 'You're teasing me again, aren't you? Anyway, what are you wearing? And you haven't told us what your role will be. You must have one. Gran wouldn't have left you out. She wouldn't dare. If Hannah and I are bridesmaids, it doesn't leave much, does it?'

Sophie fidgeted on her seat. 'Um. If you must know, she mentioned something about me being a bridesmaid too.'

Jade started to speak but turned it into a cough. Sophie looked at her levelly. 'So whatever this "edgy" outfit is that Hannah's found, it needs to suit me as well. How come I haven't been included in this trip to London next weekend? I'm beginning to feel unwanted.'

'She probably knows how busy you are, Mum. Anyway, if it suits Hannah it'll suit you. You're like peas in a pod.'

'Ha. Only if you discount my worry lines, and the floppy bits that have appeared around my bum. And this conversation has just added another worry line, I'm certain.' She yawned again. 'I think these yawns are trying to tell me something. Time for bed?'

* * *

145

The following morning, just as they were all sitting down to breakfast, the news came in. An event that shifted the whole nature of the investigation. From being worryingly vague it suddenly became a bona fide case with an obvious victim and a ready-made list of suspects. Sophie picked her chirruping mobile phone out of her bag and glanced at the caller display. It was from Rae, who should be back from Exeter by now.

Sophie frowned. Calls at this time on a Sunday morning usually meant trouble. 'Hi, Rae.'

'Ma'am, you may need to get down here. Hattie's in hospital, in a coma. She's critical, according to the doctor. She was fished out of the water down at the quayside in the early hours. It looks as though she was assaulted first before ending up in the river. She has serious head injuries and she's in a really bad way.'

Sophie frowned, thinking fast. 'Okay. Where are you? You sound as if you're still in Exeter. I thought you were due to head back home late yesterday?'

'I was uneasy about the state she was in, so I stayed on. I'll explain when I see you.'

'Fine. It should take me about an hour and a half to get to you. Can you clear access for me with the local squad? I'll call our chief now and get her to smooth my way. See you at the Exeter cop-shop.'

She ended the call and looked up. Four pairs of eyes were fixed on her. 'Sorry, everyone, I have to go. Our young target has herself become the victim of a possible murder attempt. I need the car, Martin. Can you get a hire car to get you and Jade home?'

'There's no need,' James said. 'Martin is very welcome to use ours.'

Sophie collected her things and was out of the house within twenty minutes of receiving Rae's call. Ten of those had been spent talking to her chief constable, asking for permission to join the Exeter investigation into the previous night's assault.

What on earth had been going on in Exeter? Had she seriously misjudged how vulnerable Hattie Imber was? She bit her lip, started the engine and pulled out of her grandparents' driveway. Thank goodness it was relatively early on a Sunday morning. The motorway should be quiet.

CHAPTER 26: BRUISES AND SCRATCHES

So who were the suspects? The list seemed worryingly long. It included close family members of Hattie Imber's suspected victims, as well as the people Hattie had upset. Rae reported four relationships that might have turned sour. The professor, Paul Murey, seemed to have been angered by Hattie's erratic and moody behaviour. Could she have also upset her supposed protector, George Markham, the visiting lecturer from Canada? Rae also reported on the apparent break-up of her relationship with Maria, the Greek student, who may have been more than just a close friend. Then Hattie herself had mentioned a new boyfriend, someone who didn't live locally and wasn't a student. But there were few details about this person. If he existed, was he a jealous type who might react violently when he discovered the truth about Hattie?

Sophie ran these thoughts over in her mind on the journey south. Had she been too relaxed in her approach to the investigation? But it was difficult to see how she could have justified putting more resources into it. After all, there was no direct evidence of any crime having been committed. They were just three apparent suicides. And now the case was a tangled mess with far too many suspects, and Sophie herself wouldn't even be in charge, not technically. She might well be allocated observer status only, and have to stand by and watch the case being handled by a less experienced detective from Devon. Why had Rae decided to remain in Exeter for an extra night? She was obviously worried about Hattie. Had the young student been in danger? If so, she may have been going about this in entirely the wrong way, and her team would become the focus of an internal enquiry. Sophie finally turned her car into the Exeter police station car park. She hurried across to the entrance. Rae was waiting in reception and led her to the CID offices where a local officer, DS Steve Gulliver, was waiting for her. Gulliver was a casually dressed and rugged-looking man in his thirties who had acted as Rae's local liaison. Sophie had been impressed with his precise, objective manner when she'd met him earlier in the week.

'Information is still coming in, ma'am,' he said. 'They've had a team out searching the quayside for anything suspicious but they finished an hour ago without finding anything. We've got them knocking on doors now, starting with the commercial premises, although some of them haven't opened yet. There are some residential flats on the opposite bank but the chances of the residents being able to see anything would be almost non-existent. They're all too far away from the area with the bars and cafés.'

'So what happened? Have you been able to piece anything together?' Sophie asked.

'It was about midnight, give or take a couple of minutes. A guy passing by heard a splash and decided to investigate. He was walking from a pizza place to one of the bars. The sound came from a darker spot further on. Most people would have ignored it, in which case she'd now be dead, but he decided to have a look. He saw her floating, face down. There was a set of steps down to a ferry landing stage nearby, and a lifebelt. He grabbed it and went in. He got hold of her and pulled her back to the stage. It was only later, when the ambulance arrived, that they spotted her head wounds.'

'Anyone else around?'

Gulliver ran his fingers through his dark hair. 'The guy was in a group of three. They didn't see anyone, but it was pretty dark at the time. There weren't many people about because of the rain, but from what we can tell, that area seemed particularly quiet at the time it happened.'

'You're aware of why Rae was here? That we think the student in question may have played a part in three possible suspicious deaths in our neck of the woods? I was here earlier in the week and spoke to one of your bosses.'

'I remembered that. I realised that the victim was the person you had under surveillance when I came on shift first thing this morning. That's when we tried to get hold of your DC here to see if she was still around.'

'Can we visit the victim? I spoke to her on Wednesday while I was here, and I remember her well. I know she's in a coma, but it would confirm to you that she is who you think she is. I've also been thinking through a list of some of her possible assailants. It's a long one. That girl has managed to upset the world and his dog, as far as I can tell. I met her mother a few days ago, and she was prickly in the extreme. My guess is that something's been worrying her for a long time. Have you contacted her yet?'

'Yes, but she has no way of getting here. She said that her daughter had the car, and it was here in Exeter. She was going to phone me back when she'd managed to arrange a lift from someone but there's been no word from her. Yet she has my direct number.' He shook his head.

'We might be able to help,' Sophie replied. 'I can probably get my DS, Barry Marsh, to bring her down. Give me a couple of minutes to make the arrangements. Maybe she'll open up a bit more on the drive here. To say she was unco-operative when we saw her a couple of days ago would be a major understatement.'

* * *

150

Hattie Imber was in a small room in the intensive care unit at Exeter Hospital, wired up to a bank of monitoring equipment. The top of her head was partly shrouded in a dressing, but enough of her face was showing to make her recognisable. Sophie turned to the doctor standing beside her.

'Yes, she's Harriet Imber. How is she?'

The doctor shook her head. 'Still critical. Even if she does pull through, we don't know how she'll be. There was bleeding on her brain, so there could be permanent damage. Someone gave her a really hard blow.'

'Has she been scanned? X-rayed? Are there any clues as to what caused the injury?'

'She'd been hit by a bottle, hard enough to shatter the glass. We're not sure whether the damage was compounded by her spell in the water. It's difficult to say.'

'It may have saved her life. The splash made enough noise to draw attention to her plight and she was pulled out pretty quickly, apparently. Her mother will be arriving in about an hour. One of my officers is bringing her down from Dorchester.' Sophie paused. 'I don't know whether it will be useful to you, but we were wondering if she's mildly schizophrenic, just from her erratic behaviour over the past few days. Was she on medication do you know?'

'We haven't found any, and nothing showed up in the blood tests, so I wouldn't have said so. What makes you suspect schizophrenia?'

'I interviewed her briefly on Wednesday but cut it short because she was clearly getting stressed. The way she reacted to some of my questions made me wonder. I eased off at that point. I'll see what the local police have found in her room and let you know.'

'That would be helpful. We've already tried to contact the university medical centre, and someone's due to phone us back. It's Sunday morning, so there'll only be a skeleton staff.'

Sophie left Hattie's room and returned to Rae who was waiting with Gulliver in the reception area.

'It's her,' she said. 'Apparently she was struck with a bottle, so your forensics team should have the fragments. Is that right?'

Gulliver nodded. 'As I said earlier, we've finished searching the quayside. My guess is that the rest of the bottle is lying twenty feet under. Wouldn't you chuck it into the water? Get rid of the evidence?'

'When you searched her room on campus, did you find any prescription medication?'

He shook his head. 'Not yet as far as I know. My boss is there now. Let me ask her.' Gulliver disappeared out of the reception office and shut the door behind him.

Sophie turned to Rae. 'How are they? The local team, I mean?'

Rae pursed her lips. 'Okay, I guess. I don't think the unit boss has much imagination, so things are a bit slow. They still don't know whether to reclassify it as attempted murder. It was originally logged as assault, and that still applies at the moment. I don't have the clout to influence them, ma'am, but you do.'

Sophie frowned. 'I've got to tread carefully, Rae. I was hoping it was going to be Tommy Milburn in charge, but apparently he's on a boating holiday on the Norfolk Broads. In bloody November! Needs his head examined. Anyway, I don't know his second, so I've got to be cautious. If she has any sense she'll make use of us since we're here and we know some of the background, but you know provincial cops. Prickly buggers, some of them. Me, for example. I'm at a loose end. I'd like to start seeing all these people Hattie's upset recently but we can't do anything till we've got clearance from the SIO here. Maybe we should pay a quick visit to the campus and see her. I'll let Gulliver know. I didn't like the way he shut the door on us to make his call. Don't they trust us?' She glanced at her watch. 'We've got an hour before Barry gets here with Hattie's mother. I don't want to waste any more time so we might as well get over there.'

***

152

The local detectives, along with two forensic officers, had almost finished their search of Hattie's room when Sophie and Rae arrived. Groups of students were watching, and whispering to each other. Rae pointed Maria out to Sophie.

The local detective inspector, Sue Wilding, came out of the door.

'Hi,' said Sophie. 'I hope your DS told you we were coming up here. DI Wilding, isn't it?'

DI Wilding smiled warily. She was a tall, slim woman, with her long dark hair pulled back in a ponytail. 'We're just finishing off. Not that there's much of interest. Just the usual student stuff, as far as we can tell.' Her voice was flat, and she sounded indifferent.

'You do know that we're interested in her, don't you? And that I've had one of my officers here for the past few days carrying out a low-level investigation?'

'So Steve told me. I don't know much about it because DCI Milburn made all the arrangements. I can't really see how we can help you.'

'We've got the go-ahead for full cooperation from your chief constable, so I'd like a look around in there if possible.'

Sue Wilding shrugged. 'Be my guest. It's a bit of a tip.'

'Fine. Thanks. Two things, though. I'd like to know if you found any medication. And we're keen to talk to one of her closest friends, Maria. She's the spiky-haired young woman standing over near the doorway. That's all at the moment. Harriet's mother's on her way from Dorchester and should be here before long. I want to be at the hospital when she arrives, so I need to be quick. Have you arranged for the room to be secured once we've finished here?'

'We've got a key, so we can just lock it up.'

Sophie frowned. 'I'm worried that one of the other students might have a copy of her key. Can you keep someone here until we get an extra lock put on the door? Maybe security can help. We can arrange that, if you like. Rae, my DC, has been working with them since Thursday, so it shouldn't be difficult.'

'Is it really that serious? She probably got caught up in some minor scuffle. It got out of hand and she got whacked and ended up in the water. You sound as if you think it's something far worse. That's hardly likely.'

Sophie looked at her coolly. Was she really so unimaginative? 'I think it was probably attempted murder. And if she doesn't make it, then it'll be the real thing. And on your patch, while you're in charge. My advice would be to assume that's the case right now and go through all the right procedures. If you don't, Tommy Milburn will have your guts when he gets back, take my word for it. Maybe I know him better than you do.'

Sophie suited herself up and entered Hattie's flat, along with one of the forensic team members. Despite what Wilding had said, Sophie found several items of interest which she insisted were logged and bagged up.

* * *

Maria was clearly nervous and upset. Sophie and Rae took her into a small lounge area and closed the door. They all sat down.

'How did you get that bruise on your face, Maria?' Sophie asked.

Maria shrugged and looked at the floor.

'Did you have a fight with Hattie?'

Maria burst into tears. 'She hasn't been her normal self for days. She's been really horrible, not just to me but to all her friends. I don't know why.' She looked up at Sophie. 'I thought she loved me and that we would have a future together. That's what she always said. And then yesterday she said she didn't want me anymore and that I annoyed her. I hit her and then she pushed me, and I fell over. I grazed my arm as well.' She raised her arm, and showed them the red mark.

'When did this happen?'

Maria sniffed. 'In the afternoon. We were meant to be going out, and later too, in the evening, but instead we argued.

It was all because of that boy, the one who comes up from Plymouth. He was here yesterday and she didn't tell me about him. Who does she think she is, lying to me like that?'

'She's in a coma, Maria, hanging onto life by a thread.'

Maria started crying again. 'I don't want her to die. I love her. When can I see her? I must see her, please.'

'What did you hit her with?' Sophie wondered just how many arguments Hattie had got herself into the previous day. Maria seemed to be describing a pretty low-level one.

Maria looked up at Sophie. 'Just my hand. I slapped her. It wasn't too hard. It couldn't even have hurt her that much. She didn't even fall over. It was me that got hurt when she pushed me into the wall and I fell.'

'What did she do afterwards?'

'She walked off. She didn't even look back to see if I was hurt. I don't know where she went. Maybe she was planning to see her new boyfriend. She wouldn't tell me about him but I know he came here last weekend, and someone said they were together yesterday, in town.'

'Where did you have this argument with her? What time?'

'It was about five o'clock. We'd arranged to meet up, and get something to eat before going out for the evening. It was here, outside my room.'

'Did you see her later?'

Maria shook her head. 'I didn't go out. I just felt sick at what had happened and I decided to stay in.'

Sophie checked her watch and thought rapidly. 'I have to go, Maria. I'll leave DC Gregson here with you to ask you some more questions about what happened yesterday. But we'll need a full interview with you, and you'll have to make a formal statement. Maybe that can wait until tomorrow, but we'll need to know where you were last night and who can vouch for you. And we need to know more about this boy-friend, okay?'

Sophie drove back to the hospital, hoping she'd arrive before Marsh and Hattie's mother, although she was more than ten minutes late. Barry's car wasn't in the car park. Sophie made her way to the ICU. There was no sign of the visitors there either. She entered Hattie's room and knew at once that something had changed. A young doctor was at the bedside.

'Has something happened?'

'She's becoming agitated,' he replied. 'There's no physical movement, but it's showing up on the monitors. And her mother isn't here yet.'

Sophie thought for a moment. 'Would you like me to sit with her? I've only met her once, a few days ago, but I have two daughters of her age. I know what I'd do if they were lying in a hospital bed in her condition.'

'Well, if you don't mind. There's nothing else we doctors can do for her.'

Sophie sat down on the left side of Hattie's bed, remembering the young woman's favoured hand from their interview the previous week. She took Hattie's hand in hers, and gently stroked her forehead, brushing aside a lock of hair that peeped out below the dressing that encased half of her head.

She leaned forward, and whispered. 'Hattie, it's fine. Everything will be alright. Just rest and concentrate on getting well. Your mother will be here soon.' She gently squeezed the limp fingers, and stroked the back of the slim hand. 'You're in good hands. The staff here are very experienced, so there's no need for you to worry. You've a bright future ahead of you. Just relax and rest.'

The doctor was watching the displays on the monitoring equipment. 'There's still uneven mental activity, though whether it's good or bad I can't say. She may possibly be floating in and out of consciousness.'

156

CHAPTER 27: FLICKERING THOUGHTS
IN DEEP COMA

Dark. Blackness. Nothing. Nothingness. Black as hell. Hell. Brutal. Brute. Hell. Angry. Pain. Pain. Lonely. Blackness. Lonely. Alone. Alone. Always alone.

* * *

Black. Float. Drift. Hang. Emptiness. Empty. Empty. Bare. Desolation. Godforsaken. Waste. Hell. Ruin. Alone. Lonely. Lonely. Lonely. Lonely. Alone. Always alone.

Silence. Cold. Alone. Deserted. Wilderness. Ruin. Abandoned. Alone. Lonely. Lonely. Lonely. Lost. Tired. Tired. So tired. Pain. Tears. Dark. Trapped in the dark. Lonely. So tired.

* * *

Alone. No one. Nowhere. Tears. Why? Why? Why me? Hell. Hell. Brute. Brute. Beast. Angry. Savage. Cruel. Cruel. Cruel. Hell. All hell, all of it. Force. Force me. Kick. Punch. Pain. Pain. Pain. No. No. No. No. No. No. Pain. Pain. No. No.

Scream. No. No. No. Weep, sob, cry. Tears, always tears. Blackness. Hell. Alone. Lonely.

* * *

Mummy. Bitch. Hurt me. Mummy let him hurt me. Hate. Hate. Hate you. Hate you. Mummy. Hate you.

* * *

Touch. Someone's touch. Finger touch. Forehead touch. Whisper. Whisper. Voice. Whisper. It's her. She knows. Green eyes. Witch woman. She knows. Can't go back. Pain. Always pain. Always tears. Always voices, whispering voices. Always alone. Always lonely.

* * *

Pointless. Aimless. Dream. Nightmare. Ghost. Ghosts. Voices. Lost souls. Daddy. Daddy. Daddy. Left. You left. Daddy. You left me in hell. Why did you leave me, Daddy? Why didn't you keep me safe? Why didn't you look after me?

I want to die. Cry. All my life, cry. Please, Daddy, let me die. Cry. Cry. All my life, cry. In hell. Don't want to be in hell any more. Let me die. Cry. Tears. Let me die. Oh, Daddy, let me die. Come for me, Daddy.

CHAPTER 28: SQUABBLES

Barry Marsh skidded to a halt near the staff entrance to the intensive care unit. He'd radioed ahead during the last stage of the journey, asking for a squad car escort, and had managed to cut several minutes off the journey time. Even so, he wondered if they would be too late.

He got out and hurried round to the rear passenger door to help Hattie's mother out of the vehicle. She just didn't seem able to move quickly, and he found himself silently cursing the woman. That last phone message from the boss had not been at all encouraging, yet the woman didn't seem at all agitated. A staff member met them at the door and ushered them towards the ward area, where a doctor was waiting for them. Marsh noticed his boss sitting in a side room, so he slipped away from the group to join her.

'She died five minutes ago,' she said. 'What was the hold up? What took you so long?'

He shook his head in exasperation. 'It was her, the mother. She knew exactly when I was due to arrive, but she wasn't ready. And she insisted on fussing around the house, checking unnecessary things before she decided she was ready to go. I was at least fifteen minutes late leaving. I just don't understand it. And we're too late? By five minutes? Bloody hell. I told her there might be no time to lose. It just doesn't make sense.'

Sophie saw how upset he was. 'Has anything made any sense since we stumbled on this case? Maybe it's a case of like mother, like daughter.'

Marsh was clearly angry. It wasn't often that he forgot to use an occasional *ma'am* when addressing Sophie. 'I'll tell you the other odd thing. She refused to sit in the front of the car with me. She insisted on sitting in the back as if I were a mere chauffeur. It meant we couldn't carry on a normal conversation, so all those questions you suggested I ask were non-starters. I think the sum total of her conversation was along the lines of, "the sun is shining," "isn't everything pretty."' He scowled. 'I ask you!'

Sophie poured him a cup of coffee from a flask she carried in her bag, the remnants of the drink her grandmother had made her early that morning. 'Have this. Maybe it will help you calm down. One thing is certain, we need to see Hattie's brother. Fingers crossed he's not as nutty as the rest of the family and can shed some light on their behaviour.'

'We haven't even met the father yet. Where's he, for God's sake?'

'Do you think there is one?'

'What?' Marsh looked at her.

'Think back to those photos on display at the house. None of them showed two parents, just the mother. I know she mentioned a husband, but I wonder if he's imaginary, someone she makes up to fend off awkward questions.'

He shook his head slowly as he finished the cup. 'This is all too much for me. I was hoping for a nice quiet day relaxing with Gwen. Then all this happens.'

Sophie poked him in the ribs. 'You love it really, you know you do. Listen, drive up to the campus and help Rae out. Then we'll meet for lunch before deciding what we do next. I need to be here for a while longer to speak to the mother. I was with Hattie when she died.'

Marsh opened his eyes wide. 'You were with her? What, at her bedside?'

'Holding her hand. Not just me, there was a nurse on the other side, and a doctor fussing about. But she needed someone at that moment, just talking gently to her. She had another haemorrhage, massive this time. She was gone in seconds.'

'Did she regain consciousness at all?'

Sophie shook her head. 'No. Not a sign. Not even a flicker.'

* * *

Sophie watched Mary Imber leave Hattie's room and make her way to the reception desk. She passed the small waiting room and glanced in, then stopped, frowning.

'What are you doing here?' she asked. 'Your man drove me, so I expected to see him around somewhere, but you?'

Sophie was somewhat taken aback by the sharpness in her voice. She looked pale and emotionally drained, but her tone was challenging.

'I've been here for several hours. The message reached me just after eight and I drove directly here.'

'It's scandalous. She had no one with her when she died. Why couldn't your man have got me here quicker? Why was I so late in arriving? Even the medical staff couldn't understand it.'

Sophie thought carefully. The woman was clearly on the verge of tears, but was fighting hard to hold them back. Better to avoid a confrontation just now.

'DS Marsh did everything he could to get you here on time, as did the local police. You must realise that. And Harriet wasn't alone in those last few minutes. I was with her, and so was a nurse. I held her hand and talked to her, though she probably didn't hear me.'

'Why you? What gave you the right to be with her?'

'I have two daughters of about the same age, Mrs Imber. If it had been one of them, and I couldn't get there in time, I know what I'd have wanted.'

'But what were you doing here?'

Something in this conversation jarred. 'I was in Gloucester and drove here quickly once I got the message. One of my team was in Exeter last night and called me as soon as she heard, but that was still after the local police had contacted you. Apparently you told them that you preferred to arrange a lift from a neighbour or friend, so they didn't make any further arrangements. They were waiting for a call from you. Look, can I make it clear that in my opinion the local police did everything by the book? I've checked the log. But this isn't the time to be pursuing these things, Mrs Imber. You're clearly distraught.'

'But why did the doctor let you sit with her? At her bed-side? A total stranger?'

Sophie sighed. 'I'm not a total stranger. I spoke to Harriet on Wednesday, so it seemed to be the right thing to do. What would you have preferred me to do? If you must know, I liked her. We only spoke for ten minutes or so, but we connected, if that makes sense. I was merely trying to help in a desperate situation, for goodness' sake. I'm sorry if the decision I made has upset you, but I can't see why it should.'

'You didn't tell me on Friday that you'd already spoken to Harriet. That was trickery.' Mary Imber was agitated, but still confrontational.

Sophie said nothing for a while. 'I think it would be bet-ter if we continued this conversation some other time. I can only imagine the distress you must be feeling. I'm remaining in Exeter for the rest of the day, in an advisory role. The local CID will do a thorough job of investigating Harriet's death, I'm sure of that. I shall be joining them. Look, Mrs Imber, we'll ensure that you're kept well informed about the progress of the investigation and, although the local Exeter squad will be in charge, you can rest reassured that there'll be a Dorset presence. The chief constable has made that request and it's been agreed at the highest level. We haven't been idle, far from it.'

* * *

Despite her calm appearance, Sophie was uneasy. One of her team had been monitoring the activities of the very student who'd been killed, and she knew questions would be asked. It had been done with the knowledge of Exeter's CID, but even so, how would she feel if it had happened in reverse, to a Bournemouth student being investigated by a Devon detective? She knew she'd be asking all sorts of questions. She would just have to get to the bottom of Harriet's erratic behaviour.

Sophie and Barry joined Rae on campus. The three of them were sitting in a quiet corner in a café, eating slightly stale sandwiches and drinking bottled water.

'Rae, it's time you told us why you decided to stay here an extra day. What went on yesterday?'

Rae pulled a face. 'Hattie seemed to be intent on pissing everyone off, and I mean everyone, ma'am. She had arguments with every single one of the people she's been meeting, and each row seemed to be worse than the one before. I tried to keep my eye on her as best I could. She went back to her room mid-evening and I thought she was okay. I hung around for another hour but she stayed put. She must have gone out after I went back to my lodgings and met Craig. It was about nine o'clock and we were both starving.'

'It's alright, Rae. What's happened isn't a reflection on you. You were here to do intelligence gathering and had already gone way beyond what I'd asked you to do. So, take us through the sequence of events.'

'My guess is that there were a couple of preliminary spats before I even arrived here yesterday morning. I caught up with her mid-morning, here on campus, and she was in the middle of a real humdinger of a row with a young man I haven't seen before, someone called Matt, although the argument was a bit one sided. She was hurling abuse at him, while he just stood rooted to the spot. I felt a bit sorry for him.'

'Do you think he might have been this boyfriend we've heard about?'

'He's not a student, that's for sure. I spent a couple of hours checking up on him, but I couldn't find anyone of that name that looked like him on any course here. I got the impression they only met about a week ago in a city centre bar.' Rae paused for a moment. 'Maybe *met* is the wrong word. I think she picked him up and my guess is that they had sex pretty soon after that and maybe a couple of times since, from the few comments he managed to get in. I don't think he's local though. Once he found his voice yesterday he said he'd come up from Plymouth specially to see her and that he loved her. She just laughed at him. I felt really sorry for him, hard-bitten soul that I am. She ridiculed him, right in front of the other students that were milling around. He looked distraught and completely out of his depth. Shell-shocked would be a good description.'

'But would he be affected enough to react in an extreme way? Once he'd had time to think it all over?'

Rae shrugged. 'It's possible. Maybe he's the quiet, deep type and it took a while for the anger to boil over. He didn't react much at the time though, he just slid away.'

'Any reaction from the other students?' Sophie was wondering how many witnesses there were to this argument. Maybe the local police should be rounding them all up to get their statements.

'Not as much as I expected. But maybe they'd seen her tantrums before. They looked a bit embarrassed by it all and most just hurried by, looking the other way.'

'What about the other fights you mentioned?' Barry asked.

Rae pursed her lips. 'Well, from what this Matt said, she'd already had a run-in with Markham in his driveway.

164

He'd seen it on his way up from the station. That makes sense if he got the train here. Markham's flat is on one of the roads leading up from St David's station. Hattie kept her car at Markham's place. Apparently she spat at him and called him an unmentionable pervert, that's how Matt described it. The thing is, he seemed genuinely puzzled by what he'd witnessed, and just wanted to understand. He wasn't criticising her. Oh, the other thing is he was confused by her appearance, that's what he said. He wondered why she'd changed her hairstyle so radically. I think he was being genuinely nice about it, but Hattie didn't take it that way. She reacted really viciously, and it all blew up from there.'

Sophie shook her head. Yet another person to add to the ever-growing list of Hattie's possible enemies. It seemed probable that she was even more troubled than they'd suspected.

'And Maria? The spiky-haired friend?'

'They had a row later in the afternoon, and it turned really nasty. I was on my way back after trying to find out whether this Matt was a student. I could hear them screaming at each other as I came up the stairs, and when I turned the corner Maria was on the floor crying and holding her arm. Hattie was walking away. She disappeared up the stairs at the far end. I helped Maria up and went after Hattie, but she wasn't anywhere to be seen. I've no idea where she went, which is really curious. The only explanation is that she went into some other student's room. I only saw her once more, when she came back in, mid-evening.'

Sophie was making a list in her head of all the people to be interviewed during the coming afternoon. They'd need to talk to every student with a room in the vicinity of the altercation. 'This Matt, her boyfriend, does live in Plymouth. She told us that when we interviewed her last week. You said she'd had a row with all of them. Does that include the professor? Murey, or whatever his name is?'

Rae nodded. 'Yes, I think so. A student heard her shrieking at him outside his house yesterday morning. She was really bad-mouthing him. The other students are starting to gossip about it.'

'In what way?'

'Well, just speculation really, I think. To be honest, I don't think anyone really knew her that well, not even Maria. Do I see Maria next?'

'We're not in charge of this investigation, Rae. Those kinds of decisions have to be made by the local squad, and it worries me that Tommy Milburn isn't here. He's the CID boss. I've known him for years, since we were in the West Midlands force together. I wonder if the locals have called him to let him know what's going on? Maybe I should try to find out, but the local DI, Sue Wilding, seems a bit prickly and I need to be careful. To be honest, I can understand her attitude. Here we are, gathering intelligence on someone on their patch and she suddenly ends up dead. She must be wondering if there's more to this than meets the eye.'

They finished their lunch. Sophie re-joined the local CID group, who allocated several people for her team to interview.

CHAPTER 29: MISTRESS PANDORA

Sophie and Barry called on George Markham at home in the middle of the afternoon. Looking ill at ease, he invited them in and took them to a rather disorganised sitting room. Books and periodicals were scattered over almost every surface. He told them he knew of the assault on Hattie, and her subsequent hospitalisation, but he did not know of her death. Sophie asked him how he'd learned of the incident.

'One of the students in the organ music society called me this morning. We were all devastated enough already when we learned she was in hospital, but now this.' He shook his head.

'We need the name of the person who phoned you, Doctor Markham,' said Sophie.

Barry made a note of the details.

'Am I a suspect then?' Markham asked.

'Of course,' she said. 'You were seen having an argument with her yesterday morning. What was that about?'

Markham shrugged. 'Quite honestly, I don't really know. She seemed almost frantic with tension and just lashed out at me. I don't have a clue what had happened earlier to get her into that state. Her car wouldn't start, so I went out to lend a hand and she just exploded.' He described the venom-filled abuse that Hattie had hurled his way. 'Completely unwarranted by the situation, and also out of character as far as I'm concerned. I'd never seen any hint of a temper before.'

Sophie had been watching him carefully. She leaned back. 'Now's the time to come clean about your relationship with her, Doctor Markham. There was clearly more to it than you admitted when we saw you a few days ago. So what was going on between the pair of you?'

'I don't know what you mean.' He kept his eyes fixed on Sophie and ran a hand through his already tousled hair.

'We know you lied to us. You gave her an alibi for that Sunday morning a couple of weeks ago, but key details were wrong. You went to the cathedral for the evening service, not the morning. So why did you lie?'

He shrugged. 'Because she asked me to. Simple as that.'

'So is this something that you're willing to do as a matter of routine? Lie for students you hardly know, when they ask you to? It doesn't wash, Doctor Markham. Maybe I need to remind you that your career is on the line here. Somehow that vulnerable young woman had enough of a hold over you to force you to provide an alibi for her when needed. You, a visiting lecturer on a Commonwealth exchange programme, with all the conditions that would apply to your post here. Do you think we're stupid? The fact is, the more you waste our time and the more you make us dig out the truth from other sources, the deeper you'll be in the proverbial. Cut your losses and tell us now.'

Silence.

'She was here on Thursday for much of the evening. She left shortly after ten. What was the reason for that visit?'

He fidgeted in his chair, and ran his fingers through his hair again. 'I cooked a meal — chicken casserole if you must know. She left shortly after we finished eating it. That's all.'

Sophie nodded slowly. 'So that's the way you want to play it. Well, this is when things get serious for you, Doctor Markham. You see, we already know that you didn't start eating until nine. That leaves a clear hour when she was in your house and you were up to something. What was it? For God's sake show a bit of courage and tell us.'

'She spanked me.' The words came out as a whisper.

Sophie was silent for a moment while she took this in. 'Where did this take place?'

Markham spoke in a low voice. 'In my bedroom. Look, do you think this is easy for me? Telling people that I like being spanked by attractive young women? For Christ's sake, if this gets out, my name's mud on campus. Can't you just see it in the local press? "Middle-aged male academic in spanking scandal."'

'How did it start?'

'Everything else I told you is true. We met through the church organ society. We all went for a drink one night after a recital. I was a bit clumsy and spilled some beer over her and she slapped my backside. I was taken aback that a student would do such a thing to a staff member. I joked about her doing it again and, to my astonishment, she did. She recognised something in me, and I her. It suited us both. It gave her a bit of extra pocket money and some decent food. I like cooking. I really liked cooking for Hattie, she was always so appreciative. It became a fairly regular Thursday evening thing.' He shrugged again. 'And that's the extent of it. She asked me to give her an alibi for that Sunday morning, and implied that she would end our Thursday evenings if I refused. So I did as she asked.'

Sophie said nothing.

'Look, I'm not proud of this. But I would never have harmed Hattie. I really liked her and, until yesterday morning, we hadn't had a cross word.'

'Where were you late yesterday evening?'

'Here. I had a meal out with a friend, then a couple of drinks. We were back here at about eleven, I'd guess.'

'And then? Were you alone?'

'She stayed for a while, and then left before midnight.'

'Can you be more precise?'

He shook his head. 'No. I'd had a few drinks. Maybe Val might remember more. She was driving, so she hadn't had any alcohol.'

'Details of your friend Val, please?'

'She's my secretary, Val Matthews. Look, please don't tell her about my relationship with Hattie, not the . . . spanking thing.' He jotted an address and a phone number on a slip of paper and handed it to Sophie. 'I didn't have anything to do with Hattie's death, Chief Inspector. Please believe me.'

'Someone killed her, Doctor Markham. Maybe someone with too much to lose if some sordid truth were to come to light. You're on that list, near the top. So, before I leave, I want your passport. As they say in those Wild West movies, don't leave town.'

* * *

Sophie could see that Sue Wilding was struggling to stay on top of all the information that was coming her way. She was new to her DI post, and had plenty of experience of routine, drink-fuelled violence, even murder. But this was a very complex case and far from routine. Not only that, it had a history stretching back several years, possibly more than a decade.

'Should we bring him in? Charge him? What do you think?' Wilding said.

Sophie shook her head. 'We don't have any evidence against him, not yet. And there are all these other people still to see. We have these two young friends, Maria, the other student, and the young man from Plymouth who we know nothing about and who seems to have vanished completely. Gone back home, I expect. Then, at the top of the list, we've got this professor, David Murey. Will Barry and I talk to him? I'd like to compare him with Markham, and weigh the two up, if you're happy with that. We can leave Rae to talk to Hattie's friend, Maria. There's a whole layer of murk here, just under the surface, and Hattie was involved. Maybe she was the focus of it. Whatever it was, we've had a glimpse from what Markham owned up to. There was stuff going on in Hattie's past before she came to Exeter that makes me wonder.' Sophie looked grimly at Sue Wilding. 'Have you kept Tommy informed?'

Wilding nodded. 'Yes. He might be here tomorrow. Apparently in the meantime, I have to do whatever you suggest. I'm not happy with that. Does he think I can't cope?'

Sophie refused to be drawn. 'So shall we split the load as I suggested? And it *is* only a suggestion. I'm here only in an advisory capacity, despite what Tommy may have said.'

'But you're not, are you? Not in reality. You're running the show until he gets here.' She paused. 'And even when he does get here, you'll still be trying to call the shots, won't you? I could tell from what he said on the phone. Jesus. I know the two counties are planning to merge their forensic services, but this is way beyond that.'

Wilding turned her back and walked away.

* * *

It was late afternoon. Sophie and Barry stepped up to the ornate porch of Professor Paul Murey's large house and rang the doorbell. They heard a dog bark in some distant room. How would this play out? Sophie wondered. Hattie's dubious link to a visiting junior lecturer was one thing, but a possible connection to one of the university's most illustrious and senior professors was something else entirely. Sophie knew she'd need to tread carefully. A middle-aged woman opened the door and smiled at them. She was tall and shapely, with dark curly hair framing her round face. She wore jeans, a loose cream-coloured shirt and soft shoes.

'Hello. What can I do for you?' Her Scottish accent was just discernible.

Sophie explained who they were and said they would like a few words with Professor Murey.

'You're in luck. We're both at home for once. He's in the utility room at the back, racking some plum wine that's been fermenting for a while. Come through.'

They followed her through the hallway into a spacious, well-fitted kitchen. A thickset man with dark brown hair was just entering the room from a side door, wiping his hands on a cloth. He looked at them enquiringly.

'Two police officers, dear. They want to talk to you. Maybe it's that gravel-throwing incident I reported.'

Murey's expression became wary. 'Shall we go into the front sitting room? I think this is a university matter, Fiona. From what I can tell, it may have been a student. Leave it to me.'

Fiona Murey looked puzzled for a moment, then shrugged. 'In that case, I'll make a pot of tea.'

The two detectives followed the professor back to the front of the house and entered a small, comfortable lounge. He gestured to a sofa and an armchair, and lowered himself into a second armchair on the opposite side of a low table.

Sophie decided to take the bull by the horns. 'Harriet Imber died this morning after being assaulted late last night on the quayside. I'm aware that you knew Harriet, so I require some information from you. Firstly, the nature of your relationship with her and, secondly, where you were yesterday evening and last night.'

Murey put his hand to his mouth and stroked his lips. 'Yesterday evening, Fiona and I were out with some close friends. They were celebrating a wedding anniversary. We had an early meal with them and then we all went to a concert in the Great Hall on campus. A chamber orchestra was playing.'

'And that finished when?'

'Ten fifteen? Maybe eleven when we finally left. We had another drink in the bar after the concert, and then walked back here.'

'Did you stay in after that?'

He shook his head. 'No. We took the dog out for a walk a little later on, rather later than usual. About midnight.' Murey paused, looking as if he already knew the importance of that particular time. 'That's when the assault took place, wasn't it? I've been in touch with the university welfare services today. I contacted them when I heard the news this morning.'

Sophie waited, but he said nothing further. 'That leads on to my other request. The nature of your relationship with Hattie.'

He looked at her warily. 'You called her Hattie rather than Harriet.'

'Yes, I did. Barry and I interviewed her a few days ago. I was at her bedside this morning when she died. I'm still waiting, Mr Murey.'

This time he spoke more hesitantly. 'The nature of our relationship was a professional one. I paid her for services.'

'Sexual services?'

He shook his head. 'Not precisely. I never had sex with her. She was a dominatrix, Chief Inspector, and those were the services I paid for. I didn't even know she was a student at the university until a few days ago. I would never have got involved with her if I'd known that.' He paused. 'My life is in turmoil at the moment, as I'm sure you can imagine.'

Sophie met his gaze. 'Her life is over, Professor. It ended in a brutal way. Don't look to me for sympathy.'

'No. But you do need to know that she'd started harassing me for extra money.'

'So did you kill her? To keep her quiet?'

'No. Absolutely not. And I'd really appreciate you not mentioning the exact nature of the relationship to Fiona, not unless it's absolutely necessary. She has her suspicions about my needs but can't bring herself to play the role herself, not to the extent I require. But she's been edgy for the last couple of days, since that stone-throwing incident.'

'So she's completely unaware that you took Hattie to Cambridge for the weekend a couple of months ago?'

His mouth fell open. 'You know about that? But no, how could she know? But it wasn't sex, Chief Inspector, I want you to understand that. It's never been sex. It's different.'

173

'So was Harriet blackmailing you? Is that what you're saying?'

He hesitated. 'It hadn't reached that stage, not formally. But she was beginning to push me for extra money, testing the boundaries of our agreement. I began to see what might happen. That gives me a motive, doesn't it?'

'As you say. How did you first meet her?'

'She has . . . had a website. It had an email contact form, so I used that. I had no idea she was a student. There wasn't a hint, even after she found out who I was. She was very sharp, very in control.'

Fiona Murey entered, carrying a tray of crockery, and set it down on the low table. Her husband looked up at her. 'She was a student, Fiona. The young woman who was killed. It happened at the time I was walking the dog.'

Very astute, Sophie thought. Puts the ball back in my court. Well, two can play at that game.

'She was the young woman who flung gravel at your windows on Friday evening, Mrs Murey. Have you any idea why she would have done that?'

Fiona Murey paused, then sat down on a hard-backed chair a little back from the others. 'No. What I can say is that my husband wouldn't have hurt her, Chief Inspector. It's not in his nature. I do believe that he'd have seen his career ruined rather than do anything like that, particularly to a student at his university. Whoever assaulted that young woman, it wasn't him.'

174

CHAPTER 30: TROUBLED LITTLE GIRL

Monday morning dawned bright but cold. A north wind had started up overnight, and Sophie shivered when her car door opened and Rae climbed in. The three of them had returned home the previous evening, but Sophie and Rae were making another visit to Exeter this morning. Barry was to remain in Dorset in order to try and find out more about Harriet's past.

Rae settled into the passenger seat. 'So what's on the agenda for today, ma'am?'

'It depends on what time Tommy Milburn gets here. I really need to sit down with him and figure out how we best split our efforts, where we overlap and where we stay separate. It worked fairly well yesterday, but Sue Wilding was getting irritated. She feels she's losing control. Maybe I need to be a bit gentler, a bit more restrained.'

Rae was about to speak, but thought better of it. It was hard to imagine a restrained and gentle Sophie Allen. She clamped her mouth firmly shut and fastened her seat belt. They set off back to Exeter and the tangled knots of Harriet Imber's life.

As it turned out, DCI Milburn wasn't due to arrive until noon, having decided to travel back from Norfolk by train.

He was clearly less worried than his second in command by having two Dorset detectives in the investigating unit. But then, according to the boss, she'd worked with him before, earlier in their careers. Sue Wilding was a good team leader, Rae thought, but there was a lack of clarity and too much abrupt decision-making, which Sophie put down to inexperience. 'She'll learn with time,' had been her only comment during the return to Dorset the previous evening.

Rae, with two local detectives, began interviewing people who'd been near the quayside at the time of the assault on Hattie. The area was popular with the students but, despite the Saturday night crowd, only a handful proved to be of use as witnesses to the events of that night, and that included the three students who'd managed to pull Hattie out of the water. The other four had merely spotted Hattie some fifteen minutes earlier when she'd arrived in the bar. Rae was puzzled. Her own observation of Hattie's behaviour the previous evening, Friday, had shown a flamboyant young woman who'd seemed to be the life and soul of the party. Yet it was obvious that Hattie's behaviour had been muted and restrained during her brief spell in the bar on Saturday. She had sat quietly at the bar until she received a text message. Then she left, leaving her drink unfinished. She had left more than half of her large glass of red wine when she'd slipped outside. Who had sent that message? The phone was probably now several feet underwater, and Hattie's mobile network provider would take days to find the sender's number. Divers would be searching the riverbed today, but the water at the quayside was notoriously mucky.

Rae was speaking to one of the students who'd been at the club the night before. 'You say that she didn't seem her usual self. Did you know her well?'

'Not really, but well enough to notice. She was much quieter than other times I'd seen her and she seemed nervous. She was chewing her fingernails right down, you know? She seemed totally different. It was kind of weird. Then after a bit she just seemed to vanish.'

No one had witnessed the assault itself. Hattie wasn't seen again until the three students fished her unconscious body out of the murky quayside water. How she ended up there remained a mystery.

* * *

Barry Marsh walked past the Imbers' empty cottage. Hattie's mother was staying with a family friend in Exeter. Not that the Imber house would be on his visiting list. He was in the village to find out more about the Imber family and possible explanations for mother and daughter's erratic behaviour. Sophie was convinced that something had happened in the past, something that had blighted their lives, particularly Harriet's.

An hour later, Barry was no further forward. Most of the neighbours were newcomers. They did tell him, though, that there had been no regular male visitor or resident for many years. The next door neighbour told him she could remember seeing a man there many years ago, but he'd been gone for more than a decade. Barry was about to leave when he remembered that the village allotments lay just behind the properties. A couple of elderly people were out working their patches. Worth a try? Barry got out of his car again.

Half an hour later he was sitting on a rickety bench sipping a small plastic mug of strong tea, poured from a flask by Charlie Neath, and talking to both Charlie and Denise Kirk, who'd been digging the neighbouring allotment.

'We were both here before the Imbers arrived, weren't we, Charlie?' Denise said, pouring a generous slug of rum into her cup. 'My patch butts up against their back hedge so I've been seeing them on and off since they moved in nearly twenty years ago. Harriet was just a small baby then. She worshipped her dad. It was always her dad out in the garden playing with her when she was tiny. He built her a swing that hung from a branch of the apple tree. They spent a lot of time out in the garden when he was home on leave.'

Marsh waited.

'He was in the army — a lieutenant, I think. Isn't that right, Charlie?'

Neath slowly nodded. 'Yeah. But I never found out exactly what he did or how he died, just that he was awarded some medal or other. That would have been when Hattie was about four or five, I think. It was tragic. She was never the same again, that little lass. Whenever I caught sight of her after that, she always looked sad.'

Denise took up the story. 'She still used to talk to him, her dad, even though he wasn't around. I could hear her through the hedge. It made me feel terrible, as if I was eavesdropping or something. But she used to sit in a little den that she'd made, in a hollow in the hedge. And she'd have conversations with herself. I felt so sorry for her. I used to try and chat when I saw her around the village, but she was very guarded and wouldn't open up. Course, I didn't realise what was going on then.'

'What do you mean?' Barry asked.

'It might have been all just rumours, but there was another man around shortly after. He was here for a few years.'

Neath looked worried. 'Better let sleeping dogs lie, Denise,' he said.

'No,' said Barry. 'If something happened, I need to know. We have a duty to get to the bottom of Hattie's death, and whatever happened back then might be relevant. Her behaviour's been erratic recently, and we're trying to find out why. Go on, please, Mrs Kirk.'

'Well, there was talk of things going on, you know. He was a bit peculiar, this new bloke. I could never put my finger on it. He was kind of smarmy and creepy, you know? Anyway, Hattie got really withdrawn and wouldn't speak to anyone. She got thinner and thinner. I used to hear her crying in her little den, but if I tried to speak to her she ran off. I was about to have a word with her mum, but suddenly the guy did a runner with some girl he'd met at a pub in Dorchester. I kind of sensed that things calmed down after that, but Hattie was still troubled.'

'Do you think there was some kind of abuse going on?'

Denise looked at him. 'What do you think? He was a creep, and she was such a pretty little thing, and so lost in the years after her dad's death.' She shook her head. 'Tragic. Bloody tragic.'

'What was his name? Can you remember?'

Denise shook her head, but Charlie said, 'Hoggart, or something like that. First name was Sean. But you won't find him. I heard that he died in a motorbike crash a few years after he left the village.'

* * *

Barry looked up from his desk and saw Sergeant Rose Simons approaching. He smiled. 'Hello, Rose. Thanks for popping across to see me. I want to pick your brains about a few things.'

She snorted. 'Brains? Me? Are you mad? It's barrel scraping time, obviously. That's why I'm still in uniform. Most people have neural networks in their heads. I have neural knot works.' She lowered herself into a nearby chair, stretched out her legs and yawned. 'And you're in danger of becoming a replica of your boss. That's exactly the expression she used when she saw me a week or two ago, picking my brains. You'll be wearing a grey skirt suit and heels next.' She watched the startled expression on Marsh's face. 'You know, Barry, I could quite fancy you dragged up. Shall we make it a date? No tight rubber, mind. It brings me out in a rash.'

'Tiring shift last night?' Barry asked.

Rose nodded.

'You've been working in the Dorchester and Blandford area for a while now. A few things have happened over the past fifteen years or so that we're thinking might be connected in some way. That's what I wanted to ask you about. The link might be this young woman who's just been killed in Exeter, which is where the boss is right now.'

'Okay. Fire away.'

'So we start when she was four or five. Her family lived in a cottage in Bridgeford St Paul. The father was an army officer who'd been killed in action a year or two before. It's possible the mother had a relationship with someone going by the name of Sean Hoggart. Maybe he was a lodger? Anyway, he may have abused little Harriet, but he's long dead and there's nothing on record.'

'Okay. And the second event?'

'The family were still living in the same house. When Harriet was fourteen or fifteen she may have been groomed and abused by a man called Lawrence Jackson. He lived in the village and was the church organist, although he worked as a senior civil engineer. He committed suicide some five years ago. I think he was found by his wife and the children when they came home after school. He was hanging from a beam?'

Rose sank down lower in her chair.

'Around that time the Imbers seem to have become friendly with someone called Edwina Davis. Apparently she lodged with them for a few weeks when she started her job as a community midwife, until she bought her own home. Eddie took her own life six months ago, as you'll remember. Just before she died, she may have had a passionate affair with Harriet, but we think Harriet made all the running.' He paused. Rose made no comment.

'You'll be aware of the recent death of Mark Paterson at Dancing Ledge, two weeks ago. We all assumed it was an accident, but we now think Harriet was there with him that Sunday morning. And that's it. You'll have been aware of most of these events, but not the person connecting them all. So we're trying to tap into people's memories, and the boss thought of you.'

'Well, it's good of her to think of little old me. She forgot my birthday last week, though, so the love can only be skin deep. Listen, I need some food. How about coming down to the cafeteria for something? My brain works better when there's some fuel going into it. Will they still be serving bacon butties at this time in the morning, or is the canteen here at HQ too posh for that?'

Five minutes later they were sitting in a window seat, enjoying an early lunch. Or was it a late breakfast? Barry sipped his tea and watched Rose finish her first round of bacon sandwiches, liberally splattered with tomato ketchup. She licked her fingers.

'Okay, here goes. I came across your guy, Sean Hoggart, a couple of times. This was when I was a keen young rookie, out to save the world and the people in it. He was a slime-ball, talked of nothing but having it off with anything in a skirt. His speciality, according to rumour, was getting teenagers completely pissed, then screwing them while they weren't aware of what was going on. Couldn't prove anything though, and the girls involved were so drunk they didn't remember a thing. It solved a lot of our problems when he drove his motorbike into a tree doing about ninety, coming home from the pub one night. He used to do odd jobs and gardening around that area, so maybe that's how he got to know the Imbers. He had a few different lodgings, so he may have stayed with them for a short while. The thing is, when he wanted to, he could smarten himself up and come across as a half-decent human being. He could well have soft-talked the Imber woman into letting him into her house, maybe even her bed. As for your story about him abusing your Hattie when she was small, I never heard of it or anything like it. But that doesn't mean it didn't happen. He was a complete toad.' Rose took a gulp of tea. 'I remember Jackson's suicide. It was pretty tragic, but there was nothing to indicate that anyone else was involved. Nothing of what you said about him ever came to our attention.'

'No, but did you ever see a teenage girl hanging around? And was there any indication that someone had been in the cottage after he died but before his wife found him?'

Rose looked troubled. 'No, not as far as I remember. His wife didn't say that there was anything out of place. Why do you think that?'

'We found a sketchbook at Harriet's flat in Exeter yesterday. It had a sketch of a man's body hanging from a noose. I've got a scan of it here. Can you take a look?'

He extracted a sheet of paper from a folder he'd brought with him and pushed it across the table. Rose peered at it closely then, after a sharp intake of breath, looked up at Marsh.

'That's exactly how we found him, in that room. Christ, Barry. This is worrying.'

Marsh took a second sketch from the folder and showed it to Rose. She looked horrified. 'That's Eddie Davis, isn't it? I recognise her from a photo her brother had. And that's how she was found a few months ago. The exact position.' She stared at Marsh. 'What kind of a person was this girl?'

'A very troubled and sick one, by the looks of it. And here's the third.'

He pushed the final sketch towards the concerned-looking Rose. It showed a clifftop scene that looked like Dancing Ledge. Two figures were drawn with their backs to the artist. The male figure was just about to topple forward into the water, his arms were outstretched as if he were trying to regain his balance. The girl's long curly hair was blowing in the wind. And her hand was resting in the small of his back.

Rose slowly shook her head. 'Incredible. If you'd just told me this and I hadn't seen these sketches, I'd never have believed you. I'd have thought you were crazy even to consider a connection. So, your boss is . . .?'

'In Exeter, trying to get to the bottom of it all. A bit of a tough call, now that the girl's dead.'

CHAPTER 31: TOO CLINGY

Sophie Allen spotted Tommy Milburn coming through the doorway of the CID office and waved. A decade earlier, Tommy would have arrived in a flurry of witty comments and banter, but now he looked tired and careworn. He merely lifted his hand.

He made his way slowly past the logjam of desks, chairs and filing cabinets. *He's lost weight*, Sophie thought, *but he seems to have lost something else as well*.

She smiled at him. 'Sorry to ruin your holiday. It's all my fault, as I'm sure you're aware.'

'I was getting bored anyway, so a short day trip back here will be just what I need to set me up for the weekend. Sandra dropped me off at Norwich station. She's going to spend the day shopping, so was full of bounce this morning. To be honest, I'm not really sure that a holiday on a narrowboat suits either of us.'

Close up, Sophie could see the lines on his face and the tiredness in his eyes. Illness? Or is he ready for retirement at last? she wondered. He was a good fifteen years older than her but they had made the rank of DI at about the same time. Maybe the years of accumulated stress were at last taking their toll.

'Shall we go into my office?' Tommy suggested, looking first at Sue Wilding then at Sophie. 'I've got a rough idea of what's been going on but not the full details.'

Sophie let Sue take the lead. When she had finished, Milburn turned to her. 'You've always had a good nose, Sophie. Who do you think did it?'

'I'm not ready to stick my neck out yet. Logically, we have the obvious four suspects. I'm holding back until we've talked to this Plymouth boyfriend, but I will say that Markham is not my choice for front runner. His alibi for Saturday night, out for a meal with his secretary, Val Matthews, seems to be holding firm. In fact she says she was with him for longer than he seemed to think. If she's right, he couldn't have got to the quayside in time.'

'If something is going on between them, that might give him a motive for killing Harriet,' Sue interjected. 'If he was hoping to get serious with her, she might not have taken kindly to finding that he has a kink. So he removed the potential source of that information. She might be covering for him just 'cause he asked her to.'

'That did occur to me until I met Valery,' Sophie replied. 'She's old enough to be his mother, and to say that she feels maternal towards him would be an understatement. No, I'm pretty sure there's no romantic entanglement there. Apparently the meal out was a thank you for some extra work that she did for him, and they went back to his flat because she and her husband are planning a holiday in Canada. She wanted to see photos. So, he's currently the least likely of our suspects.'

'So what would your thoughts be for the next move?' Tommy interjected.

'Exactly what Sue has already suggested. It's possible that there may be other people with a motive for wanting Harriet dead, what with her history, but I don't think any of the families I told you about suspect anything untoward in their loved ones' deaths. Eddie Davis's brother knows a bit more than the others, but he seems content to let us get on with finding the truth about her death. So we keep plugging away at these four, cross-checking everything we find out about them until we get the snippet that opens the door.'

'No gut feeling then?' Tommy asked.

'No, Tommy. Sorry to disappoint you. Listen, Rae and I want to interview this latest boyfriend, Matt Brindle. Rae's already met him briefly. Are you alright with us going down to Plymouth to see him, or do you want one of your own team to do it? Or I could collect someone from Plymouth CID if you want. We could be there in an hour. We think he works in an estate agents' there, so one of your squad could trace the office and get the information to us while we're on the road.'

Tommy seemed undecided, but Sue Wilding broke in angrily. 'One of us needs to be there, boss. He's in the running for being our prime suspect, for God's sake. We can't leave all the juicy stuff to them, surely? I want to go.'

Tommy nodded somewhat wearily. 'You're right. This is our baby. Sorry, Sophie, but it needs to be Devon led.'

'Fine,' said Sophie. 'But can Rae go? She's got the background. Would you be happy with that?'

Sue Wilding grudgingly agreed. She glanced at the clock on the wall. 'As long as she's ready to go in ten minutes. I'm not hanging around for anybody.'

Sophie watched Rae head off for Plymouth in Sue Wilding's car, and then made her way back towards the campus. Tommy had decided to remain in the office and plough through the reports on Hattie Imber's background, many of which originated from Sophie's unit. Maybe she should make herself scarce for an hour or two, and try to get to the bottom of Hattie's relationship with Maria.

* * *

Maria proved to be an easy person to talk to. Even though she was still distraught at the events of the previous couple of days, she seemed open and honest. She confirmed that she was a second-year student and had occupied the room next to Hattie's in the previous academic year. They had become close friends, a relationship that soon blossomed into an on-off romance. This year they had moved to more upmarket, self-catering accommodation. They often shared cooking and laundry duties, and ate together more often than not. She admitted that they sometimes spent the night together, but less frequently of late.

'Hattie changed,' she said sadly. 'Maybe it's been going on longer than I thought and I didn't realise it. But it's been more obvious recently. She always teased me, said I'm too serious, but it was always gentle before. This term she's been getting crueller, and it made me really unhappy. But she's been bad-tempered with everyone, not just me.' Maria looked intently at Sophie, as if seeing her for the first time. 'Are you the one who spoke to her last week?'

'Yes. I interviewed her on Wednesday. Why do you ask?'

'She told me. She said you were a witch, trying to trap her. She said you had green eyes, and that was a sign of a witch in olden times. I told her she was talking nonsense and that someone with her intelligence shouldn't believe such things. She said the voices in her head were telling her that it was true.'

'So she heard voices?'

Maria nodded. 'She only told me a few weeks ago. I told her she should see the doctor, so she did. I think she got some medication for it. Do you think it could have been schizophrenia?'

'I think so, Maria. I spotted the drugs for it in her bathroom cabinet, and the doctor here on campus confirmed that she prescribed them several weeks ago. She'd started seeing a counsellor here and was waiting to see a specialist. I think it explains a lot about the changes in her behaviour. She seems to have been doing lots of other erratic things recently, and that can be a sign. I expect the drugs would have calmed her down given enough time, though it doesn't look as though she was taking her medication consistently. There are too many tablets left in the pack. What we have to remember is that her illness didn't cause her death. Someone killed her, probably someone she knew, and our job is to find out who. So I need to know exactly what you did on Saturday evening, and who can vouch for you. Can we start with your argument? You told me it was because Hattie broke up with you. Did she tell you why?'

Maria sighed and looked even more forlorn. 'She told me I was too clingy, and that I was trying to control her life. It was all over that new boyfriend. We'd agreed to tell each other if someone else came along, but she didn't. I know she wasn't the same as me. I'm just not interested in men, but she was more mixed up and didn't know what she wanted. Maybe that was the problem. Still, she should have told me and she didn't. She pretended there wasn't anyone else, but I knew she was lying. And then when I saw him on Saturday, I knew she would treat him just like all the rest. Like a toy. Just like me.' Tears started rolling down her cheeks. 'I feel so empty now she's gone.'

'But why did you hit her, Maria?'

'She told me I was a leech, trying to suck the life out of her. I was really upset and angry, so I slapped her. But it wasn't hard, I told you yesterday. She pushed me and I hit the wall and fell over.'

Sophie's stomach tightened. These were almost the same words that her own daughter, Jade, had used the previous weekend when describing her argument with her boyfriend. Thank God that in Jade's case, the violence hadn't escalated further.

'So what did you do after Hattie left?' she asked.

'I told you. I stayed in for the evening. Two of the others in our block weren't going out, so I watched TV with them.'

'Until what time?'

'Midnight or so, then we went to bed. We shared a bottle of wine first.'

187

'I'll need their names, Maria.' She paused. 'So you didn't go out again that night? You didn't walk down to the quayside, wait in the dark for Hattie to come out of the club and attack her? Just for revenge?'

Maria looked at Sophie, her eyes still wet. 'No. How could I do that? I loved her. I miss her so much.'

* * *

Sue Wilding's car drew up outside the Plymouth offices of Dart Valley Estate Agents. She and Rae peered in the window before going in. A bored-looking member of staff looked up in anticipation, only to be disappointed when Sue showed her warrant card.

'I'm looking for Matt Brindle? I understand he works here.'

The woman smiled nervously. 'He's not in today. He phoned in sick, but he said he intends to be with us tomorrow. I hope everything is alright?'

'His address, please?'

The agent reeled off the address from memory. 'It's only a short distance away. You can walk there in ten minutes.'

She was rewarded with a chilly smile. Sue turned on her heels and left. Rae gave the woman a smile. 'He's just a witness, that's all. No need to worry.' She hurried after Sue, wondering why she'd been so unpleasant, but not really surprised. During the hour-long drive from Exeter, Rae had made several attempts at conversation, but it was clear that Sue Wilding resented her presence and probably, as she saw it, their meddling in what was clearly a Devon-based investigation into an Exeter crime.

They drove into the cul-de-sac where the young man lived. A middle-aged woman opened the door and eyed them suspiciously. Her suspicion increased when Sue Wilding told her the reason for their visit.

'Matthew's not well. That's why he's not at work.'

'But his work said that he'll be in tomorrow, so he can't be that bad, can he? I want to see him for twenty minutes at the most, so please let us in.'

Reluctantly, Mrs Brindle opened the door and gestured for them to go into the sitting room. They found Matt sitting in a soft chair, a magazine on his lap. He looked scared, and his hands were shaking.

CHAPTER 32: ARREST

'She did *what*?' Sophie Allen stood with her mouth open in utter disbelief.

'She arrested him, and I don't think she has enough evidence to go on. He's in the custody suite at Plymouth, waiting for a security van to bring him here. What it'll do to his mental state, I dread to think, and his mother'll be frantic. But there was nothing I could do, ma'am. The thing is, he lied about getting home from Exeter on Saturday night. He said he got one of the last trains, after ten o'clock, but we knew that was impossible. There was some kind of engineering work beyond Newton Abbot, and everyone had to go by bus the rest of the way. He knew nothing about it. Either he got an earlier train, or he found some other way home. I don't see why he would lie about it unless he was guilty, but it still doesn't square up. He just doesn't seem to be the type.'

'It would make sense, Rae, if her death was some kind of accident, or an argument that escalated out of control. We know he'd had a barney with her earlier. Maybe they had a second round on the quayside and things got out of hand. But from what you've said about him, it doesn't seem likely, does it? Whoever assaulted Hattie deliberately left her in the water to drown instead of trying to fish her out or get help. That tends to suggest it was either predetermined or the assailant was cool and callous enough to realise that it provided a convenient solution to their problem, whatever it was. Is Matt Brindle like that?'

Rae shook her head. 'I wouldn't say so. The other thing is, I wonder if he's got some kind of emotional issues. Maybe he's a bit autistic or something, but he really struggles in social situations. I thought that when I spoke to him on Saturday afternoon. He was a bag of nerves when we saw him today, and Sue saw it as a sign of guilt, despite the fact that he denied any involvement. He was getting really mixed up in his account of what he did on Saturday evening, and in the details of his relationship with Hattie, and she immediately jumped to conclusions. But they're a really strait-laced family. The place is full of religious paraphernalia. I think whatever he got up to with Hattie after he met her a week or so ago has completely knocked away his foundations, added to which he probably feels a strong sense of guilt just because she's dead. He really doesn't know where he is.'

'He already knew about her death, then?'

Rae tucked her dark hair behind her ears. 'Yesterday afternoon he heard on the local news that an Exeter student had died, and listened to the bulletins from then on. Her identity was released in a late evening bulletin, wasn't it? He told us he didn't sleep at all last night.'

'He could be guilty though, Rae. He's in the frame, isn't he? We know that. Maybe Sue saw something that you missed.'

'I realise that. But I can't help feeling she's jumped the gun. There's no substantive evidence against him. Okay, it's true that his account was all mixed up and muddled and, frankly, a mess. But there was nothing in what he said that could pin the assault definitively on him. I think she's one angry cop, and she's gone for the easiest target. I tried to ask her what her reasons were on our way back, but she just told me to keep my nose out of local matters.'

Sophie frowned. 'I was worried about this kind of thing happening. And Tommy's just left to get his train, not twenty minutes ago. I think he's seriously ill, so he's decided to leave it all to her. From their point of view it's open and shut, isn't it? Hattie's a local student. She was knocked on the head then tipped into the water, and died from her injuries. They've decided to ignore the back story that we've brought along with us, because it adds too many complications.' Sophie stood up and went to the window.

'So where does this leave us, ma'am?'

'Maybe not much different than before. Sue Wilding can't override her chief constable's decision to allow us access to the investigation. We've got a legitimate reason for being here because of the three deaths we're investigating. In a way, she's freed us to get on in our own way.' She turned back to Rae. 'So, my response is, let's get busy. We'll dig deep, make some more visits, rattle a few more cages and see what happens. You okay with that?'

Rae smiled broadly. 'Of course.'

Sophie had managed to get a desk allocated to her and Rae. It was situated in a corner of the CID room, as far away from the incident board as it was possible to be.

'It cuts both ways,' Sophie said to Rae while they filed statements in the desk drawer. 'We're being frozen out of the local investigation, but no one's supervising us. We've got the advantage of all the prior knowledge we've built up. We've been open with it so far, but I'm not sure how much they've really digested.' She sighed. 'This is totally ridiculous and so unnecessary.'

'We can still work with Steve Gulliver, can't we? He seems a decent bloke and tries to be as helpful as he can be. That's the impression I've got of him since I've been here. I've had to use his local knowledge a few times since Thursday.'

'I'm happy with that. We're not in some stupid competition with them, for goodness' sake. Let's get busy.'

* * *

192

Rae called the Plymouth office of the Dart Valley Estate Agency and spoke to the manager. He confirmed that Matt Brindle was mildly Aspergic, but was a reliable and conscientious worker. The only obvious signs were his inability to look people in the eye when talking to them, his awkwardness in conversation and his anxiety when he had to make decisions under stress. Rae thanked him and sat pondering. These were also common signs of guilt and it was all too easy to mistake one for the other. Of course, it didn't mean that Matt was completely absolved of all guilt, but it did make it more doubtful. But if he wasn't guilty of the assault, why had he lied about his journey home? What was he hiding?

She stuffed a photo of Matt into her bag and made her way to St David's station. She spoke to five staff members before she found one who remembered Matt Brindle from Saturday. He'd arrived in the morning, and returned to Plymouth in the middle of the evening on the last train scheduled for Plymouth before the line closure came into effect.

'Are you sure?' Rae asked.

'Absolutely. We had a chat about the engineering works due on the line, then about property prices. He told me he worked in an estate agents' in Plymouth.'

'And he definitely got on the train?'

'Yep. I whistled it off. Bang on time.'

Rae walked away, shaking her head. Why hadn't Matt told them he'd got this train? What was he covering up?

She returned to the CID office and told Sophie of her findings. Sophie looked just as puzzled.

'Did you get this account verified? Could anyone at the station confirm that our young man was definitely on that train?'

'Not at Exeter, no. But I phoned Plymouth and someone there remembers him getting off the train and going through the barrier at the right time. Apparently Matt Brindle is a regular, and some of the staff know him. He was chatting to a young woman. I really can't see why he didn't tell us this himself.'

'Who else was there while this interview took place? It was at his home, wasn't it?'

'His mother was lurking. She was very nervous, as far as I could tell. She didn't hide the fact that she hadn't seen him on Saturday evening. Clearly he arrived home either very late that night or not at all. She couldn't offer an alibi for him until Sunday morning. He was there at breakfast time.'

'What's she like?'

'Pretty grim. I'd guess she's a hellfire and damnation type. There are loads of Old Testament bits and pieces around the house.'

Sophie glanced at the clock. 'We'll need to see him. He's due to arrive shortly. Meanwhile, we'd better go and tell all this to our shoot-from-the-hip DI, before she makes a complete fool of herself. Brace yourself, 'cause she ain't gonna be happy.'

* * *

To say that Sue Wilding was unhappy at this latest development was an understatement, but there was nothing she could do about it. Not only was the new evidence coming from a senior officer, but she knew she had acted too hastily and had been found out.

'Get a quick coffee or tea and give yourself a few minutes to calm down,' said Sophie. 'We'll then see Matt Brindle together. All you need to do is tell him that a mistake was made and new evidence has come to light. I'll back you up all the way. I'll drive him back to Plymouth to give Rae and me a chance to get the truth out of him. I want to know why he lied.' She paused. 'Look, don't worry. I won't let Tommy or any other senior officer know, as long as you let things rest over the fact that Brindle lied. I don't want him charged with any trumped up offence, okay?'

And so the confused young man was taken to an interview room and told he was free to go in exchange for making a full statement within two days, to be given at his local CID office in Plymouth. Sophie bought him a cream cake to have with his large mug of tea, then she and Rae led him out of the police station and into Sophie's car. Matt sat in the front passenger seat in silence.

'Okay, Matt. Rae here has worked like fury to find out what time you really returned to Plymouth on Saturday, and that's how we've been able to free you. But you've wasted a lot of our time with those lies you told, time that could have been spent hunting down Harriet's killer. So, here's the chance to redeem yourself. We want to know what you did and why you lied, and if we're not satisfied, you may well find yourself back in custody for wasting police time. Do I make myself clear?'

Matt nodded reluctantly.

'So what time did you arrive back in Plymouth?'

'At about nine thirty. I got a train from Exeter just after eight.' He paused. 'I decided at the last minute. I didn't know what to do. I really wanted to stay and see Hattie again, but in the end I thought it was hopeless.'

'What did you do until then?'

He hesitated. 'I wandered around. I went to the places we'd been to together, her and me. A couple of bars. Then I sat in the cathedral for a long time. That was where we'd been happiest, listening to the organ playing. She loved organ music. It was there I made up my mind to go home. I felt miserable, but then the walk to the station made me feel better, and a porter at the station cheered me up. We had a chat while I waited on the platform. I was starving hungry so I got a pie from the café.'

'And the train arrived at Plymouth on time?'

'It was pretty fast most of the way, but sat outside Plymouth for a while. The train was busy for that time of night. I s'pose it makes sense. I found out it was the last one to go straight through, but I didn't know it at the time.' He sighed.

'Right. That's the background sorted. Now tell us who you met and what happened later.'

Brindle squirmed in his seat. 'Someone I know was on the train, so I sat with them.'

'Singular or plural? You said *them*.'

There was a pause. 'One person. A friend.' He said nothing more.

Sophie was growing angry. She was about to give the young man a verbal lashing when she felt Rae's hand gently touching her shoulder. That was how Sue Wilding had reacted, and look where it got her. Rae was right. If Matt was indeed on the autistic spectrum he would just clam up if pushed too hard. She took a deep breath, grateful to Rae.

'Her name, Matt?'

There was another long pause. 'Sally. She's been a friend for a long time, since primary school.'

'You like her? She's a close friend?'

He seemed to relax a little. 'She's always been really nice. She's a student at Reading now, so I don't see her much. I didn't know she'd be on the train. It wasn't arranged or anything.'

Sophie began to see how to get Matt to open up. Follow up on the little clues he dropped, but in a completely non-threatening way.

'So was she on her way back home?' she asked quietly.

'Yeah. She'd been to some exhibition in London and was going home to visit her gran. Her parents live near us, but they're away on holiday. Her gran lives next door to them, but she's not well. Sally had arranged to spend the day with her yesterday, and cook her meals.'

Sophie and Rae both saw where this was leading.

'So you walked home from the station with Sally?'

He nodded.

'And you didn't go home until much later?'

Another nod. Sophie realised that it was easier for him to respond by body movements and facial expressions rather than with words, but she needed confirmation of her suspicions.

'Did you spend the night with Sally, Matt?'

His face was bright red. 'No,' he said indignantly. 'How could you think that? I've always found it easy to talk to Sally, so I told her about Hattie and me. She made some coffee and we sat talking for a long time about relationships. We hugged but that's all we did. I felt really mixed up and didn't feel like going home, so she let me sleep in the spare room. I couldn't talk to Mum about Hattie. She thinks sex outside marriage is a sin. So does Dad. But it was so special, with Hattie. It can't be a sin, can it?'

Sophie smiled gently. 'No, Matt. I don't think it's a sin. Not unless you choose to make it one.'

The two detectives were taken by surprise when Matt began to cry. 'But I let her down,' he sobbed. 'At the time Hattie was attacked I was in Sally's house talking and drinking coffee. I should have been there to protect her. I keep imagining her, bleeding, splashing into the water and sinking. I'll never forgive myself.'

Sophie shifted uneasily in her seat. To this young man, Harriet Imber had been almost saint-like, full of vigour and life, someone to be worshipped. No wonder he was distraught at the thought that he'd let her down when she'd needed him most. The problem was, this very same young woman had deliberately engineered the deaths of three people, one of whom had been universally respected. Now wasn't the time to tell him, but would it ease his own sense of guilt if he discovered the truth about Hattie at some point in the future?

CHAPTER 33: SOMETHING BAD

Back in Dorset, Barry received an email from the computer graphics department's administration office at Bournemouth University, headed 'Recent Conferences Attended by Mark Paterson.' Barry opened the attachment and scanned down the list of academic events that the programming specialist had visited. There it was: Exeter University, in July, a mere four months earlier. He needed to follow this up.

He phoned Exeter University and spoke to a secretary at the computing department about the July conference. It had lasted four days, had been focussed on computer graphics and had been addressed by several experts from universities across Europe. She confirmed that Mark Paterson from Bournemouth had attended and presented a short paper. Marsh thought for a moment. The dates didn't overlap with standard term dates. By then, Hattie should have returned home for the long summer vacation, so how could they have met?

He asked about accommodation for the delegates, and was told that they often stayed in the better student blocks, vacated for the summer.

'Do you use any of your own students to help out during the conference?'

'Yes,' she said. 'We always need a pool of helpers at these events. They work as general assistants and guides, and also serve coffee and meals. We post adverts up in the student union building several months in advance. The students like it. It's a good way of making a bit of money.'

'Do you have a record of the students who helped at that particular conference?'

'Sure, I'll look out the list. What name are you looking for?'

'Harriet Imber.'

There was a silence. Then the secretary said quietly, 'She's the young woman who died at the weekend, isn't she? I'll be as quick as I can.'

His hunch confirmed, Barry decided to go a step further. 'Can you tell me if Maria Katsaros is also on the list?'

It was. Something else to be followed up in Exeter.

* * *

Sophie had managed to get hold of an office in the university administration block for interviewing students. It was far less intimidating than the formal interview rooms in the police station, although they would be needed later for formal questioning. She unlocked the door and shepherded Maria inside. They sat around a low table, Rae ready with her notebook.

'Maria, you were seen walking down to the quayside late on Saturday night. Someone recognised you as you came out of the underpass. It's time to tell me the truth. Why were you there and why didn't you tell us before?'

Maria lowered her eyes. 'How would it have looked? You would have thought it was me that pushed Hattie into the water, but it wasn't.'

Sophie stared at her. 'Why were you there, then?'

Maria sniffled, and dabbed at her nose with a tissue. 'I wanted to see her. I'd asked a few friends to let me know if they saw her, and one of them sent me a text telling me that's where she was. No one had seen her for hours, and I was getting worried about her. I know we'd had a fight earlier, but I'd calmed down. I needed to see her to tell her that it was alright, and I'd forgiven her for hitting me.'

'So what happened when you saw her?'

'I didn't. I got to the quayside just as an ambulance arrived. I was up on the top path, looking down and I saw them putting someone on a stretcher into the back, then driving off. I felt sick. Somehow I knew it was Hattie. I went down and hung around for a while, trying to find out what had happened. I heard that someone had been pulled out of the water. I went to the hospital to try and find out if it was her. I asked at reception and they told me she was having a brain scan. That was as on the reception desk. I told them I was her best friend.'

Sophie decided to change tack. 'There's something else I must ask you about, Maria. I understand that you and Hattie worked as support staff at a computing conference back in July. Is that right?'

Maria looked puzzled. 'Yes, we did several conferences. The university runs a lot of them during the holidays, and we helped out at three. It meant we could stay together and earn some money. Why?'

'I want to know about that particular conference. There was a young man there from Bournemouth University, Mark Paterson. He seems to have met Hattie there and saw her again afterwards. Is that right?'

There was a pause as Maria gathered her thoughts. 'I think we went out with a group of them one evening. We often do, if there are any younger delegates. We know all the good places to go, the clubs that are open late. I think I remember someone who spent a lot of time talking to Hattie. Was that him? Do you think it was him who killed Hattie?'

'He couldn't have done, Maria. He died two weeks ago in Dorset. We're investigating his death. Did Hattie ever mention him?'

Maria sat in silence for a while, then inhaled. 'She told me she was seeing a friend when she went back home at weekends.

I thought he was just a family friend. Was it more than that? Is that what you're saying?'

Maria looked desperately unhappy. She was being forced to take a long hard look at her friend and lover. What she was seeing must have been pretty hard to take.

'We don't know,' said Sophie. 'But it's important that we find out. There's another person from her past that we need information about. Did Hattie ever talk about a friend back in Dorset — a midwife?'

Maria dabbed at her eyes with the tissue. 'I know she went to stay with someone for a while last Easter. She had become anorexic again, and her mum didn't want her left alone when she went abroad. She went to stay with a friend of her mum's. I think she was some kind of health worker.'

'Did Hattie talk about it with you afterwards?'

Maria looked puzzled. 'Why would she? We didn't talk about every little thing that happened to us.'

'It's just that Hattie may have gone away with her for a long weekend just a couple of weeks later. To Majorca. Did you know about that?'

'I remember her saying she had a lovely weekend there, but I don't know who she went with.' Maria paused, looking puzzled. 'Are you saying that she was involved with all these people? That can't be right. She'd have told me. Surely she'd have told me?'

'Did she ever talk about her childhood, Maria? About things that might have happened to her when she was younger?' Sophie spoke gently.

'No. What are you saying?' Maria put a hand to her mouth. 'You mean something bad happened to her when she was a child? No, she never mentioned anything like that to me. But she wouldn't. You didn't know Hattie. She wasn't like other people. Everything was on her terms. If anyone asked her something she didn't like, she'd lash out at them or walk away.'

'She was touchy about particular things? Or she had a short fuse generally?'

'She was always unpredictable but sometimes it was worse than others. It was a bit like living with a whirlwind. I never got to know much about her childhood or her family. She did say once that she didn't get on with them.' Maria looked at Sophie as if she was wondering whether to say anything more. 'She hated her mother but she wouldn't tell me why. Yet whenever we met her, Hattie was always really polite. I was a bit puzzled but I didn't dare ask about it.' Maria looked at her watch. 'Can I go? I'm so tired I can hardly think straight. I haven't slept since Friday night. I feel ill and so . . .' Maria burst into a storm of weeping.

'Have you seen a doctor, Maria? Maybe you need something to help you sleep.'

Maria looked up, her cheeks streaked with tears. 'Yes. She gave me a tablet for tonight.'

Sophie watched her carefully. 'DC Gregson here will walk back to your room with you. But I may need to talk to you again very soon.'

CHAPTER 34: SERVICES OFFERED

It was time to delve a little deeper into the muddy waters of Harriet's life. While the Exeter detectives were interviewing their other suspects, Rae spent some time searching the internet and found the 'Mistress Pandora of Exeter' website. Mistress Pandora was able and willing to dispense suitable physical punishment to any man or woman who felt they deserved it and were willing to pay her hourly rates. Mistress Pandora offered spanking, flogging, blindfolding and bondage, as well as several other services that caused Rae's eyes to widen. Three photos showed Hattie dressed in tight black leathers and posing with a riding crop. Hattie had worn a similar outfit when Rae saw her at Markham's house.

'The site's a bit amateurish, ma'am, compared to some of the others, but I guess it did the trick. She probably produced it herself, it's got that unsophisticated look. Plus it's hosted by a free website service.'

Sophie went to take a look. 'Can you tell when it first appeared, Rae?'

'It looks as though it was last March, which was just before she went to stay with Eddie Davis. We might be able to get the statistics and some background from the hosting service. Leave it with me.'

'It sheds some light on her liaisons here in Exeter, but I don't think the three suicides in Dorset had anything to do with this side of her life. Not even Mark Paterson. If he was that way inclined, he'd have visited someone in the Bournemouth or Poole area, not way across here in Exeter. It seems odd, but the liaisons she formed through her Pandora persona probably didn't affect her all that much. It was the people she connected to emotionally who seemed to end up dead.'

'Do you think she really felt close to that organist then, ma'am?'

'I'm sure she did. At that age, teenage girls can become totally infatuated very easily. When it ends, their whole world comes crashing down. It had probably happened to her before, when she was abused as a child. That second time, with Jackson, she was a teenager and more prepared, so she was ready to take action. He ended up dead.' Sophie looked at the website again. 'Copy it onto a stick or something to keep as evidence. I've seen enough for now.'

DS Steve Gulliver appeared, looking excited. 'Thank goodness for our police diving team. They recovered a phone from the sludge at the quayside. Oh, and they've got a broken bottle as well.'

'That's fantastic,' Sophie replied. 'Keep that bottle safe. I was just reading a couple of weeks ago that it's now possible to lift fingerprints off submerged glass, given the right reagents and a bit of luck.'

Gulliver looked surprised. 'Really? We were thinking the phone was the important thing and the bottle was just a bonus.'

'The phone is important, Steve, but only if your forensic people can rescue the data from it. But don't mess with that bottle. It's been in the water, so much of the fingerprint residue will have washed off, but not all of it. It could be vital. That's if it's the one used to clobber that poor girl.'

Sophie visited the labs with Gulliver and as she expected, she was told that the focus was on trying to dry out the phone and tease some usable data out of it. Sophie asked the forensic officer to prioritise tests on the bottle as well.

'We'll let you know once we've got something from the phone,' the forensic chief said. 'But I'll push ahead with the bottle too. It looks as though it's the one used in the assault, judging from the fragments of glass extracted from her head, but we'll be more certain after some spectroscope work. Once we're sure, I'll get the fingerprint expert to look for residues.'

Sophie looked around the lab. 'Where's the phone then?'

The forensic chief pointed at the lab bench. 'Right in front of us.'

Sophie looked again at the disassembled object in front of her. 'That's not Harriet's phone. Hers was a deep red smartphone. No student would be seen dead with a cheap one like this.' She looked at the parts again. 'But keep working at that one. We know she was lured to the waterside somehow. What better way to get rid of the evidence than to toss it in the water along with the bottle?' Sophie turned to Gulliver. 'I hope the divers haven't started packing up yet. Harriet's phone is probably still down in the water, along with her bag.'

* * *

Sophie and Rae were back in Dorset after a long and tiring day. 'The diving unit is coming back tomorrow to continue the search. It was a stroke of good fortune that we happened to see Hattie's phone last week,' Sophie said.

Barry frowned. 'They should have checked. Surely it's basic procedure?'

'Well, it's all turned out for the good. That cheap black phone could be a vital piece of evidence if it was the one used to lure her outside. What colour was Hattie's bag, Barry? Can you remember?'

Marsh ran his fingers through his hair, making it stick up. 'It was a knitted bag, wasn't it? A sort of sandy colour?'

'That's what I remember,' Rae added. 'It had tassels. But she also had a really cute black one. I saw her with it on Thursday evening.'

'That one's accounted for. It was in her room when I searched it on Sunday morning. The knitted one is missing. If it's down there in the mud it wouldn't stand out, would it? It would look like some soggy bit of material.' Sophie looked at her team. 'Well done both of you, but we're all exhausted and need to go home and get some sleep. Barry, is there anything else going on here that needs you? If not, shall we all head back to Exeter tomorrow? It may be time to flex our muscles a bit.'

CHAPTER 35: JIGSAW PUZZLE

After a few good days the malevolent side of the Devon climate now kicked in with a vengeance. Driven by a stiff wind from the Atlantic, rain was hampering the efforts of the diving team on the Exeter quayside. Obviously the weather would make little difference to the divers, but the surface crew were drenched. At least the rain kept the onlookers away. Sophie and Barry Marsh made a quick visit to check on progress but the divers had not yet gone down.

A ruddy-faced man came out of a glassblowing workshop close to the scene and introduced himself as the owner. 'My daughter was down here on Saturday night,' he told them. 'She says that someone rushed past her as she was coming down the steps from the street, just there, behind my workshop. Probably nothing to do with the assault, but I told her I'd mention it to the police.'

'Well, it could be useful and we'll need to check it out. Why didn't she tell you earlier?' Sophie said.

The man looked embarrassed. 'She's only sixteen and we've forbidden her from coming down here late in the evenings. As far as we knew, she was at a friend's house for the evening. It took her till breakfast this morning to pluck up the courage to tell us.'

'Scared?'

The man nodded grimly. 'Not of me, mind. My wife. She really tore into her.'

'Is she at school today?'

'Yeah. Northside Academy.'

While Barry noted the details Sophie returned to the cluster of officers standing around the diving equipment. She picked out Steve Gulliver and told him the news.

She went back to Barry. 'Let's go. Now's our chance. Gulliver's been told to remain here with the divers, and Sue Wilding is in court for the morning. We'll leave Rae with the CCTV team.'

She and Barry drove through the city to the northern suburbs and pulled into the car park of a large school. Heads down against the rain, they hurried inside and spoke to the receptionist. The deputy head came to speak to them. He was a tall, bony individual, and Sophie wondered if he'd honed that cold stare over many years. It was enough to intimidate anyone, young or old. He went out and after a few minutes returned, accompanied by a thin young girl who he introduced as Lizzie. The girl looked terrified. Her pale face looked white against the dark ringlets that framed it. Sophie gave her a reassuring smile and held out her hand. The girl's palm was icy cold. The deputy led them into a vacant office.

'Lizzie, your father said you told him someone hurried past you on the steps leading down to the quayside on Saturday night. You did exactly the right thing to tell your parents about it this morning, so I want to thank you on behalf of the police. Were you really worried about speaking up?'

Lizzie nodded.

'There's no need to be. What you saw may make a big difference to our investigation, so are you happy to answer a few questions?'

'Yes,' Lizzie replied hesitantly. 'But I really didn't see much.'

'Everything helps, Lizzie. I'll ask the questions and Sergeant Marsh here will take notes.' Lizzie nodded.

Sophie dropped her voice to a stage whisper. 'His writing is better than mine.'

This elicited a faint smile.

Sophie continued. 'Now, can you remember what time you were on the steps to the quayside?'

'I think it was about five past twelve. When Emma and I passed the cathedral the bells rang for midnight. It was only a few minutes from then.'

'That's good. Was it just you who saw this figure or was it your friend Emma as well?'

Lizzie chewed at her fingernail. 'Just me. We met up with some of Emma's other friends near the cathedral and they decided to go down to the quay. I didn't want to, so they all went on without me. I didn't know what to do. I didn't want to go home on my own, so I went after them. They must have gone down Coombe Street and through the underpass, but I didn't want to go down there by myself. It's really dark and scary. I went across the main road and took the steps.'

'And was it on the steps that this person came past you?'

Once Lizzie embarked on her story, she grew more relaxed. 'Yeah. I was halfway down, just turning a corner, when whoever it was nearly knocked me over. They came rushing round the corner.'

'Can you describe them, Lizzie? Their clothes?'

'All I remember is that they were dark. He wore a hoodie with the hood up. I couldn't see much.'

'What about the height? Were they taller than you?'

Lizzie frowned. 'I don't think so. When they bumped into me, I think their face was about level with mine, or not much higher.' She hesitated. 'It's hard to be sure.'

'Don't worry. You're what? About five foot five?'

Lizzie nodded.

'Now, do you remember anything about this person's face? Could you see very much of it under the hood?'

Lizzie was chewing her nails. 'It was only a second. But it was pale. I thought it was a ghost. It scared me.'

'I'm not surprised. Lizzie, you said *he* just now. Are you sure it was a man?'

Lizzie thought for a moment, then shook her head. 'Not really. I s'pose it could've been a woman.'

'I'm going to give you my card. It's got my contact details on it. You must phone me if you remember anything else. Do you promise?'

'Yes,' the girl nodded solemnly. 'I will.'

'So tell me what you did after this incident on the steps.'

'I went to my grandad's. He lives quite close to the quay. He drove me home and promised not to tell Mum or Dad. Mum would have shouted at me, I know.'

Sophie thanked the girl for her help, fished around in her bag and pulled out a small badge, inscribed with the words 'Dorset Police Young Helper.' She handed it to a noticeably calmer Lizzie. 'We did a project with our local schools a few months ago and that badge was left over. I just knew there must be a reason for keeping it all this time, and here you are, helping us. It's just a little something as a thank you.'

* * *

Sophie and Barry drove back to the city centre. 'What do you think, Barry?' she said.

'It could be whoever whacked Hattie. Then again, there could be any number of other reasons why someone might be hurrying up those steps. As for who it was, if she was right about the height then it rules out Markham and Murey. They're both tall and would have dwarfed her. So that leaves Maria and Hattie's boyfriend, Matt Brindle. But we've ruled him out, haven't we?'

'Not entirely. We still need to speak to this Sally person he claims he spent the night with. He could have come back to Exeter by car and got here in time. We know he didn't get home until the next morning but until we get direct corroboration for his alibi, he's still in the frame. I was hoping to speak to her by phone last night but I couldn't get through.'

Marsh was quiet for a few moments. 'Tell you what, ma'am. Why don't I go to Reading right now? There's a fast train service from St David's. With a bit of luck I could be there by late morning.'

'That would certainly speed things up. Okay, but we'll give her mobile another call to check she actually exists and will be there. And be extra careful. Matt will have had plenty of time to prime her with a suitable story. You'll need to probe a bit.'

They were in luck. A fast train to London Paddington was due from Penzance in ten minutes, with Reading as its first stop. Sophie returned to the quayside, where the rain had settled to a thin drizzle. On the way she stopped at a nearby coffee shop and bought half a dozen takeaway coffees and some fruit biscuits.

The diving support crew were thankful for a hot drink and something to eat. Sophie peered into the murky water, trying to spot a movement. Just after the last biscuit had been eaten, the rope was tugged three times, and the attendant started drawing in the line. Slowly the divers reappeared. One of them had a squelchy mass covered in green slime slung around his waist in a net bag.

The forensic team slowly teased the object free of its weed and mud coating, to reveal a sodden, sandy-coloured, knitted bag. Hattie's? It could be. Sophie watched a forensic officer open it and tip the contents into evidence bags. There it was. A deep red mobile phone. Sophie caught the eye of the officer and smiled. She hurried back to the café and bought another tray of coffee for the divers, and thick chocolate biscuits. It was the least she could do.

Sophie drew a half bottle from her shoulder bag. 'Anyone want a slug of scotch in their coffee?'

She wasn't short of takers.

* * *

'CCTV's a wonderful thing, ma'am, but it takes forever to work through all the recordings. At least what that girl saw on the steps helps narrow it down a bit.'

'And? You're stringing me along, Rae. You're picking up bad habits from the local squad. Just tell me what you've found.'

'We may have something. There's a camera near the quayside, on the outside wall of one of the bars. At first we didn't think it showed anything, but I took another look.'

Rae started the sequence. The image was dim but some lights could be seen further down the quayside.

'Is that the pizza place?' Sophie asked.

'Yes. Now look just past it.'

Sophie could just make out someone walking past the restaurant and disappearing into the darkness beyond. Then she seemed to see another slight movement, and a figure flitted across the corner of the picture, heading quickly away from the waterside.

'That's just where those steps would finally reach the quay,' Rae said. 'And look at the time. Five past twelve. I think that might just show Hattie being assaulted and pushed into the water, then the assailant running for the steps.'

Sophie smiled. 'So if we get forensics to do some measurements of the distances and the height of those buildings, it should give us an idea of the height of that shadowy figure? That's great, really. Well done, Rae.'

* * *

Barry phoned from Reading at lunchtime. He'd managed to interview Sally Pullman, and she'd confirmed Brindle's story.

'I've got her statement and I think we can trust her, ma'am,' he said. 'She seems to be a pretty honest sort of person. And why would she lie? What would she gain from it?'

Sophie agreed with him. 'Can you come back now? Phone when you're almost here and I'll pick you up from the station. Things are moving quickly, by the way. We might have a witness, we've got some useful CCTV and Hattie's bag and phone have just been pulled out of the water. The weather might be foul but it's been a good day for us so far.'

The forensic team had managed to get some data from the cheap black phone found in the water on the previous day. Its last contact had been a text message sent at midnight on Saturday.

'That's to Harriet's phone,' Sophie commented. 'Look at the number.' She turned to the technical chief. 'What's holding up those people at the phone company? Why haven't we been able to see the content yet?'

'It's coming, ma'am. We were promised access to her log by this afternoon. There's still a while to go.'

'Well, it had better be here by two or they'll get a mouthful from me.' Sophie took hold of Rae's arm. 'Come on, Rae. Grab your waterproofs. We've got time to interview some of my favourite people, those nosey neighbours.' She looked out of the window. 'Bloody Devon weather. I bet it's not raining like this in Dorset.'

In fact the rain was easing again, reducing its intensity once more to a fine drizzle. Sophie drove to a residential area south of the university campus and parked her car in a street covered in sodden, slimy leaves.

'Is this the place?' she asked.

Rae looked across at the building that housed Markham's apartment. 'Yes.'

'Well, let's get started. It'll probably start bucketing again soon and I'd like to be back in a warm room with a hot coffee when it happens.'

Several neighbours had witnessed the short altercation between Markham and a young woman on Saturday morning, and they all agreed that the abuse had come from her. It seemed Markham had shown commendable restraint.

They returned to Sophie's car and drove the short distance to the avenue where Professor Murey lived. They were in luck again.

An elderly man living across the road had been out in his front garden raking leaves from his lawn at the time in question, and had witnessed the ill-tempered exchange. He described the confrontation in some detail, including the fact that the scene had been witnessed by others.

'It was, how shall I put it? Very undignified,' he said. 'That young woman ended up spitting at him before she left. I ask you. Is that any way to behave in public?'

The two detectives grabbed a quick lunch in a city centre café, then retraced young Lizzie's footsteps late that Saturday night, timing sequences and matching them against the whereabouts of Professor Murey and his dog, as shown in the grainy CCTV images Rae had examined. These were taken from the few cameras in the vicinity of South Street, near the White Hart. It all fitted. All they needed now was corroborating evidence from Hattie's phone. The pieces of the puzzle were finally beginning to fit together.

CHAPTER 36: TIME TO GO HOME

'What's the verdict?' Sophie asked. They were back in the forensic lab, standing with a small cluster of technicians grouped around one of the bench tops. The contents of Hattie's shoulder bag lay spread out across it. Her phone had been opened up, the case resting on a layer of absorbent paper, a fan gently blowing warm air over its exposed circuitry.

'You're probably in luck,' replied the chief. 'It wasn't a cheap bag. It had a PVC lining under the stitching and a good-quality zip. The stuff inside was damp but water had been seeping in only slowly. There was still air inside.'

'How come it sank, then?' Rae asked.

'Money in her purse. It was weighed down with coins. Once we're sure it's dry we can charge it up and switch it on. It might be completely undamaged.'

They were joined by Sue Wilding. She listened in silence to Sophie's report on the morning's developments.

'Steve didn't tell me any of this when I called him mid-morning,' she grumbled.

'It was only conjecture at that point,' said Sophie. 'That phone should have the midnight text message on it. And who knows what else we'll find. It might turn out to be an Aladdin's cave.'

It was another hour before the phone was dry. The technicians clustered around the bench with bated breath while the phone was plugged in and powered up. It beeped at them, just as a normal phone would, then showed them its home-screen of icons, with a photo of a laughing Harriet Imber, her long red hair blowing in the breeze.

'Can we look at the contents first, then get it all downloaded somewhere for analysis? Would that be sensible?' Sophie asked.

The forensic chief opened the log of text messages. The last one was received at 11:58 p.m. on Saturday.

'That's the one,' Sophie said. 'Let's have a look.'

They read the words that led Hattie to her death. *I have your money. I'm close by, at the quayside beyond the glassblowing workshop but I'll only wait five minutes. Come alone.*

'Yes, that would have done it,' Sophie whispered. 'Let's look at the photos now. Surely she'll have taken some on her phone.'

In silence they looked at a series of several hundred images. Mixed in with the usual cluster of selfies taken with friends were the significant ones. The body of Mark Paterson, face down in the wild sea at Dancing Ledge, his blue jacket clearly identifying him. Several photos of someone resembling Paul Murey, face down on a bed, bound, gagged and blindfolded, with red weals across his buttocks. And, finally several photos that eliminated any notion that Harriet Imber had somehow been accidentally caught up in the events of the past year and so deserved some sympathy. Two of the photos showed the body of Edwina Davis, hanging from a noose in her home. Close up shots of the protruding tongue and distorted features.

'She went in,' Sophie whispered. 'Either she was there when Edwina hanged herself or she went in afterwards just to take these photos. God, she might even have murdered the poor woman.'

'Unbelievable,' breathed Rae.

Sophie stared bleakly at the phone display. 'According to the university medical centre, she'd only just begun receiving treatment for schizophrenia. I wonder if it started months before, at about the time of Edwina's death. What other explanation is there for these photos?'

***

Barry arrived at St David's station shortly afterwards. His cheerful greeting trailed away when he saw Sophie and Rae's set faces. They told him of the photos on Hattie's phone.

Barry shook his head. 'So maybe whoever killed her did society a service. What do we do with this information now we have it? It's confirmation for us, and it shows the powers that be that we were right to investigate her. But where do we go from here?'

'It doesn't appear that anyone else was involved in these deaths, just Hattie. I'll have to present it all to the CPS and let them decide. Good luck to them. But I can't see them taking the cases any further. What would be the point? The families of Eddie Davis and Mark Paterson will need to be told. In Eddie's case, it's likely that the coroner's suicide verdict will be reversed, which will please her brother.' Sophie stared at the ground. 'What a complete and utter mess that girl created. I just can't fathom what was going on her head, and now we'll never know.'

'Well, we've still got to nail whoever killed her,' Barry said. 'How's that going?'

'Sorted, Barry. We're moving in twenty minutes. Well, not us. The local squad are doing it, but we've been invited along. What a wonderful thing CCTV is. Not only does it prove where people are, it also proves where they aren't. We've got a sequence that shows Murey walking down South Street with his dog at the time Hattie was assaulted. He was nearby, but not near enough.'

'So?'

'Wake up, Barry. He was pretty close but not actually there. What does that imply?'

'Ah.'

***

217

The leafy avenue was still covered with sticky leaves. A pale face appeared briefly at the front window and then vanished as the police vehicles disgorged their occupants.

DI Sue Wilding rang the bell and the woman opened the door immediately. Her face was white.

'Did there have to be so many of you? Did you have to turn it into a circus?'

'If it's a circus, then you're the ringmaster, Mrs Murey. The show started on Saturday night, when you broke that bottle over Harriet Imber's head and left her for dead in the water. Now, let us in.'

Sophie looked at Sue Wilding with renewed interest. That was exactly the response that she would have made.

* * *

Sophie paid a visit to George Markham in his campus office and then walked to the residential block where Harriet Imber had lived. Maria listened to the account with tears streaming down her face.

Steve Gulliver and his team were going through Professor Paul Murey's office, searching for further clues. Had he been involved? Sophie thought it likely, but there was no direct evidence against him. Traces of his wife's DNA had just been found on the cheap phone salvaged from the water. Had she acted alone, in an attempt to save her husband's reputation without his knowledge? Sophie thought it highly unlikely. Even if he hadn't been at the actual scene of the assault he'd been in the vicinity. The incident bore all the hallmarks of a carefully staged attack. Paul Murey was the major beneficiary of Hattie's death. At a single stroke all threat of blackmail had been eliminated. There was enough suspicion to justify a charge against him as well as his wife. It would then be up to a jury to decide. Maybe the search of the Murey house would show that Fiona Murey knew of her husband's masochism. She might well have been involved herself. After all, Hattie's threats put his career in danger, not his marriage.

Sophie returned to the CID car park, where Barry and Rae were waiting, leaning against a wall, enjoying a brief break in the clouds.

'You know, I've suddenly had a thought. We haven't yet seen the younger brother. What's his name? Richard? Didn't Mary Imber say she didn't want us to contact him directly and she'd make the arrangements herself?'

'That's right, she did,' Barry replied. 'Another odd bit of behaviour. I told her we'd keep it low key, but she seemed uneasy. I was only trying to save her more worry.'

'We'll need to follow it up tomorrow,' Sophie said. 'Time to go home.'

CHAPTER 37: CHILDHOOD TRUTHS

Sophie woke with a start. It was pitch dark and the only sound was Martin's breathing. She listened intently, but there was no other sound, not even an owl hooting or a fox crying. What had made her wake up so suddenly? Had she been dreaming? All she could remember was something involving Mary Imber. Strange. Why would she be dreaming about that odd woman, with her cold, belligerent attitude? Something about Mary Imber struck her as false. That must be it. The woman was a puzzle, and Sophie realised she'd been uneasy about her ever since they'd first met. It was as if she were living on an emotional high wire and any false move, however slight, would cause her to fall. Sophie wondered if Hattie was the cause of that tension. Then another thought struck her, and kept her awake for another hour.

* * *

Yesterday evening Sophie had told her two assistants that they could have a late start, considering the long hours they'd put into this case. After all, Hattie's murder had been solved and the circumstances surrounding the deaths of Mark Paterson and Eddie Davis had been largely resolved. All that remained was the paperwork and administration. Wasn't it?

Barry and Rae arrived in the office at about the same time, shortly before ten o'clock, to find their boss in her office with the door closed and the blinds partly down. They could see her talking on the phone. Sophie waved vaguely in their direction.

'Is she up to something?' Rae asked.

Barry shrugged. 'Looks like it. And judging from the stuff on her desk, she's been up to it for a couple of hours at least. She'll call us in when she's good and ready.'

They sat at their desks and discussed the report they'd be working on. It was a good ten minutes before the inner door opened and Sophie appeared. She was clearly very animated.

'That bloody woman isn't Hattie's birth mother,' she announced. 'She was the father's second wife and they married just before Hattie's second birthday. Hattie's mother died in childbirth. The boy, Richard, is Hattie's half-brother. He really is her child. Did you pick up on any of this during that drive on Sunday morning, Barry?'

He shook his head. 'No. Like I said at the time, she hardly said a word. Maybe that explains her attitude.'

'Well, it makes it even more imperative that we visit the brother and get his take on things. Could one of you phone his school, check if he's in today and if he is there, push hard for us to visit this afternoon? I doubt he'll remember anything from the time when Hattie was abused, he'd have been too young. But he could provide an insight if we ask the right questions in the right way. Okay?'

* * *

They drove up the broad, gravel driveway to the front entrance of the school building. Barry's feelings of resentment resurfaced. He didn't have a problem with the rich having material goods and luxury items, but this was something else entirely.

How could most of the youngsters coming to a private school like this ever understand what it meant not to know where the next meal or the money for the next rent instalment was going to come from? He sighed and shook his head.

Sophie steered into the car park. 'I can guess what you're thinking, Barry. I met a lot of people from this kind of background when I was at Oxford. Most of them are perfectly nice people, but they've never had to face any real hardship, even if they're not as arrogant as they seem. Those Hooray-Henry types are just a small, nasty minority. They suffer the same emotional pressures as the rest of us. Marriage breakdowns, family bust-ups and all the rest are as common at the top of society as at the bottom. Half of these kids will be miserable here. I couldn't have faced sending my two to a boarding school for months at a time, even if we could have afforded it. And Martin and I both saw the effect it had on some of our friends at university. We saw too many cases where people sent to places like this were haunted by it, even into their twenties.' She looked at her watch. 'Time to go. He should be waiting in reception.'

The contrast with her visit to the state school in Exeter on the previous day struck Sophie immediately on entering the ornate hallway. Northside Academy had a colourful, vibrant atmosphere, its walls covered with displays of artwork produced by the pupils along with certificates and copies of awards. There had been a buzz of conversation, a feeling of energy. Sophie had been struck by one sleepy-looking lad who had passed them wearing odd shoes, one black and one brown. She couldn't imagine that happening here. The hall seemed overly austere, and much too quiet.

The receptionist looked up as they approached her desk.

'I'm Detective Chief Inspector Sophie Allen. We're here to speak to Richard Imber?'

'Oh yes,' came the reply. 'I think the deputy head wants to be in on your meeting with him.'

When the deputy head appeared a minute later, Sophie nearly did a double take. He had the same kind of tall, bony, austere look as the deputy the previous day. It made her wonder for a second what persona Martin adopted at his school. No, he wouldn't be able to project that austere image, no matter how hard he tried. He was just too funny.

The deputy head held out his hand to Barry. 'Good morning, Chief Inspector.'

Sophie stood stock still for a few moments, her mouth open. So the age-old assumptions of male privilege and dominance still held sway in places like this. Poor kids.

'That would be me, Mr Tweddle. As you can see from the badge I'm wearing, prominently displayed on my lapel. I'm the DCI, mere woman that I am. Life's a bugger sometimes, isn't it? Letting a woman through into a senior role, despite all the mass of evidence that we're far too frivolous to take on such a responsibility.'

Tweddle looked embarrassed. 'I'm so sorry. I didn't mean to cause offence.'

'No. Idiots rarely do.' Sophie caught sight of a broad grin spreading across the previously strained face of the young man standing behind Tweddle. This was a perfect way to get Richard Imber on her side.

'Um, can we start again? Good morning, Chief Inspector.' Tweddle looked as if he wished the ground would open up and swallow him.

She grasped the outstretched hand, gave him a bright smile and deliberately fluttered her eyelashes. 'And good morning to you, Deputy Head. Am I right in assuming that this is Richard Imber?'

The young man nodded, still smirking slightly, and offered his hand.

Sophie clasped it in both of hers. 'Richard, I want you to know how much I feel for you over the tragic loss of your sister. I was at Hattie's bedside when she died, holding her hand. I'll try to answer any questions you have about her death.' She turned to the deputy. 'Can we go somewhere more private?'

'Of course. Come along to my office. I'll ask for coffee to be sent in. And I am sorry for the slip-up, really I am.'

He led the way along a wood-panelled corridor, the sound of their footfalls echoing from the polished timber. Tweddle's office was rather more welcoming than Sophie had been expecting. It was warm and carpeted, and there were a few photos of his family on his desk, positioned behind the ubiquitous computer screen.

'This is Richard's first day back at school since the weekend,' Tweddle said. 'He's been home with his mother until this morning, but with A levels looming it's a question of how much work he can afford to miss.'

'Do you have a destination in mind, Richard?'

'Well, I'm hoping to study law at Sheffield. It's going to be tough to get the grades though.'

'He underestimates his abilities,' Tweddle said. 'From what I hear he should manage the entry grades quite easily.'

Ignoring Tweddle, Sophie said, 'That's my subject. I took a degree in law, then did a master's in criminal psychology later. It's stood me in good stead, so well done you for choosing it. But let's concentrate on why I'm here. I'll do my best to answer any questions you have about Hattie's death, as long as it doesn't put the court case in jeopardy. You may have heard that we charged someone with her murder late yesterday. I expect your mother told you?'

Richard nodded. He's a good-looking young man, Sophie thought. Those dark curls and olive skin tone would bowl anyone over. He could go into film if he wanted. His voice was gentle and considered. 'Yes, but she didn't say much.'

'All I can tell you is that it's a couple from Exeter. Hattie knew the man but it's the wife who is being charged. Exeter police haven't decided what to charge the man with. It may be murder or it could be accessory to murder. The CPS will consider all the evidence before they decide.'

'So it wasn't just a brawl?' Richard said.

'No. We think it was deliberate and planned in advance, but I can't say any more than that. What I can do is reassure you about Hattie's death. As I said earlier, I was at her bedside for an hour before she died, along with an intensive care nurse. She died peacefully, Richard. I'm sure she didn't suffer. Your mother arrived a few minutes later. Sergeant Marsh here drove her down to Exeter. He did his very best to get her to the hospital in time, but it just wasn't to be.'

'I still can't believe it. I still think Hattie will phone me for a chat or to get my opinion on something stupid. She was always doing that.'

'So you were close to her?'

'Yeah. Who else did she have? She kept telling me that I was her only real relative. That's because Mum was only her step-mum. Hattie was my half-sister.'

Sophie leaned forward again. 'We found that out this morning. Do you feel like telling me more about it, Richard?'

'Hattie and Mum were at loggerheads a lot of the time, but I never really found out why. Maybe they kind of resented each other. Hattie was always saying that she was alone in the world apart from me, but even when Mum tried to be really nice to her she brushed her off. Hattie used to shriek at her that she was just trying to trick her by being nice. She used to make Mum cry.'

'How did that make you feel?'

'I sneaked out and went to my room. Sometimes Hattie followed me. She said she hated Mum, but she never really told me why. That was when we were older. When I was small, Hattie had a secret den in the hedge at the bottom of the garden and she used to hide in there. I wasn't allowed in. She used to tell me that she'd got a witch to put a curse on it and if I ever went in my skin would turn to warts.'

'Why did Hattie need a den, do you think?'

'We had a lodger and he used to creep about the house. Hattie hated him, but she wouldn't say why. She used her den a lot when he was around. I didn't mind him. He used to buy me sweets.'

'When did you last see Hattie, Richard?'

He thought for a moment. 'I was home a few weeks ago, that stormy weekend. It was Mum's birthday on the Saturday and she was planning to take us out for the evening. But Hattie changed her mind at the last minute. She came for the afternoon, but then said she had to see someone in Bournemouth that evening. Mum was really upset about it and they had another row. Then Hattie drove off in the car. In the end we just stayed in. Mum cancelled the restaurant.'

Sophie thought for a moment and decided to try her luck.

'Richard, do you remember a woman called Eddie Davis? She may have been a friend of your mother's.'

He frowned. 'Yeah. She stayed with us for a while a long time ago, when I was still in primary school. I think she was a nurse or something. Why?'

'Did your mum have any other lodgers besides Eddie and the man you talked about?'

'No. There was a big gap after him. Hattie said she'd run away if Mum had any others. Mum only took Auntie Eddie in because she already knew us.'

Sophie tried hard not to appear surprised. 'She was your auntie?'

'She wasn't a real aunt. I think she'd been at school with Mum. She was really nice. When we were small she'd send us birthday cards, but Hattie said we shouldn't trust her. She said Eddie might be a witch.'

'Did you know that she took Hattie away for a short holiday last spring?'

'Yeah. I thought it meant Hattie had finally got over her stupid ideas. Eddie was one of the nicest people we knew. I went to her funeral with Mum.'

Richard was thoughtful, so unlike his sister. But, of course, he'd had his mother to cherish him along with Hattie herself, and it was unlikely that he'd been abused as a child.

'I think Hattie was ill again. That last time we saw her, she was different somehow. She was anorexic, did you know? It started when she was about fifteen. She could be really bad when she got into one of her moods.'

'Did she often talk about witches, Richard?'

'Not all the time. It was really only during her bad spells.'

Sophie thought for a moment. This might be the only opportunity to find out what the family had known about Hattie's possible relationship with Lawrence Jackson. But how best to go about it?

'There was a church organist in your village, Richard. He gave lessons to teenagers. Did you ever come into contact with him?'

'I think I know who you mean. He taught Hattie but I was too young. Well, that's what Mum told me.'

'Can you remember whether your mum was ever concerned about him teaching Hattie?'

Richard thought for a moment or two before replying. 'I don't think so.' He frowned.

Sophie wondered if she'd raised an issue that had long been buried. 'I have a responsibility, Richard. I'm a senior police officer, and if someone shows certain patterns of behaviour I really should uncover them.'

'Can't you ask Mum?'

'She refused to talk about it. I think she feels that she's somehow responsible, even though that's not the case. If you could shed any light on what went on, it would be a great help. There's no one else, you see. It won't help any prosecutions, of course. The man's dead. But it will help to explain Hattie's strange moods.'

Sophie gave him a gentle smile.

'There may have been something. There was one time when Hattie was missing until really late. We went out looking for her. I was only taken along because Mum didn't want to leave me by myself. We saw Hattie coming out of his house with him. They were holding hands but he let go as soon as he saw us coming. Mum and Hattie had a screaming match in the middle of the road. I can't remember much else.' He paused and looked at her keenly. 'Do you think they were . . . you know?'

'We'll never know for sure. How old was she then?'

'That's easy. It was her fifteenth birthday. She'd had a few friends round earlier for tea and after they went home, she just vanished. We thought she'd gone with them and Mum only found out she hadn't much later, after she got worried and phoned them. And that's all I remember.'

That was it. The situation Richard described meshed so well with what they'd learned from talking to Jackson's first wife, Caroline. A seduction on the girl's fifteenth or sixteenth birthday. Well, he would have quickly found out that he'd bitten off more than he could chew with Hattie. She'd been abused before and would have recognised him for what he really was. The blackmail would have started soon afterwards. The one thing that could be said in his favour was that he'd killed the right person — himself — rather than his young victim. Unlike the Mureys.

The two detectives thanked Richard and Tweddle. The latter looked more than a little shell-shocked. Sophie wondered whether a school like this ever had to deal with these kinds of issues. Maybe the preferred policy was to brush such things under a conveniently situated carpet.

They walked back to the car.

'I think that's it, Barry,' Sophie said. 'I'm content that we have something close to the whole sorry picture. I feel desperately sad about Hattie's life. So much of it seems to have pivoted on three key events. The loss of her father, the probable abuse by that creepy lodger when she was small, and Jackson's manipulation of her, even if it did turn on him and bite him back. Those experiences were formative. To say it was a tragedy is an understatement.'

Barry climbed into the passenger seat of Sophie's car and they both sat in silence.

Barry coughed. 'I know we usually have some kind of celebration after we wrap up a case, ma'am. I'm not sure I feel that way about this one.'

'No. The Exeter mob are doing something tomorrow evening and we're invited. But I've already sent our apologies. Like you, my feelings about it are too mixed up.'

'Do you think Rae might want to go? She's spent far more time down there than us.'

'No. She told me just before we left the office. She'd heard about it from Steve Gulliver. He probably doesn't realise that she's already got a bloke and thinks he's in with a chance. I wonder if Rae ever imagined that she'd have men queuing up for her like this.' Sophie swung the car out of the parking slot. 'Tell you what. Why don't we go out at the weekend for a pub meal? Martin's always up for an evening out. You can bring Gwen and we'll ask Rae to bring her young man. Craig, isn't it?'

'That might terrify him, ma'am. You can be pretty intimidating, you know.'

She laughed. 'Oh, I know, alright. I've been working on it for years.'

THE END

ACKNOWLEDGEMENTS

This is a work of fiction, and none of the characters and situations described in this novel bear any resemblance to real persons or events. I would like to emphasise my great respect for all of the staff I've met at Exeter University.

However, many of the places mentioned in this novel do indeed exist. In particular, Dancing Ledge is a wonderful spot on the coast path in Dorset, a couple of miles west of Swanage. Durlston Estate is a beautiful country park with spectacular coastal views, and its castle functions as a visitor centre with a great cafe/restaurant that serves Palmer's Dorset Gold ale on hand-pump. Swanage people know it well.

If you have never visited the city of Exeter in Devon, I would recommend it. It's a bustling, thriving place, full of history. Sophie Allen, of course, likes it for its pubs. Readers who have never been to Exeter may wonder why I refer to Exeter St David's railway station by its name. Exeter has two main stations: Central and St David's. St David's is the larger of the two, and is one of the main stops on the fast Paddington to Penzance line. Central has slower long-distance trains to Salisbury and London Waterloo.

I must thank many people for their help and support during the writing of this novel. Firstly, the staff at Joffe Books.

My thanks to the editorial team, particularly Anne Derges, the crime editor. Any errors that remain, and I'm sure there are some, are entirely my responsibility. Next, some friends who listened to my ideas and made useful comments. Particular thanks go to Rachel, who suggested a way out of a very early dilemma while we were having a drink in a pub in the lovely Wiltshire town of Bradford On Avon. Also to Eleanor and all her friends, particularly Sylvie and Ava. To my curry companion, thank you. Lastly to my wife Margaret, always supportive.

Samaritans offers support for people in the UK going through tough times
www.samaritans.org/how-we-can-help-you/contact-us

And in the USA, Lifeline offers support
www.suicidepreventionlifeline.org/help-yourself/

CHARACTER LIST

Detective Chief Inspector Sophie Allen is Dorset's acknowledged expert on murder and violent crime, appointed to run the county's Serious and Violent Crime Unit. She is now 44 years old, and lives with her family in Wareham. Sophie has a law degree and a master's in criminal psychology. Sophie may appear at first to be somewhat of a 'cold fish,' over-intellectual and too clever by half, but conceals a dark past.

Detective Sergeant Barry Marsh is in his early thirties and is now the permanent number two in the unit. He's quiet, methodical and dedicated, the perfect foil for Sophie's hidden fragility.

Detective Constable Rae (Rachel) Gregson joined the team in book 3, to replace Lydia Pillay. She is astute and hard-working. Rae is transgender with a troubled past.

Sergeant Rose Simons is a uniformed officer, now based at Dorchester in Dorset. Rose can appear to be rather cynical about her work but in reality she is a reliable, hard-working and scrupulously honest officer. She lives alone with her young son and has a wacky sense of humour.

Constable George Warrander is a young officer in his second year with Dorset police, working under Rose Simons. George appeared as a civilian in novel 1, Dark Crimes, interviewed by Sophie Allen and Barry Marsh when they were investigating the death of Donna Goodenough. During that interview he indicated his wish to join the police.

DCI Tommy Milburn is the senior officer in Exeter CID. Sophie Allen has known him since they worked together in the Midlands a decade earlier. He is on holiday during the events described in this novel, only making a quick visit. Sophie spots that he is ill.

DI Sue Wilding is Milburn's deputy. She shows some inflexibility in her approach to the investigation.

DS Steve Gulliver is also a member of Exeter CID. He is rather more relaxed than his boss.

Martin Allen is Sophie's husband. He is Deputy Head at a large secondary school in Dorchester. Martin has a minor, but very supportive, role in the novels. He and Sophie met while at university.

Hannah Allen is the couple's elder daughter, now 22 and a drama student in London. She has an apparently calm approach to life, although some events in novel 4, Buried Crimes, hinted at a deeper complexity.

Jade Allen is the younger daughter, now 18 and in her final year at school. Jade is academically bright but has an unpredictable and quirky personality.

Susan Carswell is Sophie's mother, now 60. She became pregnant with Sophie while a teenager. Sophie's father vanished during the pregnancy. The story is told in novel 2, Deadly Crimes.

Florence and James Howard are Sophie's paternal grandparents only discovered by her and Susan in novel 2. They live in Gloucester and have become very close. Sophie is their next of kin.

THE JOFFE BOOKS STORY

We began in 2014 when Jasper agreed to publish his mum's much-rejected romance novel and it became a bestseller.

Since then we've grown into the largest independent publisher in the UK. We're extremely proud to publish some of the very best writers in the world, including Joy Ellis, Faith Martin, Caro Ramsay, Helen Forrester, Simon Brett and Robert Goddard. Everyone at Joffe Books loves reading and we never forget that it all begins with the magic of an author telling a story.

We are proud to publish talented first-time authors, as well as established writers whose books we love introducing to a new generation of readers.

We won Trade Publisher of the Year at the Independent Publishing Awards in 2023 and Best Publisher Award in 2024 at the People's Book Prize. We have been shortlisted for Independent Publisher of the Year at the British Book Awards for the last five years, and were shortlisted for the Diversity and Inclusivity Award at the 2022 Independent Publishing Awards. In 2023 we were shortlisted for Publisher of the Year at the RNA Industry Awards, and in 2024 we were shortlisted at the CWA Daggers for the Best Crime and Mystery Publisher.

We built this company with your help, and we love to hear from you, so please email us about absolutely anything bookish at feedback@joffebooks.com.

If you want to receive free books every Friday and hear about all our new releases, join our mailing list: www.joffebooks.com/free-books

And when you tell your friends about us, just remember: it's pronounced Joffe as in coffee or toffee!